DRAGFIRE
THE USURPER KING

Neftali Hernandez

DRAGON'S FIRE

Book 1: Rise of the Elementals

Book 2: The Usurper King

DRAGON'S FIRE

THE USURPER KING

Neftali Hernandez

Dragon's Fire: The Usurper King

By Neftali Hernandez

Published in the United States by "Self-Published".

Copyright © 2024 by Neftali Hernandez. All rights reserved.

This book is a work of fiction. Names, characters, places, and incidents either are products of the author's imagination or are used fictitiously. Any resemblance to actual persons, living or dead, events, or locales is entirely coincidental.

No part of this publication may be reproduced, stored in a retrieval system, or transmitted, in any form or by any means, electronic, mechanical, photocopying, recording, or otherwise, without the written prior permission of the author.

ISBN: 9798883268549

First Edition: March 2024

For Denise, my guiding light, and Camila, my brightest star. This book is a humble tribute to the endless joy you infuse into every moment of my existence.

Acknowledgements

In the journey of bringing this book to life, I have been fortunate to have the unwavering support of those closest to me. First and foremost, I extend my deepest gratitude to my wife, Denise, and my mother, Sonia, who have been my first audience and my most honest critics. Their insights and feedback have been invaluable.

To my daughter, Camila, thank you for the gift of time— granting me those precious, uninterrupted hours in my office. Your remarkable ability to understand that Daddy needed to write, rather than play peek-a-boo or hunt for the elusive remote control, has allowed the world of this book to unfold. Your deep appreciation for your afternoon naps (she's not even two), has been a tremendous ally in this journey.

And to you, the readers, who have embarked on this journey with me, your enthusiasm and engagement mean the world. This book is not just my story; it is ours. Thank you for believing in this world and its characters, for every page turned and every moment lived within these chapters.

This book is a culmination of love, support, and shared dreams. To everyone who has been a part of this adventure, thank you from the bottom of my heart.

DRAGON'S FIRE

THE USURPER KING

1

Anger and Pain

With all the force I could muster, I swung my fist, landing a punch square on his jaw. The sound reverberated through the silent garden, a sharp, startling echo that seemed to hang in the air. Gaianor took the hit, staggering slightly but making no move to retaliate.

"Why?" My voice was raw, filled with the sting of a thousand unshed tears. "Why come now, after everything that's happened? After we begged you for help, after we lost so much?" The words tumbled out, a torrent of accusations, of bitterness, and of deep-seated anger.

"We needed you," I spat out, my hands clenched into tight fists at my sides. "We asked for your help, and you turned your back on us. You left us to fight alone, to die alone. And for what? For the safety of your village? For the illusion of peace?"

Gaianor remained silent, taking my words, my anger, my grief. But his silence only fueled my rage further. "You're just as guilty as the Dragon Slayers," I hissed, the words tasting like venom on my tongue. "You had the power to help us, to make a difference. But you chose not to. You chose to watch from the sidelines while our world fell apart."

My words, sharp and harsh, seemed to cut through the air, shattering the silence that hung heavy over us.

Slowly, ever so slowly, Gaianor raised his gaze to meet mine. His jaw tightened, a slight grimace betraying the pain from my punch. But he did not turn away, did not flinch. He stood there, a monolith amidst the storm, weathering the barrage of my words, the vehemence of my fury.

"Ezekiel," he finally murmured, his deep voice barely a whisper in the garden. "I... I had hoped to shield Terra, to protect my people from the wrath of the Dragon Slayers." He paused, a sigh escaping his lips as he lowered his gaze. "But in doing so, I failed to see the larger picture. I failed to realize that you were right. That we were all in this together... I failed you."

His words hit me like a punch, the regret and guilt in his voice almost palpable. But it did nothing to quell my anger. The wound was still fresh, as was the pain.

"We could have used your strength, Gaianor," I retorted, my voice trembling with the sheer intensity of my emotions. Tears now streaming down my face.

He nodded slowly, accepting my words, my anger. There was a weight to his silence, a burden of guilt and regret. He had made a decision, made a choice, and now he was living with the consequences. The sorrow in his eyes spoke volumes of his regret, but it did little to soothe the searing sting of betrayal.

As if to punctuate the tension in the air, a flurry of movement disrupted our solemn exchange. The sudden arrival of a villager, panting heavily with eyes wide and frantic, intruded upon the silence. The young man skidded to a halt on the cobblestone pathway in front of us, heaving for breath as if his life depended on it.

He glanced warily at us, his eyes momentarily falling on Gaianor before darting away, clearly not eager to intrude on our confrontation. He was a blur of disheveled hair and dirt-smudged cheeks, but his expression bore a note of urgency that was impossible to ignore.

"There's... someone," he stuttered, doubling over as he fought to catch his breath. "He arrived at the village gates just moments ago. Says... he can help with the Dragon Slayers... Wants to see you all."

The villager straightened, an expectant look in his eyes as they darted between us. The question hung in the air, tangible amidst the stillness of the garden. Who could it be, appearing out of nowhere with such a bold claim? An ally, an enemy, or perhaps another player altogether in this unfolding saga?

"What should I tell him?" The villager's voice pierced the silence, a simple question that echoed the uncertainty of our current predicament.

"It's alright," Gloria said while wiping away tears, her words carrying a calm authority that cut through the thick tension in the air. "Bring him in."

The villager nodded, relief washing over his features, before he turned to do as instructed. As he disappeared, I found myself holding my breath, not knowing what to expect.

It wasn't long before the villager returned, but he wasn't alone. As the new figure entered the garden, the world around me seemed to slow, each beat of my heart echoing loudly in my ears. An all-too-familiar face emerged from the shadows, a face I hadn't expected to see.

Shock coursed through my veins like a jolt of electricity. "Papa Yamah?" The words tumbled from my lips, barely more than a whisper, yet they hung heavily in the air. His eyes met mine, and in them, I saw a reflection of the disbelief that must have mirrored my own.

"Ezekiel," he said, his voice a low murmur that felt like a ripple through the silence that had descended upon us. And with that singular utterance, the world seemed to shift beneath my feet, signaling the end of one chapter and the uncertain beginning of the next.

Before I could even process the weight of Papa Yamah's presence, a blinding beam of light shot towards him. Gloria, her face contorted with anger and suspicion, had unleashed her power, aiming directly at him.

Almost simultaneously, Gaianor lunged at Papa Yamah with a speed that defied his size. His hand clamped onto Papa Yamah's face, and with a powerful leap, they were airborne, disappearing from the gardens.

"No!" I shouted, my voice raw with desperation. "Gaianor, stop! He's not our enemy!"

But my plea was lost in the chaos. I sprinted towards the village's edge, desperate to intervene before Gaianor did something irreversible. The villagers, sensing the danger, began to scatter, their panicked voices creating a cacophony of fear.

As I reached the outskirts, I saw them: Gaianor, his form illuminated by the bright daylight, was locked in combat with Papa Yamah.

"Amilcar!" Gloria shouted, trying to be heard over the sounds of their fierce duel. "How dare you!"

Amilcar? The name was unfamiliar to me, but it seemed to hold significance for Gloria and Gaianor.

Gloria, who had followed closely behind, skidded to a halt beside me. Her eyes were wide, her breathing ragged. "Stay back Ezekiel, we'll protect you from Amilcar!"

I nodded frantically, though I didn't understand the connection. "But he's Papa Yamah! He's the one I spoke to you about, the one that raised me!"

Papah Yamah and Gaianor were locked in a battle. The ground beneath them cracked and shifted with the force of their blows, sending dust and debris into the air. Suddenly, Gaianor's demeanor changed. His eyes, once filled with rage, now glowed with a different kind of intensity. They shun a golden hue. His body began to tremble, and I could see scales forming on his exposed skin. The Earth Elemental was on the brink of transforming into a dragon.

Seeing this, Papa Yamah's eyes widened in alarm. "Gaianor, please!" he pleaded, his voice filled with urgency. "I come in peace. I am not the Amilcar you once knew."

Gloria hesitated for a moment, her gaze darting between me and the ongoing battle. Then, with a determined expression, she raised her hands, summoning her powers once more. But this time, instead of a beam of light, she conjured a barrier of radiant energy, separating Gaianor and Papa Yamah.

The sudden intervention caught them off guard. Gaianor was momentarily disoriented. The scales that had begun to form on his skin receded, and the fierce golden glow in his eyes dimmed. He stumbled back, his breathing ragged, a mix of anger and confusion evident on his face.

Papa Yamah, on the other hand, seized the momentary respite to regain his footing. Dusting off his clothes, he straightened up, his eyes never leaving Gaianor's. "Gaianor," he began, his voice calm but firm, "I understand your distrust. But I am here in peace."

Gaianor's eyes narrowed, his hands still clenched in fists. "Dragon Slayers," he spat with evident disdain, "all the same. Killers of our kind. And you, Amilcar, are no different."

Before Papa Yamah could respond, I rushed over, positioning myself between the two. "Gaianor, please," I pleaded, my voice filled with desperation. "This is Papa Yamah. He raised me. He's not our enemy."

Without a moment's hesitation, I turned towards Papa Yamah, the distance between us closing with a few, quick steps. "Papa!" The word escaped me, a cry that was both a greeting and a plea, a sound laden with the pain of separation and the joy of reunion. "I thought you were dead!"

My arms wrapped around him tightly.

Papa Yamah's initial stiffness at my sudden embrace melted away as he returned the gesture, his arms wrapping around me with a strength and warmth that spoke of protection and a deep, enduring affection. "Ezekiel," he whispered, his voice heavy with emotion, "there's so much I need to tell you. So much that has been left unsaid."

As I stood there, enveloped in the warmth of Papa Yamah's embrace, the chaotic world around us seemed to pause. Gaianor's hostility, the whispers of the forest, the uncertainty of our future—all of it receded into a distant murmur. In that moment, there was only the profound relief and joy of having Papa Yamah alive, a feeling that eclipsed all fears and doubts.

"Papa Yamah," I said, my voice choked with emotion, "I thought I had lost you. To know you're alive... it's more than I could have hoped for." The words barely scratched the surface of the tumultuous sea of feelings within me, but they carried the weight of my gratitude and love.

However, the shadow of Papa Yamah's past loomed large, a specter that had haunted me since Vajra's revelations. "Papa, Vajra told me about your past," I continued, the words heavy on my tongue. "About the Dragon Slayers... about who you were."

Papa Yamah's expression shifted, a mixture of regret and sorrow clouding his features. "I see…" he acknowledged, his voice laced with a profound sadness. "I had hoped to shield you from that part of my life, to spare you the burden of my choices."

I looked up at him, my eyes searching his face for answers. "Why didn't you tell me? Why keep it a secret?"

He sighed, his shoulders slumping. "Because I was ashamed. Ashamed of the choices I made, of the lives I took. I wanted to leave that life behind, to start anew. And when I found you and Elijah, I saw a chance for redemption, a chance to make things right."

A tear rolled down his cheek, and he quickly wiped it away. "I'm so sorry, Ezekiel. I should have told you. I should have been honest with you."

I took a deep breath, trying to process everything. The man who had raised me, who had been my rock, had a past that was so different from the person I knew. But as I looked into his eyes, I saw the same love and care that had always been there.

"Papa," I whispered, "I understand. We all have our pasts, our mistakes. But it's what we do now, how we move forward, that defines us."

He nodded, a small smile forming on his lips. "Thank you, Ezekiel. Your understanding means more to me than you'll ever know."

Gaianor, who had been silently watching the exchange, finally spoke up. "Amilcar, or Yamah, whatever you call yourself now, know this: I will be watching. If you truly have changed, then prove it."

Papa Yamah nodded in understanding. "I will, Gaianor. I promise."

The sun overhead cast a warm glow on Ash Village, its light reflecting the hope of understanding, forgiveness, and the possibility of a new beginning.

We began our solemn procession back to the shrine. A complex tapestry of emotions hung heavily in the air.

Villagers started to gather, their faces etched with lines of worry and fear, their eyes darting nervously between us and Papa Yamah. Whispers fluttered like uneasy birds, carrying words of distrust and disdain towards the man who once hunted them.

Papa Yamah bore their stares with a quiet dignity, his shoulders squared yet bearing the weight of a past marred with actions that now stood as a testament to a time of division and hatred. His eyes, once fierce and unyielding, now held a depth of sorrow and understanding that only time and reflection could bestow.

As we moved closer to the shrine, the crowd thickened, their murmurs growing louder, more accusatory. I could feel the tendrils of their fear and anger reaching out, attempting to sway the fragile trust we were building.

I glanced at Papa Yamah, his face a stoic mask, yet I could see the slight tremble in his hands, the silent battle he fought to maintain his composure. It was a painful reminder of the long road we had ahead, the bridges that needed mending, the wounds that sought healing.

As we reached the entrance to the shrine, I turned to face the gathering crowd, my heart pounding in my chest. "Please," I implored, my voice carrying across the silent square, "I know the past cannot be undone, but we have a chance here, a chance to forge a new path, one built on understanding and unity."

I could feel their eyes on me, weighing my words, grappling with the complex web of emotions that this moment brought forth.

With a deep breath, I continued, "Papa Yamah has changed. He seeks redemption, a chance to right the wrongs of his past. I ask you to look beyond the hatred, beyond the fear, and see the man who stands before you now, a man willing to fight for a future where we stand united."

From the back of the crowd, a voice rang out, sharp and accusatory. "Why should we trust a Dragon Slayer?"

All eyes turned to the speaker, a middle-aged man with a stern face and a deep scar running down his cheek. He stepped forward, his gaze fixed on Papa Yamah with undisguised hostility.

"Amilcar," he spat out the name with evident disdain. "You think we've forgotten? The dragons you've slain, the lives you've taken?"

A murmur of agreement rippled through the crowd, and more villagers began voicing their concerns and fears. It was clear that the tide of public opinion was turning against us.

Papa Yamah raised his hands in a gesture of peace. "I understand your fears and your anger. I am not proud of my past, but I have changed. I've spent years trying to atone for my sins."

The man scoffed, "Words are easy. How can we believe you?"

I stepped forward, positioning myself beside Papa Yamah. "Because I vouch for him," I declared, my voice firm. "He raised me, cared for me, and taught me the values of honor and integrity. If he had ill intentions, he had ample opportunities to act on them. But he didn't."

The man looked at me, his expression softening slightly. "Ezekiel, we respect you. But this is a Dragon Slayer we're talking about."

A tense silence swathed the crowd. It was clear that the villagers were torn, their trust in me conflicting with their fear and distrust of Papa Yamah.

Gloria stepped forward, her voice calm and soothing. "We all have our pasts, our mistakes. But we also have the capacity to change, to grow. Let's not let fear cloud our judgment. Let's give him a chance."

The crowd seemed to ponder her words, the atmosphere thick with uncertainty, their faces reflecting the internal struggle each one faced. It was clear that while some were willing to give Papa Yamah a chance, many remained skeptical, and he would be under close scrutiny.

The crowd began to slowly disperse, their hushed conversations carrying through the air. Suspicion and doubt were evident in their sidelong glances towards Papa Yamah. The weight of the situation was palpable, and it was clear that gaining the villagers' trust would be an uphill battle.

As the last of the villagers left the clearing, Gloria motioned for us to follow her. "Come," she said, her voice gentle, "let's head back to the gardens."

I couldn't help myself but be in constant awe of the shrine. The shrine itself was a marvel. Built from stones that shimmered with an ethereal glow, it stood tall and majestic, a tribute to the dragons. Intricate carvings adorned its walls, depicting scenes of dragons soaring through the skies, their wings outstretched in a dance of freedom and power.

Gloria approached the entrance, her fingers lightly tracing the carvings. "This shrine holds the memories and hopes of our ancestors," she whispered, her voice filled with reverence.

Papa Yamah, looking up at the shrine, seemed lost in thought. "It truly is magnificent."

I could sense the weight of his past pressing down on him, the juxtaposition of his former life as a Dragon Slayer and the present moment, standing before a shrine dedicated to the very creatures he once hunted.

We entered the shrine, the cool interior a stark contrast to the warmth outside. As we walked further in, the sound of trickling water reached our ears. Following the sound, we found ourselves at the back of the shrine, where a set of ornate doors led to the gardens beyond.

Gloria pushed the doors open, revealing Ytfen's Gardens in all its splendor. "This," she said, gesturing to the expanse before us, "is where Ytfen used to meditate and seek guidance. The energy here is unlike any other."

I turned to Papa Yamah, curious to see his reaction. He stood still, his eyes taking in every detail, every flower, every tree. "It's a reminder," he said quietly, "of what we're fighting for. A world where dragons and humans can coexist in harmony."

From the corner of my eye, I noticed Gaianor's gaze fixed intently on Papa Yamah. There was a hardness in his eyes, a skepticism that was hard to miss. While the rest of us were lost in the beauty of the gardens, Gaianor's attention was solely on the former Dragon Slayer. Every word, every gesture from Papa Yamah was being scrutinized.

Papa Yamah seemed to sense Gaianor's watchful eyes, and for a brief moment, their gazes locked. It was a silent exchange, one filled with unspoken words and emotions. The tension was obvious.

In the distance, I could see Camila, Oliver, and Sombra waiting for us. Their expressions were somber, a reflection of the weight of recent events. The loss of all the Warrior Leaders, Paco, Junito and David was a fresh wound.

As soon as they caught sight of Papa Yamah, their postures shifted instantly. Oliver's hand went to his daggers, his eyes narrowing with suspicion, while Sombra took a defensive stance, her body coiled and ready to strike.

"Stay back, mate!" Oliver warned, his voice tense.

Papa Yamah raised his hands in a gesture of peace, but the air crackled with unease.

"No, wait!" I shouted, rushing forward to position myself between them and Papa Yamah. "It's okay. He's with me."

Camila, her expression a complex tapestry of confusion and concern, met my gaze. Her eyes searched mine, seeking understanding in the midst of the unfolding tension.

"Who is he?" Sombra asked, her posture still guarded.

Before I could answer, Papa Yamah spoke up, his voice filled with sincerity. "I'm here to help, to make amends for my past. I know it's hard to believe, but I've changed."

Gaianor, however, wasn't as easily convinced. He stepped forward, his eyes never leaving Papa Yamah. "Sombra," he began, his voice dripping with disdain, "this man, Amilcar, or as he now calls himself, Yamah, was once a Dragon Slayer. One of the most feared."

Oliver's eyes widened in realization, and he took a step back, his hands instinctively pulling out his daggers. Sombra's face hardened.

Papa Yamah sighed, his shoulders slumping slightly. "Yes, I was Amilcar. I won't deny my past, nor the deeds I've done. But I've spent years trying to atone, to find a new path."

Gaianor snorted, clearly unconvinced. "A Dragon Slayer, seeking redemption? Forgive me if I find that hard to believe."

I felt a pang of frustration. "Gaianor, please," I pleaded, "he saved my life, raised me when I had no one. He's not the enemy."

Gaianor's gaze softened slightly as he looked at me, but the mistrust remained. "Ezekiel, I understand your feelings, but we need to be cautious. The past has a way of catching up, and we can't afford any mistakes."

Papa Yamah nodded slowly, his expression somber. "I know the weight of my past, and I'm prepared to face any consequences. But for now, all I ask is a chance to prove myself."

There was a tense silence.

Finally, Sombra relaxed her stance, though she still kept a watchful eye on Papa Yamah. "For Ezekiel's sake, we'll give you a chance. But know this," she said, her voice firm, "any sign of betrayal, and we won't hesitate to act."

Papa Yamah nodded in understanding. "I expect nothing less."

"Ezekiel," Oliver began, his voice heavy with emotion, "we've been discussing what happened. The loss of the Warrior Leaders, Paco, Junito and David... it's a pain we all share."

Sombra nodded in agreement. "They were brave, loyal, and true to the end. They deserve to be remembered and honored."

I took a deep breath, the weight of their loss pressing down on me. "We should hold a memorial for them," I suggested. "A ceremony to honor their sacrifice and celebrate their lives."

Gloria nodded. "It's the least we can do. They gave their lives to protect us, to protect the future of dragons and humans alike."

"In my time as a Dragon Slayer, I've seen many fall in battle," Papa Yamah said. "Each loss is a reminder of the cost of war, the price we pay for our beliefs and convictions. Honoring those who fell is not just a tribute to them, but a commitment to ensuring their sacrifice was not in vain."

The group nodded in agreement, the resolve to honor their fallen comrades evident in their expressions.

"We'll gather the villagers," Gloria said. "Everyone should have the chance to pay their respects."

As preparations began for the memorial, I took a moment to reflect on the journey ahead. The loss of Junito and David was a glaring reminder of the challenges we faced. But with the support of my allies and the memories of our fallen comrades to guide us, I was determined to see our mission through to the end.

2

Dragon Memorial

The sun began its descent, casting a golden hue over Ash Village. As the first stars began to twinkle in the evening sky, the villagers gathered in a clearing near Ytfen's Garden. A gentle breeze rustled the leaves, carrying with it the soft melodies of birds returning to their nests.

In the center of the clearing stood two pyres, meticulously constructed from fragrant woods and adorned with flowers and herbs. Atop each pyre lay the bodies of Junito and David, dressed in ceremonial robes, their faces serene in eternal slumber. Torches were placed around the clearing, their flames flickering, casting dancing shadows that seemed to pay their own silent respects.

Gloria stepped forward, holding a crystal vial filled with a liquid.

I watched in awe as the liquid shimmered in the moonlight, its ethereal glow casting a gentle radiance over the pyres. The sight was mesmerizing, and I found myself drawn to the vial in Gloria's hand.

"What is that?" I whispered to Camila, who was standing by me.

"I am not sure," she said.

Papa Yamah, standing to the other side of me, spoke up. "Those, Ezekiel, are Dragon Tears," he said, his voice filled with reverence.

I turned to him, my eyes wide with surprise. "Dragon Tears?"

Papa Yamah nodded. "Yes. They are one of the rarest and most sacred substances in this world. They are not tears in the way you might think. They are not borne of sadness or pain, but of deep emotion and connection."

I looked back at the vial, a newfound appreciation for the precious liquid within. "It's beautiful," I murmured.

Papa Yamah smiled softly. "Indeed. It's a testament to the deep emotions and magic that dragons possess. Their tears are a symbol of their love, their pain, and their connection to the world around them."

Gloria approached the pyres and gently sprinkled the tears over Junito and David, her voice soft as she began to chant an ancient song of farewell.

Gloria's voice began, soft and melodic, setting the tone for the ancient chant:

> "Aelora na'thul, serin vaelor,
> Whispers of wind, carry them forth.
> Brave souls departed, into the night,
> Guided by stars, bathed in moonlight."

The villagers joined in, their voices harmonizing beautifully:

> "Lorien sa'thar, valen morae,
> Through realms unknown, show them the way.
> In battles they stood, fearless and true,
> Now find them peace, in skies so blue."

The chorus continued, the melody flowing like a gentle river:

> "Aerion na'fel, serin daelar,
> Embrace them now, near and afar.
> For in our hearts, their memories stay,
> Until we meet, at break of day."

The song's haunting melody resonated through the clearing, a tribute to the fallen and a promise of hope for the future. The combined voices of the villagers created a powerful and emotional atmosphere, a proof to the bond they shared and the depth of their loss.

Oliver and Sombra stood side by side, their hands clasped tightly. Tears streamed down their faces.

The weight of the moment pressed heavily on my heart, and despite my best efforts to hold back, tears welled up in my eyes. The raw emotion of the ceremony, combined with the memories of Junito and David, overwhelmed me.

I couldn't help but think of all the loss I had experienced ever since that fateful day in Bryson Village.

I felt a hand on my shoulder and turned to see Papa Yamah. His face, bore the weight of countless memories and losses. "In every culture, in every age, we find ways to honor those who have passed," he whispered. "It's a demonstration to the indomitable spirit of life, to the bonds that tie us together."

As the song reached its crescendo, Gaianor, in his dragon form, soared overhead, letting out a mournful roar that echoed through the skies. It was a final salute, a dragon's tribute to the fallen.

With the song's conclusion, Gloria walked towards me and handed me a torch. "You should be the one to do it," she said.

I stepped forward, torch in hand. With a deep breath, I lit the pyres. Flames quickly engulfed them, reaching skyward, their warmth and light a beacon in the growing darkness.

The villagers watched in solemn silence as the pyres burned, the flames consuming all, leaving behind only memories and the promise to never forget. The night deepened, and one by one, the villagers began to depart, their hearts heavy but filled with a renewed sense of purpose and unity.

As the last embers of the pyres faded, the clearing was bathed in the soft glow of the moon and stars. The silence was profound, broken only by the gentle sounds of nature.

Gathering around the dying fires, our group found ourselves drawn together, the weight of the day's events pressing heavily upon us. It was Papa Yamah who broke the silence.

"There's something I need to share," he began, his voice low and filled with gravity. "The reason why I came."

I looked at him, curiosity piqued.

Papa Yamah inhaled deeply, seemingly ready to share his reasons, when Gloria's voice interrupted the silence. "Not now, Yamah," she said, her voice gentle yet firm. "This isn't the time or place."

I watched as he met her gaze, a hint of surprise evident in his eyes, but he nodded in understanding. "Of course," he replied softly, his eyes downcast.

"We've been through a lot today," she said. "Tonight, we need to reflect, to honor Junito, David, and all of those who lost their lives, and find solace in each other's presence. Tomorrow, you can tell us what you've come to say."

I looked around at the group, seeing nods of agreement. The weight of the day's events was evident, and the soft glow of the moonlight seemed to wrap around us, offering a gentle embrace.

As the hours passed, we sat together, some lost in thought, while others shared stories of Junito and David. We laughed at cherished memories and shed tears for the pain of their loss. The bond between us felt stronger than ever, solidified by shared grief and hope.

Gradually, members of our group began to retire. First Gaianor, then Camila.

Oliver and Sombra stepped forward. "We must leave for Furki Village immediately," Oliver announced, his voice firm.

Gloria looked at them with concern. "It's late, you should stay here for the night. It's dangerous to travel at night."

Sombra shook her head, her gaze determined. "Time is of the essence. With Chief Paco and the Warrior Leaders gone, Furki Village is vulnerable. Our place is there."

Are you sure?" I asked, hoping they might reconsider.

Oliver nodded. "We appreciate your concern, mate, but we gotta go. Every second counts."

Gloria sighed, understanding the gravity of their decision. "Very well. But please, be careful."

"We will," Sombra assured her.

With a final nod, Oliver and Sombra turned and began their journey, disappearing into the night. We watched them go, our thoughts filled with a mix of admiration, concern, and hope for the future.

"I think it's time to call it a night," Gloria said, her voice soft. "It's been a long day, and we all need some rest."

I nodded in understanding, "Thank you, Gloria, for everything. Rest well."

She gave a small smile, her gaze lingering on each of us for a moment. "Goodnight," she whispered before turning and making her way back towards the shrine.

With Gloria's departure, the atmosphere felt even more somber. I turned to Papa Yamah, who stood a little apart from me, his gaze fixed on the spot where the pyres had burned, lost in thought.

"Papa Yamah," I began, my voice gentle, not wanting to startle him from his reverie.

He turned to face me, his eyes filled with a mix of sadness and warmth. "Ezekiel," he acknowledged with a soft smile.

"I was thinking," I hesitated for a moment, searching for the right words, "would you like to spend the night in the same room? We have so much to catch up on."

He nodded, "I would like that very much, Ezekiel. It's been too long since we last spoke, and there's much I want to share with you."

We got up and started heading back to the shrine.

As we walked through the winding corridors, the soft patter of our footsteps echoed gently, creating a rhythmic cadence that seemed to lull the world into a peaceful slumber. After a few turns, we arrived at a chamber tucked away in a quiet corner of the shrine. The room was modest but cozy, with a few beds lined up against the walls, each draped with soft linens and adorned with hand-stitched quilts.

I gestured for Papa Yamah to choose a bed, and he settled on one near the window, where the soft light of the moon filtered through the curtains. I took the bed opposite him, and as we both got comfortable, the room was filled with a comfortable silence, a momentary pause before the floodgates of memories and emotions were opened.

After a few moments, I cleared my throat, breaking the silence. "It's been so long, Papa Yamah. So much has happened since Bryson Village."

He nodded, his eyes distant. "Far too long, Ezekiel."

There was a moment of silence.

"What happened that day…?" I asked.

Papa Yamah's gaze grew distant, lost in the memories of that fateful day. "There was so much chaos…so much destruction... Vajra killing Elijah. And then you... your transformation into a Dark Dragon. The sheer power, the raw, unbridled rage of your Dark Dragon form... it was terrifying."

He paused, taking a deep breath as he continued, "The ensuing battle was intense. The shock waves from the clashes, the explosions... I was caught in one of them. It sent me flying, and for a moment, everything went black. When I regained consciousness, the village was in ruins, and there was no sign of anyone. My heart refused to accept it, but my mind feared the worst—that I had lost you to the same fate as Elijah."

"Where were you all this time?" I pressed, needing to bridge the gap that time had carved between us.

Papa Yamah's gaze turned inward, reflecting on the years spent in shadow. "I sought refuge in Serenity's Edge, a place that had once been a sanctuary to me. There, amidst old allies, I sought any clue of your whereabouts. But Vajra's shadow loomed large, and my search was fraught with danger. Despite my efforts, there was no trace of you. I was convinced that I had lost you forever."

The revelation was a balm and a blade all at once, soothing the ache of abandonment while laying bare the depth of Papa Yamah's torment.

The chamber, lit only by the soft, flickering glow of lanterns, seemed to close in around us, its shadows dancing eerily on the walls. Each flicker cast a new pattern of light and darkness, mirroring the turmoil within me.

Taking a deep breath, I found the courage to speak. "I am so sorry, Papa," I said, my voice barely above a whisper. The words felt inadequate, too small to convey the depth of my regret. "Everything that's happened... it's because of me."

"You have nothing to be sorry about, Ezekiel," he replied, his voice steady and reassuring. "What happened that day was beyond your control. You couldn't have known."

The weight of Papa Yamah's words pressed heavily upon me, yet they did little to lift the burden of guilt that had settled in my heart. "But I was the one," I insisted, the words catching in my throat, "I was the one who destroyed our home, our village. Knowing that... it's like a poison in my veins, eating away at me from the inside out."

Papa Yamah's expression softened, a mixture of sorrow and understanding in his eyes. "Ezekiel, my boy," he began, his voice imbued with a gentle firmness, "the power that surged through you that day, the transformation into the Dark Dragon—it was a force of nature, untamed and uncontrollable. You were but a vessel for a power far greater than any of us could have anticipated."

I tried to absorb his words, to find solace in the idea that it wasn't my fault, but the guilt was a relentless shadow, darkening every thought. "I can't help but feel responsible," I admitted, my voice breaking under the weight of the confession. "Every time I close my eyes, I see the flames, the destruction... I hear the screams. It haunts me, Papa. How do I live with that? How do I forgive myself?"

Papa Yamah reached out, placing a hand on my shoulder, a gesture of support and solidarity. "Forgiveness, especially of oneself, is a journey, not a destination," he said, his gaze holding mine. "You carry a heavy burden, but you do not carry it alone. We will walk this path together, step by step, day by day. Healing is possible, Ezekiel, but it takes time, and it takes courage—the courage to face the past, to accept it, and to move forward."

His words, though comforting, were a balm to a wound that felt too deep to heal. Yet, in his presence, I found a glimmer of hope. Perhaps, in time, I could learn to forgive myself, to find peace amidst the ruins of my past. But for now, the journey ahead seemed long and fraught with shadows.

I looked down, grappling with the emotions swirling inside me. "Papa Yamah," I began again, my voice trembling with the weight of what I was about to reveal. "There's something I need to tell you. Something important, and... it might be hard for you to believe."

The words hung in the air between us, a confession poised on the brink of revelation. In that dimly lit chamber, with the shadows playing their silent dance, I prepared to unveil a truth that could change everything.

I took a deep breath, the weight of the revelation pressing heavily on my chest. "Elijah... he's alive."

Papa Yamah's eyes widened in shock, and for a moment, he was rendered speechless. "But... how? I saw Vajra kill him. I saw his lifeless body."

I nodded, "I thought the same. But he survived, and he's not the same."

Papa Yamah's expression grew somber. "What do you mean?"

I swallowed hard, choosing my words carefully. "Elijah is consumed with hate and revenge. He blames dragons and Dragon Slayers for everything that's happened. He's on a path of destruction, and I fear what he might do next."

Papa Yamah's face paled, the implications of my words sinking in. "We need to find him, Ezekiel. Before he does something he'll regret."

I nodded in agreement, "Yes, we do. But it won't be easy. Elijah is determined, and he won't stop until he feels justice has been served."

"Could you please tell me everything that's happened up until now?" he asked.

Papa Yamah listened intently, his eyes never leaving mine as I poured out the details of my journey – the trials, the battles, and the revelations that had shaped my path. As I spoke of Aquaria, Terra, and Ignicia, and the harrowing battle against Elijah, his expression was a mix of concern and pride.

When I finally spoke of Yrome's return, the room fell into a heavy silence, the gravity of the situation settling around us like a thick cloak. Papa Yamah leaned back against the bed rest, his gaze thoughtful, absorbing the magnitude of what I had shared.

After a moment, he spoke, his voice filled with a warmth that reached deep into my heart. "Ezekiel, you've grown so much," he said, a hint of emotion coloring his words. "You've faced challenges that would have broken many, but you've stood strong. I'm proud of you, more than words can express."

He paused, his eyes reflecting the flickering lantern light. "But this situation with Yrome... it's more dire than we could have imagined. His return marks a dark turn in our struggle. We're not just fighting for our survival now; we're fighting for the very soul of our world."

Papa Yamah's words resonated with a deep truth, echoing the fears and uncertainties that had been gnawing at me. His acknowledgment of my growth, coupled with the blatant reality of Yrome's threat, solidified my resolve.

Still, an important question haunted me. I hesitated, my heart pounding in my chest, as I wrestled with the fear and uncertainty that had gripped me. I took a moment, gathering my thoughts, before finally mustering all the courage I had. "Papa,"

I began, my voice steady but filled with emotion, my gaze meeting Papa Yamah's, "did you know? Did you know all along that Elijah and I... that we were dragons?"

Papa Yamah's eyes widened slightly, and he seemed taken aback by the question. He looked away, his gaze distant, as if lost in a sea of memories. The silence stretched on, becoming almost unbearable. I could feel my heart racing, waiting for his answer.

Finally, he let out a deep sigh, his shoulders sagging as if carrying the weight of a heavy burden. "Ezekiel," he began, his voice filled with a mix of regret and sadness, "it's... complicated."

I felt a pang of frustration. "Complicated? How? Just tell me the truth."

Papa Yamah looked back at me, his eyes filled with sincerity. "I promise, I will explain everything. But for now, all you need to know is that discovering the truth about you and Elijah... it changed everything for me. It's the reason I couldn't continue as a Dragon Slayer. You two... you were the catalyst for my change of heart."

I stared at him, trying to process his words. A whirlwind of emotions swirled within me - confusion, anger, relief. The weight of the revelations, combined with the lingering questions, threatened to overwhelm me.

"Why won't you tell me?" I pressed, my voice rising with a mix of desperation and frustration. "After everything we've been through, after all these years, don't I deserve to know the truth?"

Papa Yamah's gaze met mine, and for a moment, I saw a vulnerability in his eyes that I had never seen before. "Ezekiel," he began, his voice heavy with emotion, "it's not that I don't want to tell you. It's just... the truth is painful. It's a burden I've carried for so long, and I've always hoped to spare you from it."

I clenched my fists, feeling the heat of anger rise within me. "Spare me? By keeping me in the dark? By letting me believe lies? How is that sparing me?"

He took a deep breath, his shoulders sagging. "I wanted to protect you, to shield you from the harsh realities of our world. But I realize now that perhaps I was wrong. Perhaps you deserve to know, no matter how painful it might be."

I leaned forward, my eyes locked onto his. "Then tell me, Papa. Tell me everything."

Papa Yamah hesitated for a moment, then nodded slowly. "Alright," he whispered, his voice filled with a mix of resignation and determination. "It's time you knew the whole truth."

3

Reduced to Ashes

Papa Yamah's voice was low, almost a whisper, as if he was sharing a sacred secret. "One day, many years ago, when I was still a young man, I felt a sudden, powerful force in the land. It was unlike anything I had ever experienced. It was the power of a dragon, but not just any dragon. It was immense, overwhelming."

I leaned in, my heart pounding in my chest. This was it, the truth I had been seeking.

Papa Yamah continued, "I was the leader of the Dragon Slayers back then, and Vajra was just a young teenager, learning from me. We, along with some of the other Dragon Slayers, sensed this incredible power. We had to investigate; it was our duty."

"Wait," I interrupted. "You were the leader of the Dragon Slayers?"

Papa Yamah looked at me with sad eyes. "I was."

DRAGON'S FIRE

How could this be? The man who had shown me kindness, who had taught me about life, about survival, was once the leader of those who hunted my brethren. It was a paradox that I struggled to reconcile. The man I had looked up to, who had been a father figure to me, was also the man who had once embodied everything I had come to despise.

I simply looked down, breaking my gaze from him. "Go on…" I whispered.

He paused, his eyes distant as if he was seeing the past unfold before him. "I told the other Dragon Slayers that I would go on ahead and investigate. I followed the source of the power. It led me to a hidden cave, tucked away in a place where no one would think to look. What I found there… it changed everything."

I could barely breathe, hanging on to his every word. "What did you find?"

"I found two baby dragons," he said, his voice imbued with a sense of wonder. "Tiny, fragile creatures, curled up together. It was you and Elijah."

He paused, allowing the memory to wash over him. "There you were, so small, so innocent. The moment I laid eyes on you, I felt something shift inside me. The power that radiated from you both was unmistakable, yet there was a vulnerability that I couldn't ignore."

I listened, captivated by the image he painted – a picture of our earliest, most vulnerable selves, a beginning I had never known.

Papa Yamah continued, his gaze meeting mine. "When I approached, something remarkable happened. You both reverted, right before my eyes, back to your human forms. Little babies. It was then I knew – you were no ordinary dragons. You were something more, something extraordinary."

I could see Papa Yamah's eyes watering.

"From the moment I laid eyes on you and Elijah, I knew that my life, my purpose, had changed forever. I couldn't bring myself to harm two innocent and helpless babies. Even if you were dragons, there had to be another way. Instead, I took you in, and disappeared, never to be seen by the Dragon Slayers again. It was because of you and Elijah that I eventually turned my back on being a Dragon Slayer. You showed me that there was another way, a path of coexistence and understanding."

I stared at Papa Yamah, my mind grappling with the image of Elijah and me as infants, alone in a cave. "But how is that possible?" I asked, my voice tinged with disbelief. "How could we have been there all by ourselves? Was there no one else around? Was there anything else that could explain it?"

He shook his head slowly, his eyes reflecting the same questions that were swirling in my mind. "I don't know, Ezekiel," he admitted, his voice tinged with frustration. "When I found you, it was just the two of you, alone in that cave. There was no sign of anyone else, no clue as to how you got there or why you were left there."

His words hung in the air, adding to the mystery that shrouded our origins. The idea that Elijah and I had been abandoned, left to fend for ourselves in a cave, was both baffling and distressing. It raised more questions than answers. Who had left us there? Why were we abandoned? And most importantly, where had we come from?

"There was something else," he said, his voice tinged with a hint of mystery. "Around each of your necks, there was a necklace. Simple, yet clearly precious. On each, a name was inscribed – 'Ezekiel' on yours, and 'Elijah' on your brother's."

He paused, as if visualizing the scene once more in his mind's eye. "Those necklaces... they were like a silent message, a clue to your identities. It was as if someone, perhaps your parents, had left them there for a reason. Maybe as a way to ensure that, should you ever be found, your names and your heritage would be known."

I absorbed his words, each one adding a piece to the puzzle of my past. The idea that our parents had left us with such a personal token, a connection to our true selves, filled me with a mix of sadness and curiosity.

I felt a surge of emotions, a mix of betrayal and confusion. "So, all those stories you told us about knowing our parents, about your promise to them to protect us... was all of that just a lie?" I asked, my voice trembling.

Papa Yamah's face was etched with remorse, and he sighed deeply. "Ezekiel, I... I didn't know how to tell you the truth. I thought those stories would give you a sense of belonging, a sense of being wanted and loved. I wanted to protect you from the harsh reality of being abandoned."

I clenched my fists, feeling a mix of anger and sadness. "But why lie? Why create a false history for us? Didn't you think we deserved to know the truth?"

He nodded slowly, his voice heavy with regret. "You're right. You did deserve to know the truth. But I was afraid. Afraid that the truth would hurt you more. I thought that by giving you a story, a sense of identity, it would help you grow stronger."

I shook my head, struggling to process his words. "But it was all a fabrication. Our entire childhood, the foundation of who we thought we were... it was built on lies."

Papa Yamah reached out, as if to offer comfort, but I pulled away. "I know, and I'm sorry. I truly am. I thought I was doing what was best for you, but I see now that I was wrong. I should have been honest with you from the beginning."

His apology, sincere as it was, did little to ease the turmoil inside me. The revelation that our past, our very identity, was shrouded in mystery and falsehoods left me feeling adrift, unsure of who I really was. It was a bitter pill to swallow, and one that would take time to come to terms with.

The room felt heavy with unspoken words and unresolved emotions. Papa Yamah's revelations about his past and the truth about Elijah and me had left me reeling. I felt a mix of anger, confusion, and betrayal. The man who raised me, who I thought I knew, was a stranger in some ways. The weight of his lies and omissions pressed down on me, suffocating.

I turned away from him, my mind a whirlwind of thoughts. "We need to rest," I said curtly, cutting off any further conversation. "We can finish this tomorrow."

Papa Yamah opened his mouth as if to say something, but then closed it, nodding silently. The tension between us was palpable, a gulf that had opened up with his confessions.

I lay down on my bed, my back to him, feeling a mix of exhaustion and restlessness. Sleep seemed like an impossible luxury, yet I knew we needed it. The emotional toll of the day had drained me, and the revelations had only added to the burden.

As I closed my eyes, trying to find some semblance of peace in the turmoil, sleep remained elusive. The revelations kept replaying in my mind, each one a stab of betrayal. Just as I felt myself slipping into a fitful doze, a sudden explosion shattered the night.

My eyes snapped open, and I was on my feet in an instant. Another explosion followed, the sounds of screaming villagers piercing the night. I glanced at Papa Yamah, who was already up, his expression a mix of alarm and determination.

"We need to move, now!" he said, urgency in his voice.

We hurriedly dressed and rushed out of the chamber, the sounds of chaos growing louder with each step. The peaceful night had turned into a nightmare, the village under attack, its tranquility shattered by violence and fear.

As we raced towards the heart of the village, the flames and cries of the villagers guided our path. The night had taken a dark and unexpected turn, and we were thrust into the midst of a battle we hadn't anticipated.

As we dashed through the chaos, the village was a blur of flames and terror. We spotted Gaianor and Camila in the distance, their faces etched with confusion and concern. We ran over to them, the urgency of the situation propelling us forward.

"What's happening?" I asked, panting from the sprint.

Gaianor shook his head, his expression grim. "We don't know. It came out of nowhere. Explosions, fire... it's chaos."

Camila's eyes were wide with fear. "We can't see who is attacking. It's like they're striking from the shadows."

We scanned the surroundings, trying to make sense of the situation, but the attacker remained elusive, hidden in the darkness. The villagers were running in panic, trying to escape the sudden onslaught.

Then, without warning, a deafening roar split the night, sending shivers down our spines. We looked up, and there, soaring above the village, was a dragon. Its scales glinted in the firelight, a majestic yet terrifying sight.

It let out another roar, a sound filled with rage and power, and then it unleashed a barrage of fireballs, raining destruction upon the village.

My heart sank as I recognized the dragon. "It's Elijah," I whispered, disbelief and horror mingling in my voice.

Gaianor's eyes widened. "Elijah? How did…"

Before he could finish, another explosion rocked the village, cutting him off. We watched helplessly as Elijah's dragon form continued its assault, the village helpless against his fury.

"We need to do something," I said, determination steeling my voice. "We can't let him destroy everything."

"Elijah!" Papa Yamah shouted.

"It won't do any good," I said. "Elijah can't control that form. He can't hear you."

"I see…" Papa Yamah nodded. "Then we need to protect the villagers."

Camila's voice cut through the chaos, her tone firm and decisive. "Gaianor and I will transform. We'll try to distract Elijah, draw his attention away from the village."

Gaianor nodded in agreement, his eyes set with determination. "It's the best chance we have. We need to buy time for the villagers to escape."

I looked at them, a mix of gratitude and concern in my eyes. "Be careful. Elijah is extremely powerful and... he's not himself."

Camila gave me a reassuring smile, though I could see the worry lurking behind it. "We'll be fine. Just focus on helping the villagers."

"Ezekiel," Papa Yamah said. "We need to act fast. Every second counts."

I nodded, feeling the weight of responsibility settle on my shoulders. "Let's do this."

With a final nod to each other, we split up. Camila and Gaianor headed towards an open space, preparing to transform into their dragon forms, while Papa Yamah and I plunged into the heart of the village, where screams and cries for help echoed through the night.

The scene was one of utter devastation. Buildings were ablaze, their flames casting an eerie glow on the panicked faces of the villagers as they tried to flee. The heat was intense, the air thick with smoke and the smell of burning.

Papa Yamah and I moved quickly, helping wherever we could. We guided the villagers towards safety, carried the injured, and did our best to douse the fires that threatened to consume everything.

Above us, Camila and Gaianor, now in their dragon forms, soared into the sky, their roars challenging Elijah's. They weaved through the air, drawing his attention, their scales shimmering in the firelight.

I couldn't help but glance up, watching as they engaged Elijah, hoping against hope that they could bring him back to his senses. But deep down, I knew it wouldn't be easy. Elijah's dragon form was a manifestation of his rage, a rage that had been festering for far too long.

"We need to keep moving, Ezekiel," Papa Yamah urged, snapping me back to the task at hand.

As Papa Yamah and I continued our relentless efforts on the ground, the battle in the skies raged on with ferocious intensity. Every so often, amidst the chaos and the roar of flames, I caught glimpses of the aerial combat unfolding above.

Elijah was a formidable sight. He moved with a grace and power that was almost hypnotic, his wings cutting through the air with lethal precision.

Camila and Gaianor were locked in a desperate struggle against him. Camila's Water Dragon form was a stark contrast to Elijah's fiery presence. Her scales glistened like the surface of a tranquil ocean, and her movements were fluid and graceful. Every so often, she unleashed powerful jets of water from her maw, not only striking at Elijah but also dousing some of the flames that threatened to consume the village.

Gaianor, with his Earth Dragon form, was a bastion of strength and resilience. His earthy, rugged scales seemed to absorb the light, giving him an almost stoic appearance. He maneuvered through the air with a deliberate, calculated grace, his tail whipping through the air like a deadly weapon.

The three dragons danced a deadly ballet in the night sky, a whirlwind of fire, water, and earth. The clash of their powers sent shockwaves through the air.

Despite the terror of the situation, there was a part of me that couldn't help but be awestruck by the spectacle. The raw power, the elemental fury—it was both terrifying and mesmerizing.

But even as I watched, my heart ached with the knowledge that this was no mere display of power.

As Camila once again unleashed a torrent of water, dousing another section of the village in a much-needed reprieve from the flames, I felt a surge of gratitude. But it was quickly overshadowed by the urgency of the situation, the need to end this conflict before it claimed any more lives.

The chaos of the village was momentarily pierced by a sudden, brilliant light emanating from its center. A swirling vortex of energy materialized, its edges shimmering with an otherworldly glow. From within this portal, a figure stepped out, her presence commanding even amidst the pandemonium.

It was Aria, the Dragon Slayer known for her portal magic.

Papa Yamah's voice cut through the noise, a mixture of recognition and dread. "Aria," he uttered, his tone betraying a history that went beyond mere acquaintance.

Almost simultaneously, a scream tore through the night, jolting me with its urgency. It was a sound I knew all too well—Gloria's voice, emanating from the direction of the shrine.

Papa Yamah and I exchanged a quick, knowing glance. The unspoken understanding between us was clear. He turned to me, his expression resolute. "I'll handle Aria. You go to the shrine."

I nodded, my heart pounding in my chest. "Be careful," I said, the concern evident in my voice.

Papa Yamah gave me a brief nod, a silent promise. Then, without another word, he moved towards Aria.

I turned and sprinted towards the shrine, my legs pumping with adrenaline. The night air was thick with smoke and the cries of the villagers, but Gloria's scream echoed in my mind, urging me on.

As I neared the shrine, the sense of foreboding grew. My breath came in ragged gasps, and my muscles burned with exertion, but I pushed on, driven by a singular purpose.

Reaching the entrance, I paused for a moment, gathering my strength. Then, with a deep breath, I stepped inside, ready to face whatever awaited me. The fate of Gloria, and perhaps the fate of the entire village, hung in the balance.

The shrine, once a sanctuary of serenity and reverence, was now a scene of devastation. As I stepped inside, my heart sank at the sight before me. The once immaculate walls were marred with scorch marks, and debris littered the floor. Holes punctured the ceiling, allowing moonlight to stream in, casting eerie shadows across the chaos.

I moved quickly, my eyes scanning the wreckage for any sign of Gloria. The throne room, once a place of counsel and wisdom, was now a jumble of overturned chairs and shattered artifacts. I stepped over the remnants of what had been sacred relics, my heart pounding with a growing sense of dread.

The dining hall, where we had shared meals and laughter, was unrecognizable. Tables were upturned, and the remnants of meals lay scattered, a testament to the abruptness of the attack. I called out Gloria's name, my voice echoing through the desolation, but there was no response.

I continued my frantic search, checking every room, every corner, but Gloria was nowhere to be found. The air was thick with the acrid smell of smoke, and the crackling of flames added to the cacophony of destruction.

Then, amidst the chaos, I heard it—a distant explosion. It was coming from Ytfen's Gardens.

I turned and ran towards the gardens, my mind racing with possibilities. The explosion could mean anything, but one thing was certain: Gloria, or whoever was responsible for her disappearance, might be there.

As I dashed through the corridors, the destruction around me blurred into a whirlwind of motion. The gardens were not far, but with each step, the sense of urgency grew. The fate of Gloria, and perhaps the fate of us all, hung in the balance.

The garden was engulfed in flames, its splendor reduced to ashes and embers. The sight was a stark contrast to the peaceful haven it once was, and my heart ached at the destruction.

Amidst the chaos, my eyes found Gloria. She lay on the ground, her body trembling, her eyes wide with terror. The sight of her, so vulnerable and frightened, sent a jolt of fear through me.

Then, I saw him. Yrome. He stood there, a figure of imposing power, his red eyes glowing like embers in the night. His silver hair cascaded down his back. The air around him seemed to crackle with energy.

Panic surged within me, a tidal wave of fear and uncertainty. Yrome's presence was overwhelming, his power level beyond anything I had ever encountered. The air felt heavy, charged with a tension that made it hard to breathe.

I took a step forward, my mind racing. Every instinct screamed at me to flee, to escape the danger that Yrome represented. But I couldn't leave Gloria. I couldn't abandon her to this fate.

Swallowing hard, I tried to steady my breathing, to calm the storm of emotions that threatened to overwhelm me. Sword in hand, I forced myself to focus.

As I stood there, my mind raced through a whirlwind of possibilities, each scenario playing out with its own set of risks and outcomes.

The first thought that came to mind was to transform into my dragon form. The power and strength it would grant me could be the key to confronting Yrome. But transforming would undoubtedly draw Elijah's attention, potentially turning the situation into an even more chaotic and dangerous confrontation. Moreover, the sheer force of my transformation could harm Gloria, who lay vulnerable and terrified on the ground. The risk was too great.

Another option was to approach Yrome stealthily, using the cover of the garden's remaining foliage and the chaos around us. I could attempt to catch him off guard, to somehow incapacitate him without direct confrontation. But as I considered this, I realized the futility of such a plan. Yrome's senses were likely far too keen, and his reaction time too quick for such a tactic to succeed. It was a gamble with slim chances of success.

Could I reason with Yrome? The thought seemed almost laughable. He didn't appear to be here for dialogue.

Maybe I could distract him? Creating a distraction seemed like the most viable option. If I could divert Yrome's attention, even for a moment, it might give me a chance to get Gloria to safety. But what could possibly distract someone as powerful as Yrome? And would I be quick enough to save her?

Each scenario played out in my mind, a rapid-fire succession of possibilities and dangers. The decision I made in the next few moments could mean life or death. I took a deep breath, trying to calm the storm of thoughts.

Before I could make a decision, the air shifted, and a chill ran down my spine. Yrome had moved.

My heart pounded in my chest, a frantic drumbeat echoing the surge of adrenaline that flooded my system. I didn't dare move, didn't dare breathe. The sense of danger was overwhelming, a primal instinct screaming that I was in the presence of a predator unlike any other.

He was already behind me.

"Do you truly believe you can stop me?" Yrome said, his voice resonating with an otherworldly timbre, echoing around me like the rumble of distant thunder.

Gloria's voice, strained and weak, pierced through the paralyzing fear that held me captive. "Run, Ezekiel!" she gasped, her eyes wide with urgency. "You must flee! You're not ready to face him, not yet. You're not strong enough!"

Her words echoed in my mind, a desperate plea from a mentor who had always guided me with wisdom and strength. But in that moment, her voice was tinged with a vulnerability that I had never heard before. It was the sound of fear, of a deep understanding of the insurmountable power that Yrome possessed.

I stood there, my feet rooted to the ground, my body refusing to obey. Fear, confusion, and a sense of duty warred within me. How could I run and leave Gloria behind? How could I turn my back on the village that had become my home? Yet, her words rang with a truth that I couldn't deny—I was not ready for this battle.

As these thoughts raced through my mind, Gloria gathered the last vestiges of her strength. Her body trembled, but her resolve was unyielding. With a cry that was both a battle cry and a farewell, she unleashed a torrent of blinding light, a beam of pure, concentrated energy that shot towards Yrome with the fury of a thousand suns.

The light illuminated the garden, casting long, dancing shadows and turning the night into day. It was a display of power that was both beautiful and terrifying, a testament to Gloria's will to protect, even in the face of certain defeat.

For a brief moment, time seemed to stand still, the world holding its breath as the beam of light collided with Yrome's formidable presence. But even as the light enveloped him, I knew it was not enough. Yrome was a being beyond the constraints of mere power, a force that seemed to exist outside the laws of nature.

Gloria's attack, valiant as it was, only served as a distraction, a fleeting obstacle in Yrome's path.

As Gloria's beam of light erupted in a dazzling display of power, she quickly closed the distance between us. In a swift motion, she embraced me, and the world around us seemed to dissolve into nothingness. Suddenly, we were no longer in the burning garden, but in a place that defied all sense of reality—a mindscape where we stood facing each other, floating in an expanse of void.

The transition was disorienting, the sudden shift from the chaos of battle to this serene, almost surreal environment.

Around us, there was nothing but an endless expanse of emptiness, a space devoid of time and matter.

Gloria stood before me, her expression calm yet resolute. In this mindscape, the weariness and fear that had marked her face moments ago were gone, replaced by a clarity and strength that seemed to emanate from her very being.

"Ezekiel," she said, her voice tinged with a mixture of strength and weariness, "I've brought us here, to this mindscape, but time is a fickle thing here. It flows differently, and I can't be certain how much we have. Every moment here could be precious seconds slipping away in the real world."

I could sense the gravity of her words, the unspoken truth that lingered between us. "Gloria, what are you saying?"

She took a deep breath, her gaze unwavering. "I believe in you, Ezekiel. I believe that you have the power to stop Yrome, to change the course of this war. But not yet. You're not ready to face him, not in your current state. He is a force unlike any other, a being whose power we can scarcely comprehend."

Her words echoed in the vast emptiness of the mindscape, each syllable carrying the weight of unspoken fears and hopes. "You must survive, Ezekiel. You must grow stronger, learn more about your abilities, and gather allies. There will come a time when you'll stand against Yrome, but that time is not now."

I felt a pang of frustration, a desire to fight, to protect, but her words rang true. "How can I just leave you here? How can I run away?"

Gloria's expression softened, a maternal warmth radiating from her. "Sometimes, the bravest thing we can do is to choose when to fight and when to retreat. Your journey is far from over, and there are battles ahead that only you can fight. You carry within you a potential that even Yrome fears. Trust in that, trust in yourself."

Her words were like a beacon in the darkness, guiding me through the turmoil of my thoughts. "I'll do it, Gloria. I'll find a way to stop him."

Gloria's eyes held a depth of resolve as she spoke, "Before you go, there is something I must bestow upon you. It's crucial that you understand the truth, the full scope of our history, the very essence of the conflict that has torn our world apart."

I could feel the intensity of her gaze, the weight of the moment pressing upon us. "The truth?" I echoed, my heart racing with anticipation and apprehension.

"Yes, the truth about the war between dragons and Dragon Slayers, the origins of this endless cycle of hatred and destruction." Her voice was steady, imbued with a sense of solemnity. "You need to see it through the eyes of one who witnessed it all, one who bore the burden of those tumultuous times."

She reached out, her hand hovering just above my forehead. "I will share with you Ytfen's memories. His experiences, his perspectives, the events that shaped our world as we know it. Through his eyes, you will see the genesis of the war, the choices made, and the consequences that followed."

A sense of awe and trepidation washed over me. "Ytfen's memories? But how?"

Gloria's expression was one of determination. "As the guardian of Ash Village, I've been entrusted with the legacy of Ytfen, the wisdom and memories of the ancient Dragon King.

It's a sacred duty, one that I now pass onto you, in part. You must see the truth for yourself, Ezekiel. It's the only way you can truly understand what's at stake and find a way to stop Yrome."

I nodded, a mixture of honor and responsibility settling in my chest. "I'm ready, Gloria. Show me."

With a gentle touch, she connected with my mind, and a flood of images, emotions, and memories cascaded into my consciousness. As the memories from Ytfen began to flow into me, I found myself transported to another time, another place. I was no longer Ezekiel, standing in the present; I was Ytfen, on the most significant day of my life.

Limitless Love (5500 Years Ago)

The air was filled with the sweet fragrance of blooming flowers, their petals dancing gently in the soft breeze. The sun shone brightly, casting a warm, golden glow over the lush gardens that surrounded the ceremonial grounds. It was my wedding day, and the atmosphere was one of joy and celebration.

I stood at the altar, adorned in ceremonial robes that bore the intricate symbols of my lineage – a lineage that traced back to the ancient dragon kings. The fabric was a rich, deep blue, embroidered with threads of silver that shimmered in the sunlight, reflecting my status and heritage.

Before me was an aisle, lined with smiling faces of friends, family, and dignitaries from distant lands. They had all come to witness this union, a union that symbolized not just the love between two individuals, but the promise of a future filled with hope and unity.

At the end of the aisle, Denise appeared, her beauty taking my breath away. She was a vision in her wedding gown, which flowed around her like a cascade of moonlight. Her hair was adorned with flowers that matched those in the garden, and her eyes sparkled with happiness and love.

As Denise gracefully approached the altar, each step she took was like a verse in a love song, her presence illuminating the space around her. The guests, a sea of familiar and friendly faces, watched in silent reverence, captivated by the moment. The garden, bathed in the golden light of the afternoon sun, was alive with the vibrant colors of blooming flowers, their petals fluttering gently in the breeze.

Our eyes met, and in that gaze, I found a universe of shared dreams and unspoken promises. Her hand, delicate yet strong, slipped into mine, sending a current of profound emotion through me. It was a touch that spoke of years of companionship, of challenges overcome, and of a future ripe with potential.

We turned together to face the officiant, my mother, Sonia. Her presence was a comforting anchor, her eyes reflecting the pride and love of a lifetime. She had always been a pillar of wisdom and strength in our lives and having her officiate our union made the moment all the more poignant.

"Today, we gather not just to witness the union of Ytfen and Denise," Sonia began, her voice resonating with warmth and authority, "but to celebrate the joining of two hearts, two souls, bound by a love as deep as the roots of the earth and as enduring as the stars in the sky."

Denise and I exchanged a tender glance, our hands clasped tightly. Sonia continued, weaving the ancient traditions of our people with the personal journey Denise and I had embarked upon together. She spoke of the dragon heritage that coursed through our veins, a legacy of power and responsibility that we were now to carry forward together.

When it came time to exchange vows, Denise's voice was clear and filled with emotion. "Ytfen, in you, I have found my partner, my protector, and my best friend. I vow to stand by your side, to share in your joys and your sorrows, to support your dreams, and to build a future that honors both our heritage and our love."

As I spoke my vows in return, my voice was steady, but my heart raced with the magnitude of the moment. "Denise, you are my light in the darkest of times, my joy in moments of despair. I vow to cherish you, to respect you, and to love you with all that I am and all that I will become. Together, we will forge a path that honors the past and embraces the future."

The exchange of rings was a sacred moment, the metal cool and heavy in our hands. These rings, crafted from the rarest ores and imbued with the essence of our dragon lineage, symbolized a bond that transcended time and place.

Sonia's voice rang out, strong and clear, "By the power vested in me, I now pronounce you husband and wife. May your union be as unbreakable as the mountains and as eternal as the stars."

The crowd erupted in cheers and applause, a symphony of joy and celebration. Denise and I turned to face our friends and family, our hearts overflowing with gratitude and love. Musicians, stationed near a beautifully adorned pavilion, began to play a lively melody, the notes floating through the air like joyful birdsong.

As the musicians played, a group of dragons soared overhead. Their presence was both awe-inspiring and harmonious with the celebration below. The dragons, glided gracefully across the sky. Their wings, vast and powerful, caught the light, casting intricate patterns of shadows and light over the gathered crowd. As they flew, they let out a series of deep, resonant roars, adding a primal, exhilarating note to the symphony of the celebration.

Denise and I stood hand in hand, our eyes following our fellow dragons as they danced in the sky, before making our way to the center of the pavilion. The wooden floor, polished to a shine, reflected the late afternoon sun, casting a warm, inviting glow. Our first dance as a married couple was a moment of pure magic. As we moved together, the world seemed to fade away, leaving just the two of us, lost in the rhythm and in each other.

"You're an incredible dancer," I whispered to Denise, my heart swelling with love.

She laughed, a sound more melodious than the music itself. "Only because I have an incredible partner," she replied, her eyes sparkling with happiness.

Around us, the guests joined in, the pavilion becoming a whirl of colors and movement. Friends and family, young and old, danced with abandon, their laughter mingling with the music to create a symphony of celebration.

Tables laden with a feast of delicacies lined the edges of the pavilion. The air was rich with the aromas of roasted meats, freshly baked bread, and sweet pastries. Servers moved gracefully among the guests, offering trays of fine wines and exotic fruits.

As the evening sky turned to a tapestry of twilight hues, lanterns hanging from the trees and pavilion rafters were lit, casting a soft, enchanting light over the festivities. The garden transformed into a scene from a fairytale, a perfect backdrop for the tales of love and adventure shared by the guests.

"To the king and queen!" a voice called out, and a cheer went up from the crowd. Glasses were raised in a toast, the clinking sound like a bell of joy and good fortune.

The night deepened, but the energy of the celebration never waned. Stories were exchanged, old friendships rekindled, and new bonds formed. It was a night of unity and joy, a fitting start to a life that promised to be filled with love, adventure, and the continuation of a legacy that stretched back through the ages.

Amidst the joyous celebration, I found myself drawn to a serene pond nestled within the gardens. The water, calm and clear, reflected the starlit sky above, creating a tranquil oasis amidst the festivities. Denise, sensing my need for a brief respite, smiled understandingly and joined me by the water's edge.

As I gazed into the pond, my reflection stared back at me. The soft light of the stars illuminated my features, casting a gentle glow on my face. My black hair, which fell to my shoulders in a cascade of dark waves, framed my face, adding a touch of elegance to my appearance. My athletic build, a testimony to years of training and battles, was subtly outlined by the fine fabric of my wedding attire.

My eyes, large and dark, reflected the depth of the emotions I felt on this momentous day. They were the windows to my soul, revealing the strength, determination, and love that defined me as a leader, a husband, and a dragon.

Denise, standing beside me, placed her hand gently on my arm. "You look perfect," she whispered, her voice filled with love and admiration.

I turned to her, my heart swelling with affection. In her eyes, I saw not just my reflection, but the reflection of our shared dreams and hopes for the future. Together, by the tranquil pond, under the canopy of stars, we shared a moment of quiet reflection, a moment that captured the essence of our bond and the journey that lay ahead.

As the night of celebration continued, its vibrant energy undiminished, one of my guards approached, his expression serious amidst the revelry. He leaned in, his voice barely audible over the music and laughter.

"Your Majesty, the special guest you've been awaiting has arrived," he informed me, his eyes scanning the crowd cautiously.

I nodded, a sense of anticipation stirring within me. "Thank you. Please, lead the way."

I placed a hand on Denise's waist, as if to say, 'I'll be right back.'

Weaving through the throng of dancing and chatting guests, I felt a curious sensation, as if the world around me was beginning to flicker, the edges of my vision blurring in and out. It was a subtle reminder that these were memories, and I was still Ezekiel, experiencing Ytfen's past.

The guard led me to a secluded part of the garden, where a figure stood waiting, his presence commanding even in stillness. It was Yrome, the King of the human kingdom, his long black hair cascading down his back like a river of night. He was dressed in regal attire, befitting his status, yet there was an air of simplicity about him.

"King Yrome," I greeted him, extending a hand in a gesture of peace and unity. "Your presence honors us."

Yrome's eyes, dark and deep, met mine. "King Ytfen, the honor is mine. Your invitation is a symbol of the trust and cooperation we hope to build between our peoples."

His voice was calm, measured, yet there was an undercurrent of something I couldn't quite place. It was as if he held a secret, a depth of knowledge that went beyond the pleasantries of our conversation.

"I believe our union today marks the beginning of a new era," I said, the words feeling more significant than a mere diplomatic exchange.

"Indeed," Yrome replied, his gaze lingering on me for a moment longer than necessary. "An era of peace and prosperity, if we are wise enough to nurture it."

As we spoke, the world around me began to flicker more intensely, the static growing stronger. The sounds of the celebration seemed to fade in and out, a clear sign that Gloria's memory transfer was reaching its limit.

Before I could delve deeper into the conversation with Yrome, the garden, the guests, and the night itself began to dissolve into a whirl of colors and sounds. I felt myself being pulled back, the memory fading, leaving me with more questions than answers.

Serenity's Edge

Just as suddenly as it had begun, the memory ended, and I was back in the present, as Ezekiel. The vividness of the wedding, the conversation with Yrome, and the sense of an impending revelation lingered in my mind, a puzzle waiting to be solved.

I found myself back in the mindscape with Gloria, a newfound understanding dawning within me. "I see it now," I whispered, the weight of Ytfen's memories settling in my soul.

Gloria nodded, a look of pride and sadness mingling in her eyes. "The rest of his memories will reveal themselves in time. Go now, Ezekiel. Carry these memories, carry this truth, and find the path to peace. You have a destiny to fulfill, and a world to save. You are the onl--"

Her words abruptly cut off, her eyes widening in shock and pain. The mindscape began to dissolve, the ethereal landscape fading away as reality crashed back in with a jarring force.

I was back in the burning gardens, the heat of the flames licking at my skin. Yrome stood before me, his hand tightly gripping Gloria's throat, lifting her off the ground. She struggled, her feet kicking futilely as she gasped for air.

Yrome's other hand reached out, touching her forehead. "The Light Dragon will be mine," he declared, his voice resonating with a dark power. But as his hand made contact, his expression shifted from triumph to confusion, then to anger.

"This... this is not right," he growled, his grip on Gloria tightening. "Where is it?"

Gloria, despite her struggle to breathe, managed a defiant glare. "You will never have it, Yrome. You will never control the power of the Light Dragon."

Yrome's eyes narrowed, a dangerous glint in them. "We shall see about that," he hissed. But even as he spoke, there was a sense of uncertainty in his voice, a hint of doubt that hadn't been there before.

Without warning, a swirling vortex of light and shadow materialized behind me, its edges shimmering with an otherworldly energy. From within the swirling maelstrom, Papa Yamah emerged, his face etched with urgency and determination.

"Ezekiel, now!" he bellowed, reaching out to grab my arm. His eyes were wide, a mix of fear and steadfastness burning within them.

I hesitated for a fraction of a second, my gaze locked on Gloria's struggling form in Yrome's grasp. But Papa Yamah's grip was firm, insistent. "We have no time! We must go!"

The portal pulsed with a strange, pulsating rhythm, its colors shifting and blending in a hypnotic dance. I could feel its pull, a force that seemed to tug at the very core of my being.

As I took a step towards the portal, I cast one last look at Gloria. Her eyes met mine, and in that brief, silent exchange, I saw her message: Go. Live. Fight another day.

With a heavy heart and a sense of impending doom, I allowed Papa Yamah to pull me into the portal. The world around me twisted and turned, reality bending and warping in ways that defied comprehension. The last thing I saw before the portal enveloped us was Yrome's furious gaze, a promise of retribution burning in his eyes.

The portal deposited us in the heart of a village unlike any I had seen before. The air was heavy with the scent of damp earth and the distant croaking of frogs. The ground beneath my feet was soft and spongy, the soil rich and dark. Mist hung low over the water, shrouding the village in an ethereal veil.

The houses were perched on stilts, rising above the swampy terrain. Their structures were a patchwork of wood and reeds, with thatched roofs that seemed to blend seamlessly into the surrounding environment. Narrow wooden walkways connected the homes, snaking through the dense foliage and over the murky waters.

Villagers peered out from their windows and doorways, their faces a mix of curiosity and wariness. They were a hardy folk, their skin weathered by the elements and their eyes sharp and alert. Children clung to their parents, peeking out from behind legs and skirts, their wide eyes taking in the sudden appearance of strangers in their midst.

Papa Yamah steadied me as I stumbled, disoriented from the journey through the portal. My eyes quickly found Gaianor and Camila, both lying on a raised platform, their chests heaving with exhaustion. Their dragon forms had vanished, leaving them in their human guises, but the toll of their battle with Elijah was evident.

Then I saw her—Aria, the Dragon Slayer who had attacked our village. She stood a few feet away, her black cloak blending into the shadows of the swamp. Her eyes were fixed on me, and I felt a surge of anger and suspicion. Instinctively, I moved into a defensive stance, ready to confront her.

But Papa Yamah's hand on my shoulder stopped me. "Ezekiel, wait," he said firmly. "She's the reason we're alive. She saved us."

I turned to him, my confusion evident. "Saved us? She's a Dragon Slayer. She's our enemy."

Papa Yamah shook his head. "Not all Dragon Slayers are the same. Aria made a choice—a choice to help us. Without her, we wouldn't have escaped."

Aria stepped forward, her gaze unwavering. "I know my presence here is unsettling but believe me when I say my intentions are not to harm. The situation has changed, and we face a common enemy in Yrome. I couldn't stand by and watch him destroy everything."

Her words hung in the air, heavy with the weight of truth and the complexity of our situation. I could see the sincerity in her eyes, and despite my reservations, I began to lower my guard.

Gaianor, struggling to sit up, added his voice to the conversation. "She's telling the truth, Ezekiel. Aria opened the portal that allowed us to escape."

Camila, still lying on the ground, nodded weakly in agreement. "It's true. She saved us."

The revelation left me reeling, the lines between friend and foe blurring in a way I had never anticipated. I looked at Aria, then at Papa Yamah, Gaianor, and Camila. We were an unlikely group, brought together by circumstance and the looming threat of a powerful enemy.

"Alright," I said finally, my voice tinged with a mix of reluctance and acceptance. "If you're truly on our side, then we'll need to work together. But know this, Aria: any sign of betrayal, and I won't hesitate to act."

Aria nodded, a grim determination settling on her features. "Understood. And for what it's worth, I'm sorry for the pain my kind has caused. I hope, in time, we can find a way to mend what has been broken."

As the villagers began to emerge from their homes, their eyes filled with curiosity and concern, I realized that our journey had taken an unexpected turn.

Papa Yamah stepped forward, his gaze shifting between Aria and me. "I spoke with her in Ash Village," he began, his voice carrying a note of solemnity. "I used to lead her, back when I was a Dragon Slayer. Aria was always different, always questioning the path we were on. She had reservations, doubts about our cause, especially after I left, but she feared Vajra. His presence kept her in line."

He paused, his eyes darkening with the memory. "But now, with Vajra gone, Yrome has risen to power. And he's far worse than Vajra ever was. His methods, his goals... they're monstrous. Aria couldn't stand by and watch him lead the Dragon Slayers down this dark path. She reached out to me, seeking guidance, seeking a way out."

Aria's eyes met mine, and I saw a flicker of vulnerability in them. "Yamah is right," she said, her voice steady but tinged with emotion. "I've seen what Yrome is capable of, the destruction he brings. I can't be a part of that. I can't continue to serve under a banner that brings only pain and suffering. It's wrong, and I refuse to be a part of it any longer."

Her words resonated with a sincerity that was hard to ignore. I could see the conflict that had been raging within her, the struggle between duty and conscience.

Papa Yamah placed a hand on her shoulder, offering a silent show of support. "Aria's decision to leave the Dragon Slayers wasn't easy. It took courage to stand up against Yrome, to defy the path she's known all her life. But she's made her choice, and now she stands with us."

I looked at Aria, taking in her resolute expression, the determination that shone in her eyes. It was clear that her decision had been a turning point, a moment of reckoning that had set her on a new path.

"Thank you, Aria," I said, my voice firm but laced with newfound respect. "Your choice to stand against Yrome, to stand with us, it means more than you know. We'll need all the help we can get if we're to face what's coming."

Aria nodded, a small but genuine smile touching her lips. "I'm ready to do whatever it takes. Together, we'll find a way to stop Yrome and bring an end to this senseless war."

Our alliance was unexpected, but it was a testament to the power of change, of choosing a different path.

"Where are we?" I asked, while looking at my surroundings.

Papa Yamah's eyes swept across the village, a mix of nostalgia and sorrow in his gaze. "This," he began, his voice tinged with a hint of melancholy, "is Serenity's Edge. When I turned my back on the Dragon Slayers, I wasn't alone. There were others like me, others who questioned the path we were on, who couldn't reconcile the senseless slaughter of dragons with their own sense of morality."

He paused, his eyes reflecting the flickering torchlight that illuminated the village. "We were a small group, but we shared a common vision. We didn't believe in the complete eradication of dragons. To us, it was a senseless war, one that brought nothing but pain and destruction to both sides. So, we left. We left behind the life we knew, the comrades we fought alongside, and we founded this village."

The village, clearly nestled in the heart of a swamp, seemed to exist in a world of its own.

Papa Yamah continued, "This village became a sanctuary for those who sought redemption, for those who wanted to leave behind the life of a Dragon Slayer. Here, we live in peace, away from the conflict, away from the war. We've built a community based on mutual respect and understanding. We may have been Dragon Slayers once, but now, we're just people trying to live a life free from violence."

As he spoke, I could sense the depth of his conviction, the sincerity in his words. This village was more than just a refuge; it was a symbol of hope, a testament to the possibility of change.

"Many here have families, have built new lives," Papa Yamah added, his voice softening. "They've found a purpose beyond the blade, beyond the hunt. They've found peace. And that's all we ever wanted—a chance to live a life not defined by bloodshed and hatred."

The revelation of the village's true nature stirred something within me. It was a reminder that change was possible, that even those who had once walked a dark path could find their way to the light. In the midst of a world torn apart by war, Serenity's Edge stood as a beacon of hope, a reminder that there was more to life than conflict and destruction.

A reminder that maybe, just maybe, we'd have the old Elijah back.

A villager, an older man with a weathered face and kind eyes, approached us, his gaze shifting between me and Papa Yamah. "Amilcar! So good to see you back," he said, his voice tinged with relief. "And the boy… could it be? Oh, how you've grown!"

I stared at the man; confusion etched on my face. How did he know me? I had no memory of this place, no recollection of these people.

Papa Yamah placed a hand on my shoulder, a gentle smile on his lips. "Yes, Joren, this is Ezekiel. He has indeed grown."

Joren's eyes softened as he looked at me. "I remember when you were just a little one, running around the village with Elijah. You two were inseparable."

I turned to Papa Yamah, my mind racing with questions. "We lived here? With these people?"

Papa Yamah nodded, his expression somber. "Yes, we did. After I left the Dragon Slayers, we came here. This village was our home for a few years. You and Elijah were just children then. We lived here in peace, away from the conflict, away from the eyes of those who would seek to harm us."

I nodded, trying to grasp the flood of information. "I don't remember any of this," I admitted, feeling a strange sense of loss."

Papa Yamah's eyes met mine, filled with a mix of understanding and regret. "You were very young. Too young to form lasting memories. But this village was a part of your earliest years. The people here cared for you and Elijah as if you were their own."

Joren chuckled softly, a warm, grandfatherly sound. "You may not remember us, Ezekiel, but we certainly remember you. You brought joy to this place, even amidst the shadows that chased us."

I looked around at the swampy village, at the faces emerging from the homes, some with smiles, others with tears of joy at seeing Papa Yamah again. It was a community that had thrived on the edge of the world, away from the war that raged beyond the swamps.

"Perhaps one day, some of those memories might come back to you," Papa Yamah said, placing a comforting hand on my back. "For now, know that you are among friends, among family."

The word 'family' echoed in my mind. Here, in this hidden corner of the world, I had a history I had never known, a family I couldn't remember. It was a bittersweet realization, one that filled me with a longing to know more, to remember what had been lost to time.

Papa Yamah's tone shifted, the warmth giving way to the gravity of our situation. "As much as I wish we could indulge in this reunion, we have pressing matters to attend to," he said, his gaze sweeping over the gathered villagers before settling on Joren. "Are the other leaders present? We must convene immediately to discuss the recent events."

Joren's expression sobered as he nodded. "They're here, Amilcar. They've been waiting for your return. I'll take you to them."

We followed Joren through the village, the swampy air thick with the scent of earth and water. The villagers parted for us, their eyes filled with a mix of respect and concern. We arrived at a building that stood on stilts above the water, its architecture a blend of strength and elegance.

Inside, three individuals rose from a table laden with maps and scrolls. Their faces were etched with the lines of experience, and their eyes spoke of the wisdom gained through years of leadership.

"Amilcar, you've returned—and not a moment too soon," said a woman with striking black hair and silver streaks that was braided. "We've heard troubling rumors, but we need to know the truth of what's happening beyond our borders."

Papa Yamah nodded solemnly. "The situation is dire. Yrome has returned, and his power is unmatched. We must strategize, for the safety of this village and the world at large."

The leaders exchanged grave looks, the weight of Papa Yamah's words settling heavily in the room.

Papa Yamah offered a faint smile, tinged with the shadows of his past. "It's good to see you all, but please remember that I go by Yamah now. Amilcar belongs to a past I've left behind—a past of bloodshed and regret," he explained, his voice carrying a quiet strength.

He turned towards us, gesturing with an open hand. "You already know Ezekiel, it seems he has a destiny greater than any of us could have imagined. Beside him are Camila and Gaianor, Water and Earth Elementals respectively, allies in our quest for peace."

The leaders' eyes widened slightly as they took in Camila and Gaianor, their expressions a mixture of awe and respect. They bowed their heads slightly in a silent acknowledgment of our roles in the unfolding events.

Lastly, Papa Yamah's gaze softened as he looked at Aria, who lingered just a step behind, her posture closed off, a clear sign of her discomfort. "And I'm sure you remember Aria. She has seen the truth and has chosen a new path."

One of the leaders, a tall man with a gentle demeanor, stepped forward. "Aria, we always hoped you'd find your way to us. The past doesn't have to define us. Here, you can start anew."

The warmth in his voice seemed to reach Aria, and though she remained quiet, the tension in her shoulders eased ever so slightly. The leaders welcomed her with nods of understanding, their faces reflecting a shared history of transformation and redemption.

The first to step forward was Joren, the one who had greeted us initially. His eyes, a deep shade of hazel, held a spark of intelligence and kindness. "As you already know, I am Joren," he said, his voice resonant with the wisdom of his years. "I fought alongside Amil—Yamah, during our early days as Dragon Slayers. But the senseless violence, the endless cycle of revenge, it wore on my soul. I was one of the first to join him when he decided to leave that life behind."

Next came a woman with silver streaks running through her tightly braided hair, her stance exuding a quiet authority. "My name is Nina," she introduced herself. "I was a healer among the Dragon Slayers, saving lives on one hand and taking them on the other. It was a contradiction I could no longer live with. When Yamah spoke of a place where we could live without blood on our hands, I followed without hesitation."

The third elder was a burly man with scars that spoke of many battles. His hands, though rough, were open and inviting. "I'm called Gabriel," he said, his voice a deep rumble like distant thunder. "I was a warrior, feared and respected. But fear and respect earned through violence are hollow. Yamah showed me there was honor in peace. It's a lesson I've carried with me ever since."

Finally, a slender man with keen eyes and a scholar's poise made his introduction. "I am Caius," he stated, his tone measured and calm. "I was a strategist for the Dragon Slayers, a planner of campaigns that brought nothing but destruction. Papa Yamah's vision of a different path, one of coexistence and understanding, gave me hope for redemption. I've dedicated my life to that cause ever since."

Each elder carried the weight of their past actions, but also the light of their current purpose. They had been warriors, healers, and thinkers in a cause that they grew to see as misguided, and now they stood as pillars of a community built on the very principles they once fought against. Their stories were individual threads woven into the larger tapestry of the village's history, a tapestry that Yamah had helped to create.

"You all must have many questions," said Nina.

I looked to the group. Camila and Gaianor were clearly just as curious as I was.

"I suppose it would be wise to start from the beginning," said Joren, looking at the other Dragon Slayers.

"I think that's a great idea," said Nina. "The day was ordinary, the sun rising as it always had over the fields and forests that bordered our village at the time," she began, her eyes distant as if peering back across the years. "We, the Dragon Slayers, were vigilant, our lives dedicated to a singular purpose. But that day, the air shifted, a tremor of power rippled through the world, and we felt it—a draconic force so pure and immense it could not be ignored."

Gabriel, his face a tapestry of old battles, his eyes like flint, took up the narrative. "We gathered, as was our way, in the war room, the air thick with anticipation. What was this power? Where did it come from? And what did it portend for our sworn duty?"

Joren leaned forward, his eyes alight with the intensity of the memory. "It was as if the earth itself had shifted beneath our feet. A power, vast and overwhelming, surged through the land, and we knew, without a word, that something monumental had occurred."

"We convened to discuss," added Caius. "In that moment of uncertainty, we turned to our leader, Yamah. We were able to determine that the power had originated from a nearby cave. We all thought it would make the most sense to send Yamah as he was the most powerful one of us all, just in case."

Papa Yamah nodded slowly, acknowledging Nina's words. His eyes held a depth of emotion that seemed to reach back through the years to the moment that had defined his very being.

"I remember the stillness of that cave," Papa Yamah began, his voice a deep rumble that resonated with the truth of his tale. "The power that had drawn me there was unlike any I had encountered. It was not the dark, fearsome energy of the dragons we had been taught to hunt and slay. It was pure, almost... sacred."

Papa Yamah told everyone what he told me the night before. About finding Elijah and I in the cave.

The room was silent, hanging on every word, every breath. "I had led men into battle, had faced the fiercest of dragons, but nothing had prepared me for the vulnerability of that moment. I knew then that my path, our path, had irrevocably changed."

We all stared at Papa Yamah.

Papa Yamah's hands trembled ever so slightly as if the weight of the babes he had once held was still a burden he carried. "I could not—would not—raise my sword against you. And so, I wrapped you in the warmth of my cloak and brought you back, not as trophies of the Dragon Slayers, but as hope."

He looked at each of the elders in turn, his gaze finally resting on me. "That decision marked the end of my life as I knew it and the beginning of something new. It was the birth of hope, the first step toward a peace that I believed could be our future."

There was a moment of silence, as Papa Yamah stared off into space.

"I could not reveal the existence of two dragon infants to just anyone. The risk was too great, the potential for betrayal too high. So, I turned to the ones I knew shared a vision of a world where the sword could be laid down, where dragon and human could find a common ground."

Papa Yamah's eyes met mine again, a silent strength in their depths. "These four," he continued, "they had the wisdom to see beyond the propaganda, the courage to question the path we walked. And when I returned with you and Elijah, it was to them I revealed the truth of what I had found."

Nina nodded, her eyes reflecting the flicker of the candles. "We knew the moment we laid eyes on you both that our lives were no longer our own. We were bound to a greater cause, one that transcended the orders we had followed, the battles we had fought."

"It was a pact we made in silence," Gabriel added. "A vow etched not in the scrolls of our order, but in the very fabric of our souls. To protect you, to nurture the seed of peace you represented, became our sacred duty."

Joren's gruff voice chimed in, "We built Serenity's Edge not just as a refuge from the war, but as a cradle for a new era. An era that now, with Yrome's return, hangs in the balance."

Caius spoke last, his words slow and deliberate. "We have watched over this village, over you and Elijah, as if you were our own. And though the path has been shrouded in shadow, we have never lost sight of the light you brought into our lives."

Papa Yamah's voice took on a somber tone, the joy momentarily fading from his features as he recounted the days of uncertainty and fear. "As you both grew, it became increasingly clear that the sanctuary we had built could only hold for so long. The other Dragon Slayers, they were relentless, scouring the lands for the so-called traitors and what we had found. The risk of discovery grew with each passing day."

He paused, his eyes distant as if he could see the past unfolding before him. "We knew that to keep you in Serenity's Edge would be to tether you to a ticking time bomb. The day would come when Vajra or another like him would sense your growing power, and they would descend upon us with the fury of the scorned."

"The decision to leave was one of the hardest I've ever made," Papa Yamah continued, his voice barely above a whisper. "To uproot your lives, to sever the bonds we had formed... it was a sacrifice that pained us all deeply. But it was necessary. For your safety, for the future we dreamed of."

He looked at each of his old comrades in turn, a silent communication passing between them. "I could tell no one of our destination, not even these trusted few. The fewer who knew, the safer you would be. It was the only way to ensure that the shadows of our past did not reach out to ensnare you."

Nina's eyes were moist, and she reached out to touch Papa Yamah's hand. "We understood, though it broke our hearts. The silence was our final gift to you, a shroud to cover your escape."

Gabriel nodded. "We placed our trust in Yamah, in the hope that you would find peace in a world ravaged by war."

"We stayed behind," Joren said. "Maintaining the illusion of normalcy, all the while our hearts were with you, in that unknown village that became your new home."

"And though we remained here," Caius added, "Our spirits traveled with you. Through every challenge, every joy, every moment of your lives, we were there in spirit."

Papa Yamah's eyes met mine once more, a fierce determination within them. "We did it all for you, Ezekiel. For the hope of a better world. And now, with Yrome's return, it seems our journey is far from over. But we face it as we always have—united, steadfast, and with the courage to believe in a brighter tomorrow."

As the elders spoke, their words, though meant to comfort, felt like chains around my heart. I stood amidst them, the weight of their expectations and the burden of their sacrifices pressing upon me. I nodded to each in turn.

"I understand," I said, my voice barely above a whisper, yet it carried in the hush that had befallen the room. "And I carry with me not just your hopes, but the essence of what you've built here—peace, a respite from the relentless tides of war. But the peace is threatened now, not just here, but everywhere. Yrome's shadow looms large, and we must act, not just for ourselves, but for the future generations who deserve to live without fear."

Papa Yamah stepped forward, the lines on his face deepening as he offered a sad smile. "That's my boy," he said, his voice thick with pride. "You've grown into the leader we always knew you would become."

"We must figure out Yrome's next move," I said. "What could someone of that much power want?"

"More power," said Nina. "It's always been about more power."

The room fell silent to those chilling words.

"I believe I may have an idea of what his next move may be," said Papa Yamah.

The crowd drew in closer, the air thick with anticipation.

"The crown..." Papa Yamah continued.

The elders looked puzzled. "What crown?" asked Gabriel.

"Yrome's Crown, an object of immense and ancient power." He said. He looked at each of us in turn. "The crown gave him the ability to bestow upon humans powers that rival the dragons themselves. This was the only way to keep the Dragon Slayer lineage going."

Nina, her brows furrowed in a mix of confusion and concern, rose from her seat, her posture reflecting the gravity of the conversation. "What are you talking about, Yamah?"

Yamah's eyes held a faraway look. "The crown's existence is a closely guarded secret, known only to the leaders of the Dragon Slayers," he said.

The room grew apprehensive.

"Please elaborate," said Gabriel seeming very tense.

This conversation was taking a peculiar turn of events.

"Did you actually believe that Dragon Slayers were born with such power? Or why there were such few of us? Or why we would never find any humans with powers like ours?" said Papa Yamah. "Yrome's Crown is the reason why we exist. Our powers are a gift."

"What do you mean?" I asked, my voice steady despite the turmoil inside.

Papa Yamah regarded me with a thoughtful gaze, as if measuring the weight of the knowledge he was about to impart. "The crown," he began, his voice a low murmur, "is not just a vessel of power. It is sentient in its own right, ancient beyond our understanding."

He moved to the hearth, his hands outstretched to the warmth as he continued. "Every few years, a new generation of Dragon Slayers is chosen. They are gathered, children with the seeds of great potential within them, and the crown is placed upon their heads. It delves into their souls, finds the latent power there, and amplifies it, binds it to the elements."

A hushed awe fell over the group as Papa Yamah spoke, each of us contemplating the implications of such a ritual.

"The last group to undergo this... were the very Dragon Slayers you battled," Papa Yamah said, casting a glance at Aria, who stood with her head bowed, a storm of emotions playing across her face. "Vajra, Aria, Ignis, Cyrus, Bria... they were all touched by the crown's power, chosen for the strength of their will and the depth of their potential."

"How come I do not remember any of this?" asked Aria.

"A great question," said Papa Yamah. "The crown erases the memory of the experience. For what purpose? I do not know."

"Do you know where it is?" I asked.

Papa Yamah's gaze lingered on the flickering flames, his mind seemingly traversing realms far beyond the cozy confines of the room. "Yes," he finally said, turning back to face us, his eyes reflecting a deep, unspoken resolve. "After I renounced my allegiance to the Dragon Slayers, I knew the crown could not remain where Vajra might find it. So, I retrieved it under the cover of darkness and concealed it within the depths of the Cavern of Echoes.

"The Cavern of Echoes?" Gabriel asked, his brow furrowing. "That's a mere legend, a tale we were told as children so that we would steer clear of caves."

Papa Yamah shook his head, a faint smile playing on his lips. "Not a legend, but a clever ruse to protect one of the greatest secrets of our time. The cavern is real, veiled by powerful enchantments to keep it hidden from others. Only those who know its true nature can navigate mazes and illusions to get there."

Nina leaned in, her interest piqued. "And you believe it has remained undisturbed all this time?"

"I do," Papa Yamah affirmed, his voice carrying a weight of responsibility. "While I ensured the crown was hidden safely, away from the prying eyes of Dragon Slayers and others who might misuse it, I fear that Yrome, with his newfound powers and determination, could eventually uncover its location."

Aria's eyes widened. "If Yrome even suspects you know where the crown is, he won't hesitate to come after you," she said, the gravity of the situation evident in her tone.

Papa Yamah nodded solemnly, his expression resolute. "I'm aware of the danger," he replied. "But we can't let the fear of what might happen deter us. Our priority must be to secure the crown before Yrome has a chance to track it down. It's a risk, but one we must take for the greater good. Once we have it here, then we can figure out what to do with it."

"The crown should be safe here in Serenity's Edge," Joren said, his gaze sweeping across the room. "Our village is protected by powerful barriers, both protective and concealing.

These enchantments have kept us hidden from other Dragon Slayers and dragons for years."

Joren's words were met with nods of agreement, but it was Nina who added a crucial piece of history to the conversation. "Yes, the barriers are strong, but we must remember the sacrifice that made them possible," she said, her voice tinged with a mix of reverence and sorrow. "It was I who cast the ultimate forbidden spell to erect these barriers. In doing so, I expended all of my powers."

The room fell silent, the gravity of her revelation hanging heavily in the air. Nina continued, "The spell was our last resort, a desperate measure to protect what we had built here. But the cost was high. I lost my ability to wield magic, a price I willingly paid to ensure our safety and secrecy."

The revelation from Nina about the forbidden spells sparked a wave of confusion among us. Camila, Gaianor, and I exchanged puzzled glances, the concept of such powerful magic being unfamiliar to us.

Nina noticed our confusion and elaborated further. "In the world of Dragon Slayers, there exist spells of immense power, often referred to as 'forbidden' due to their extreme nature and the heavy toll they take on the caster. These spells are the ultimate expression of our abilities, but they come at a great cost."

She paused, a reflective look crossing her face. "My abilities were centered around healing and protection. Using the forbidden spell, I was able to extend my protective powers to encompass the entire village, creating a barrier strong enough to shield us from the outside world."

Nina's voice held a note of resignation, but also a sense of peace. "Losing my powers was a sacrifice I was willing to make. They were a constant reminder of a past I wished to leave behind. In casting that spell, I not only protected our village but also freed myself from the burdens of my former life."

Her explanation shed light on the depth and complexity of the Dragon Slayer's magic, revealing a side of their world that was both awe-inspiring and daunting. It was a testimony to the lengths they would go to protect what they held dear, even if it meant giving up a part of themselves.

Papa Yamah looked at Nina. "Your sacrifice has not been in vain, Nina. These barriers have been our shield, our protection from a world that may not have understood or accepted us. Thanks to you, Serenity's Edge has remained a sanctuary for all these years."

My curiosity piqued, I couldn't help but draw a parallel. "This barrier... it's similar to Ytfen's Barriers, isn't it? The ones that have protected and concealed the Dragon Villages for centuries."

At my words, Nina and the other leaders exchanged knowing glances, a silent communication passing between them. It was Joren who broke the silence, his voice tinged with a newfound understanding. "Ah, so that's how the dragons did it," he mused aloud, an expression of realization dawning on his face. "We always wondered about the magic that shielded the dragon realms. It seems we had a similar approach, albeit for different reasons."

Nina nodded in agreement. "Indeed, it appears that both our peoples, dragons and Dragon Slayers alike, have long understood the value of such protective magic. It's fascinating to see how parallel our solutions were, despite our differences."

The revelation that both dragons and Dragon Slayers had resorted to similar magical means to protect their respective worlds served as a reminder of our shared instincts for preservation and peace.

"It's a testament to the ingenuity and resilience of both our kinds," Caius added. "Despite our differences, we've both sought to protect what we cherish most."

Just as I opened my mouth to delve deeper into the discussion, Papa Yamah gently placed a hand on my shoulder, interrupting my train of thought. "Ezekiel, I know you have many questions, and they deserve answers," he said, his voice calm yet firm. "But we must rest now. Tomorrow, we have a long journey ahead of us. We're going to the Cavern of Echoes to retrieve the crown."

His words brought a sense of urgency back into focus. The importance of our mission, the need to secure the crown before Yrome could lay his hands on it, overshadowed my curiosity.

"You're right, Papa," I replied, nodding in agreement. "We need to be prepared for what's to come. The crown is too important, and we can't afford any delays."

Nina rose gracefully, her presence commanding yet comforting. "Come," she said, gesturing to the door. "We have prepared quarters for you."

It was still dark as we walked through Serenity's Edge, yet the village revealed itself to be a tapestry of nature and craftsmanship, woven seamlessly into the heart of the swamplands. The air was thick with the scent of wet earth and wildflowers, a fragrance that spoke of life persisting in the most unexpected places. Fireflies danced around us, their tiny lights flickering like stars brought down to earth, casting an ethereal glow over the winding paths.

The houses were built on sturdy stilts, rising above the marshy ground, their wooden structures melding with the natural surroundings as if they had grown there.

The pathways were laid with smooth stones, their surfaces worn smooth. The sound of our footsteps on the stones was a comforting rhythm in the stillness of the night, a reminder of the village's enduring presence in this secluded haven.

As we approached the cluster of cottages at the village's edge, the soft murmur of the swamp waters became more pronounced, a symphony of nature's whispers. The cottages themselves were nestled among tall cypress trees, their gnarled roots like the fingers of ancient guardians clutching at the earth. Each cottage was a sanctuary in its own right, with walls that seemed to breathe with the life of the swamp, windows framed with hanging moss, and doors carved with symbols of protection and peace.

Nina took the lead in guiding Camila, Gaianor, and Aria to their respective cottages while Papa Yamah walked with Caius. Gabriel approached me with a warm, inviting smile.

"Ezekiel, you'll be staying with me tonight," he said, his voice friendly and welcoming. "It's not much, but I hope you'll find it comfortable."

I nodded in appreciation, grateful for the hospitality. "Thank you, Gabriel. I appreciate it," I replied, feeling a sense of relief at the prospect of a quiet place to rest and gather my thoughts.

As the others headed to their accommodations, I followed Gabriel to his cottage. As Gabriel and I entered his cottage, the warmth and simplicity of the interior offered a comforting contrast to the complexities of the day. He gestured towards a small but inviting area set up for me to sleep.

"Make yourself at home, Ezekiel," Gabriel said, his tone friendly but respectful of my need for space. "If you need anything, just let me know."

I nodded, appreciative of his hospitality but too exhausted for extended conversation. "Thank you, Gabriel. It's been a long day. I think I'll just go to sleep now."

Gabriel seemed to understand my need for solitude. "Of course," he replied, giving me a reassuring smile. "Rest well. Tomorrow is another day, and you'll need all your strength for the journey to the Cavern of Echoes."

With that, he quietly excused himself, leaving me to my thoughts. The room was peaceful, the soft sounds of the night outside providing a soothing backdrop. Despite the comfort, my mind was restless, replaying the day's events and the challenges that lay ahead. Eventually, fatigue overtook me, and I felt myself drifting off to sleep.

As sleep began to claim me, the familiar sensation of Ytfen's memories seeping into my consciousness took hold. The world around me faded into darkness, and I found myself being drawn into another time, another place.

The Dragon Kingdom

I found myself seated on a grand throne, its design intricate and majestic, befitting the ruler of the dragons. The throne room was vast, with high ceilings adorned with murals depicting dragons in flight, their forms intertwined with the elements they represented.

Before me stood my highest-ranked commanders, each a Pure Elemental for the five Elemental Kingdoms. The five elemental kingdoms, each a bastion of its respective element, were divided into seven distinct military outposts. These outposts were more than mere settlements; they were thriving communities, home to hundreds of Elementals. Each outpost, with its unique characteristics and strengths, functioned not only as a sanctuary for its inhabitants but also as strategic military outposts.

These outposts played a crucial role in the grand scheme of the overarching Dragon Kingdom. They were the first line of defense, safeguarding the hundreds of dragon villages scattered across the world. The dragon villages, teeming with innocent lives, relied on the protection and guidance of these elemental strongholds.

The Elementals, skilled and powerful, pledged their allegiance to their king, to me. They were the guardians of peace and stability, ensuring the safety of the dragon populace.

In contrast, the dragon populace, while deeply connected to the elements, did not possess the same level of mastery or combat prowess as the Elementals. Their connection to the elements granted them a harmonious existence, allowing them to live in tune with the natural world, but it did not extend to the battlefield. They were artisans, scholars, and farmers—keepers of ancient knowledge and traditions, not warriors.

While some among them held a modest ability to manipulate the elements, these powers were often limited to tasks that aided in daily life or the enrichment of their communities. A farmer might coax a gentle rain to nourish crops, or a craftsman might use a whisper of flame to shape metal, but these were not powers wielded in defense or aggression. Their magic was proof to their deep bond with the world around them, a connection that was spiritual rather than martial.

This distinction was crucial in understanding the dynamics of our realm. The Elementals stood as our protectors, a specialized force that bore the weight of defense, allowing the dragon villages to flourish in peace and safety. Their role was not just to fight but to shield the innocent from the horrors of war, to be the strength that guarded the gentle hearts of our people.

To my left stood Zephyra, the Pure Wind Elemental, commander of the Wind Kingdom which consisted of the following villages: Galegrove, Zephyrfield, Breezehollow, Aerovale, Whirlwind Bluff, Skywarden, and Tempest Terrace. Her eyes, sharp and clear, mirrored the endless sky. "King Ytfen," she began, her voice as soothing as a gentle gust, "the Wind Kingdom stands ready. Our dragons soar high, watching over the lands."

Next to her was Pyrus, the fiery leader of the Fire Kingdom which consisted of: Emberfall, Flamecrest, Pyrocliff, Ignicia, Inferno Ridge, Scorchwood, and Blazeburgh. His presence was as intense as the flames he wielded, his eyes burning with a passion for his people. "The Fire Kingdom's might is yours to command," he declared, his voice resonating with the crackle of a roaring fire.

Beside Pyrus was Glacius, the Ice Kingdom's stoic commander. He was overseer of: Fostvale, Glacial Hollow, Snowspire, Wintercrest, Icicle Reach, Chillwind Haven, and Crystaline Glade. His demeanor was as cool and composed as the frost-laden realm he oversaw. "The Ice Kingdom remains vigilant," he stated, his tone as crisp as a winter morning.

To my right stood Aquarion, the serene commander of the Water Kingdom and its villages: Aquaria, Rippleton, Streamvale, Cascade Hollow, Dewshore, Tidemarsh, and Floodhaven. Her calmness was as deep as the oceans, her wisdom as vast. "The Water Kingdom's tides flow in harmony with your will," she assured me, her voice flowing like a tranquil river.

Beside Aquarion stood Tarn, the Earth Kingdom commander. His presence was as solid and reassuring as the element he represented. He oversaw the seven Earth Villages. These villages were: Stonepeak, Ironwood, Claymore, Granitegrove, Terra, Mudvale, and Boulderhaven.

Lastly, there was Joaquin, leader of the Lightning Kingdom and its villages: Voltara, Thunderhaven, Sparkstone, Boltspire, Electra Peak, Stormridge, and Thundara. His energy was palpable, his presence like a charged storm. "The Lightning Kingdom is poised to strike at your command," he said, his voice crackling with raw power.

As I looked upon these formidable leaders, a sense of pride filled me. They were not just commanders; they were the embodiment of the elements they represented, a testament to the diversity and strength of our kingdom.

"The distrust between our kingdoms and the humans has reached a critical point," I stated, my voice echoing through the grand hall. "Their fear of dragons, though rooted in misconceptions, poses a real threat to the peace we cherish."

Pyrus, his hands clenched as if holding back his inner fire, added with intensity, "We must extinguish these flames of mistrust. But how do we reach out to those who see our very nature as a threat?"

"An act of goodwill, perhaps." Joaquin suggested. "A gesture that demonstrates our commitment to coexistence and mutual respect. We need to find a way to communicate our intentions clearly and calmly."

"Direct confrontation of these issues might be necessary," added Glacius. "We should face these challenges head-on, with strength."

"I agree with Glacius," said Tarn.

I absorbed their counsel, each piece adding to the mosaic of our strategy. "I believe a personal meeting with King Yrome could be a turning point. Our recent interaction at my wedding showed potential for a deeper understanding. A direct dialogue might help dispel their fears and misconceptions."

Zephyra nodded thoughtfully. "A face-to-face meeting could indeed change the winds of perception. But tread carefully, Your Majesty."

Pyrus leaned in, his voice a low rumble. "Such a meeting could either ignite a new era of understanding or fan the flames of conflict. We must prepare for both possibilities."

Glacius added, "Your approach must be balanced, my king. Show them our strength, but also our willingness to forge a peaceful path. The Ice Kingdom will support your efforts."

Aquarion's calm voice was reassuring. "The course of diplomacy is never straight, but always necessary. We trust in your wisdom."

Their advice echoed in my mind as the meeting ended. The task ahead was daunting, yet essential. The future of our kingdoms, both human and dragon, hinged on the success of this meeting with Yrome. It was a monumental task, but one I was ready to undertake for the greater good of all.

After absorbing the wisdom and perspectives of my commanders, I stood from my throne, a gesture signaling the end of our council. "Thank you, each of you, for your counsel and unwavering loyalty. Your service to our kingdoms is invaluable. You may now return to your duties."

One by one, the commanders bowed respectfully and exited the throne room, their steps echoing softly against the marble floor. The room, once filled with the energy of our discussion, now settled into a quieter, more reflective state.

As the last of them departed, Denise, my queen and confidant, approached me. Her presence was like a soothing balm, her grace and wisdom always a source of comfort and strength. She reached up, placing a gentle kiss on my cheek, her touch light yet filled with love.

"Thoughtful as always, my love," she said, her voice laced with affection. "I can see the weight of these decisions upon you."

I took her hand, feeling the warmth of her touch. "It's a burden made lighter by your presence, my queen. Your support means more to me than you can imagine."

She smiled, her eyes reflecting the depth of our shared journey. "Ytfen, remember that strength is not just in the might of your arm or the power of your command. It's also in the kindness of your heart and the wisdom of your decisions."

I nodded, her words resonating within me. "I know, and yet the path ahead is fraught with uncertainty. I fear the consequences of my choices, not just for us but for all our people."

Denise's gaze was steady, her resolve clear. "Uncertainty is a part of life, my love. But I have seen you face it with courage and grace time and again. Trust in yourself, as I trust in you. Your heart will guide you rightly."

Her words were a beacon in the tumultuous sea of my thoughts. "Your faith in me gives me strength. I will do all in my power to ensure a future where our people can live in peace and harmony."

She squeezed my hand, a silent vow of enduring support. "Together, we will face whatever comes. For in unity, there is strength, and in love, there is power."

As we stood there, hand in hand, the challenges ahead seemed less daunting. With Denise by my side, I felt ready to face whatever the future held, guided by love, wisdom, and the unwavering commitment to our people's well-being.

As Denise's reassuring words echoed in my heart, the world around me began to blur and shift.

The vividness of Ytfen's memories started to fade, like a dream dissolving upon waking. This gradual fading served as a poignant reminder that the full breadth of his past would not reveal itself in a single moment but would instead unfold gradually, piece by piece, over time.

The Whispering Woods

As the last traces of Ytfen's world vanished, I opened my eyes, finding myself once again in Gabriel's cottage in Serenity's Edge. The morning light filtered through the gauzy curtains of the cottage, casting a soft, golden glow across the room. The scent of freshly baked bread and brewed tea wafted through the air, gently coaxing me awake. Gabriel was nowhere to be seen.

There was a soft knock on the door, and a young villager entered, balancing a tray laden with a simple yet inviting breakfast. "Good morning," she said with a shy smile. "The elders sent this for you. They thought you might need a hearty meal."

The tray was set on a small wooden table in the center of the room. There were loaves of crusty bread, a pot of honey, a bowl of fresh fruits, and a steaming teapot with cups. The simplicity of the meal was a reminder of the village's harmonious and unpretentious way of life.

Camila, Gaianor, and Papa Yamah soon joined me, each taking a seat around the table. The atmosphere was one of quiet contemplation, the weight of our task ahead not lost on any of us.

Papa Yamah broke the silence, his voice steady and resolute. "Today, we must plan our next steps. The journey to the Cavern of Echoes will not be easy, and we must be prepared for whatever Yrome might throw our way."

Camila nodded, her eyes reflecting determination. "We also need to consider Elijah. We can't forget that he's still out there, possibly under Yrome's influence."

Gaianor, his expression thoughtful, added, "And we mustn't overlook the villagers' safety. Serenity's Edge is a haven, but it could become a target if Yrome learns of our presence here."

I listened to their words, feeling the responsibility of leadership heavy on my shoulders. "We have many challenges ahead," I said, taking a sip of the warm tea. "But together, we have the strength and the will to overcome them. We'll start by securing the crown and then find a way to reach Elijah. We can't let Yrome continue his reign of terror."

The conversation continued as we ate, each of us contributing ideas and strategies.

As we cleared the breakfast dishes, Papa Yamah leaned back in his chair, his gaze distant as if he were visualizing the journey ahead. "The Cavern of Echoes," he began, his voice tinged with a mix of reverence and caution, "is not an ordinary cavern. The journey itself is a test, a gauntlet that challenges the very essence of those who dare to enter."

"The cavern is located deep within the Whispering Woods," he continued. "The woods themselves are a labyrinth of ancient trees, their roots entwined with the magic of the land. Many have lost their way amidst its deceptive tranquility."

Camila interjected, her tone serious. "I've heard tales of the Whispering Woods. They say the trees speak to those who walk their paths, revealing truths and fears."

As Papa Yamah spoke of the Cavern of Echoes, I felt a mix of apprehension and curiosity stirring within me. The way he described it, as a place that tested the essence of those who entered, made me wonder about the challenges we would face. Would they be physical, mental, or something more mystical?

"The Whispering Woods," I thought to myself, "a labyrinth of ancient trees." The idea that the woods could be both beautiful and treacherous intrigued me. What secrets did they hold? What truths might they reveal about us?

Camila's mention of the trees speaking to those who walked their paths sent a shiver down my spine. It was both fascinating and unsettling. What would the trees say to me? What fears or truths would they unearth from the depths of my soul?

Papa Yamah picked up the thread of the conversation. "Once we navigate the woods, we'll find the entrance to the Cavern of Echoes."

"And the crown," I asked, "where in the cave is it?"

Papa Yamah paused thoughtfully before responding. "The crown should be relatively close to the entrance of the cavern," he said, his tone suggesting a mix of caution and certainty. "However, our path won't be without its perils. There's a guardian within the cave, a formidable protector of the crown."

Camila leaned forward, her expression serious. "A guardian? What kind of guardian are we talking about?"

Papa Yamah's eyes met each of ours in turn. "It's not a creature we can simply overpower or outmaneuver. This guardian is deeply connected to the crown, perhaps even a part of it. It's said to be a manifestation of the ancient magic that binds the crown's power. It is the very creature that has granted us Dragon Slayers our powers. I don't know much about it, but I am certain it will not let us take the crown so easily."

Gaianor, who had been listening intently, added, "So, it's not just about reaching the crown. We need to be prepared to face whatever this guardian is and prove our worth."

Aria, who had been quiet, spoke up with a hint of concern in her voice. "And if we fail to prove ourselves?"

Papa Yamah's response was solemn. "Then we may not only fail in retrieving the crown, but we could also face consequences far graver. This guardian serves as the very essence of the crown's power. It will not yield easily."

The room fell silent as we each contemplated the journey ahead. The path to the Cavern of Echoes was fraught with danger and mystery, but it was a path we had to take. With a deep breath, I stood up, determination steeling my resolve.

"Then we have to prepare," I declared. "We'll gather supplies, map our route, and ready ourselves for the challenges ahead. Together, we'll face the Cavern of Echoes and get the crown. For the future of our world, and for the peace we all seek."

The revelation of the Cavern of Echoes and its mystical nature left me in a state of disbelief. I leaned back in my chair, my mind racing with the implications of what I had just learned. "It's hard to believe," I said, my voice tinged with wonder and skepticism. "All this time, living a normal life, and now I find myself in a world where dragons, Dragon Slayers, and magical places exist."

Papa Yamah chuckled softly, a knowing look in his eyes. "The world is far more wondrous and complex than we often give it credit for, Ezekiel. Magic has always been a part of it, just hidden from the eyes of those not meant to see."

Camila leaned forward, her eyes sparkling with excitement. "This is going to be quite the adventure. The world is so full of mysteries waiting to be uncovered."

Gaianor nodded, his expression thoughtful. "Magic is like a hidden melody in the symphony of life. It's always been there, subtly influencing the world around us. It's only when you start paying attention that you begin to hear its tune."

Papa Yamah leaned back, a twinkle of ancient knowledge in his eyes. "Did you really believe that dragons were the only things out there?" he asked, his voice carrying a hint of mystery. "Dragons are but one aspect of the magical tapestry that makes up our world. They are ancient, yes, but they are not alone in their antiquity or their connection to the deeper magics of the earth."

He paused, allowing his words to resonate in the quiet room. "Consider the vastness of our world, the unexplored depths of the oceans, the unreachable heights of the skies, and the mysteries that lie hidden beneath the earth. Each of these realms holds its own secrets, its own ancient magic."

"The world is far more complex and wondrous than most can imagine. Dragons, while majestic and powerful, are just one part of this greater whole. There are forces, entities, and realms that exist beyond the common understanding, each with its own role in the grand design of nature."

I absorbed his words, feeling a sense of wonder and curiosity stirring within me. "So, the guardian of the crown... it could be something beyond our comprehension?"

Papa Yamah nodded solemnly. "Precisely. It's a reminder that the world holds mysteries and powers far beyond what we see on the surface."

The conversation opened my eyes to the broader spectrum of magic and mystery that our world held. It was a humbling and exhilarating realization that our quest for the crown was not just a journey through physical space, but a venture into the deeper, hidden realms of magic and ancient power.

I mulled over their words, feeling a mixture of awe and apprehension. "I guess I've been living with my eyes closed," I admitted. "But now, it's as if a whole new world has opened up to me. A world filled with danger, yes, but also with endless possibilities."

Papa Yamah reached across the table, placing a reassuring hand on my shoulder. "We've got this, Ezekiel."

His words bolstered my spirits, and I felt a renewed sense of purpose. "Lets do this," I said, a determined smile forming on my lips.

The Cavern of Echoes awaits us, and I'm ready to face whatever secrets it holds.

"Alright, let's get moving," Papa Yamah announced, his voice carrying a note of determination. He rose from his seat with a purposeful air and made his way towards the door. "Follow me," he added, glancing back to ensure we were ready.

We promptly stood up, gathering our belongings and preparing ourselves for the journey ahead. As Papa Yamah stepped outside, we fell into step behind him, ready to embark on the next phase of our quest.

As the morning sun cast its golden rays over Serenity's Edge, the village awakened to a day filled with vibrant energy. The thatched roofs of the cottages glowed warmly in the sunlight, harmonizing with the lush greenery that surrounded the settlement. The air, fresh and invigorating, carried the symphony of nature – the chirping of birds, the gentle rustling of leaves in the breeze. The village, which had been shrouded in darkness the night before, now revealed its breathtaking beauty in the daylight.

Papa Yamah, leading us through the winding pathways of smoothly worn stones, began to share insights about the village. "Serenity's Edge has always been a place of peace and harmony," he said, his voice filled with pride.

The pathways meandered through the village, leading to quaint structures that served as homes and communal spaces. Each building, constructed with a harmonious blend of natural materials, seemed to have sprung organically from the earth itself.

Villagers, adorned in simple yet colorful attire, exchanged smiles and warm conversations as they commenced their daily routines. Some tended to vibrant gardens, bursting with strange herbs and exotic flowers, while others carried baskets brimming with fresh produce, likely destined to be shared with neighbors.

Children's laughter echoed near the water's edge, where the swamp lent a mystical quality to the landscape. The water was clear and serene, with lily pads floating gently and small fish darting below the surface. The occasional croak of a frog or the splash of a water bird diving for its breakfast added to the chorus of morning sounds.

Papa Yamah gestured towards the mist-covered swamp in the distance. "The swamp is both a natural barrier and a source of life for us. It provides resources and a unique connection to the natural world. It's part of what makes Serenity's Edge special."

Walking through the village, I was struck by the profound transformation of its inhabitants. Once Dragon Slayers, these individuals had chosen a path of peace, their former lives a stark contrast to the tranquil existence they now embraced. It was a demonstration to the possibility of change and redemption, and I couldn't help but feel a deep sense of awe at their journey.

The villagers, going about their morning routines, paused to observe us as we made our preparations. Their gazes held a mix of curiosity and respect, a silent acknowledgment of the gravity of our quest. It was clear they understood the significance of our mission, and their expressions conveyed a quiet support, a hope that we would succeed and return safely.

As we finished gathering our gear and weapons, the atmosphere was one of quiet anticipation. It was then that Camila turned to Aria with a question that had been on all our minds. "Aria, why don't we just use your power to open a portal directly to the Cavern of Echoes?" she asked, her tone indicating both curiosity and a desire for efficiency.

Aria, her expression serious, shook her head slightly. "I can only create portals to places I've physically been to," she explained. "I've never been to the Cavern of Echoes, so I can't open a portal there."

Papa Yamah nodded in understanding. "It's a limitation we must work with," he said. "But Aria's ability will still be invaluable on our journey."

As we prepared to leave, Nina, Gabriel, Joren, and Caius, emerged to bid us farewell. Their faces were etched with a mixture of pride and concern.

Nina stepped forward, her wise eyes meeting each of ours. "We would join you if we could," she said, her voice tinged with regret. "But our duty is here, to protect Serenity's Edge and maintain it as a sanctuary for those who seek refuge from the war."

Gabriel nodded in agreement. "We played our part many years ago. You are the new generation, the ones who must confront this threat head-on."

"We will keep the village," Joren added. "Your journey is crucial, and knowing Serenity's Edge is secure will give you peace of mind."

Caius spoke last. "Remember, you carry with you not just our hopes, but the essence of what we've built here. Peace, understanding, and a chance for a different future."

Papa Yamah nodded solemnly. "We understand, and we're grateful for your support. We'll return as soon as we can."

Nina's voice carried a gentle concern as she bid us farewell. "Please be safe," she implored, her eyes reflecting the care and worry of a mother.

"We will," Papa Yamah assured her with a confident nod, his tone conveying a sense of determination.

With that, Papa Yamah guided us through the village, leading us towards the swamp that bordered Serenity's Edge. The path gradually gave way to the wetlands, where the air was thick with the scent of earth and water. At the edge of the swamp, a small, well-maintained dock came into view. Moored to it was a boat.

The boat, with its broad base and stable structure, seemed perfectly suited for our journey through the swamp. As we approached the boat, ready to embark on the next leg of our journey, the reality of our mission settled in. The Cavern of Echoes awaited us, and with it, the challenges and mysteries we were yet to face.

"We'll need to cross the swamp to reach the Whispering Woods," Papa Yamah explained, as he helped us load our supplies onto the boat.

Gaianor looked at the boat with a hint of apprehension. "I've never been fond of water travel," he admitted, his tone dry.

I couldn't help but smile at his discomfort. "Come on, Gaianor, it's just a bit of water. What's the worst that could happen?" I teased, giving him a friendly nudge.

Aria, who had been quietly observing, cautiously took a seat in the boat. She glanced around at the swamp's edge, her curiosity evident. "So, anything we should look out for in these waters?" she asked casually. "You know, swamp monsters, giant leeches, that sort of thing?"

Her question, though light-hearted, was a valid one, considering the unknowns of the swamp. We all looked to Papa Yamah, expecting his experience might provide some insight into what lay beneath the still surface of the swamp waters.

"I've honestly never had any issues in these waters."

Well, that's a relief.

As we set off, the boat glided smoothly over the water, parting the thick green algae that coated the surface. The air was heavy with the scent of damp earth and decaying vegetation.

The swamp was a labyrinth of waterways, with tall reeds and drooping willows lining the banks. The sound of our boat slicing through the water was the only disturbance in the otherwise silent expanse.

Papa Yamah navigated expertly, steering us through the maze of channels. "The swamp is ever-changing," he said. "Paths that were clear yesterday might be impassable today. But no worries, I can manage."

As we traveled deeper into the swamp, the light dimmed, filtered through the dense canopy of trees overhead. The water beneath us darkened.

I turned to Papa Yamah. "Back in Serenity's Edge, Nina talked about how she used her powers to create the barrier around the village, using her forbidden spell. Can you tell us more about that? What are these forbidden spells exactly? And do all Dragon Slayers have access to them?"

Papa Yamah glanced at me, his eyes reflecting a depth of knowledge and experience. "Forbidden spells," he began, his voice low, "are powerful magic that comes with great risks. They're called 'forbidden' for a reason. As I previously mentioned, they can have devastating effects, not just on the target, but also on the one who casts them."

He paused, steering the boat around a particularly dense clump of reeds. "Not all Dragon Slayers have access to these spells. They require a deep understanding of magic and a strong will to control them. In the wrong hands, they can cause irreparable harm."

Aria, who had been quiet, spoke up with a hint of curiosity in her voice. "There is still so much that I don't know about being a Dragon Slayer. Are these spells truly that powerful?"

Papa Yamah nodded solemnly. "Yes, they can bend the laws of nature, but at a cost that is often too high. That's why they are forbidden and taught only to those who have proven their wisdom and restraint."

As the boat gently rocked on the swamp's murky waters, I pondered over Vajra and his group of Dragon Slayers. "Papa Yamah, Vajra and his group never used any forbidden spells. Why is that?"

Papa Yamah's expression turned thoughtful as he navigated through a particularly narrow passage. "That's because they were never taught about these spells. Forbidden spells are closely guarded secrets, passed down only to a select few. Usually, it's the leader of the Dragon Slayers who decides who learns them."

He glanced back at me, his eyes holding a mix of regret and relief. "When I left the Dragon Slayers, I took that knowledge with me. I chose not to pass it on to Vajra or any of the others. It was a deliberate decision. Those spells... they carry too much risk, too much potential for destruction. I couldn't in good conscience allow such power to fall into hands that might misuse it, even unintentionally."

Camila chimed in, "So, in a way, your departure helped prevent further misuse of magic."

Papa Yamah nodded. "Yes, you could say that. It was part of my effort to change the course we were on, to seek a different path that didn't rely on such dangerous powers."

There was silence as the boat continued to glide through the swamp.

"So, every Dragon Slayer has the potential to unleash one of these so-called forbidden spells?" I asked, curiosity laced in my voice.

Papa Yamah nodded, his gaze fixed on the path ahead. "Yes, with the right training and knowledge," he confirmed.

"Do you know your forbidden spell?" I asked, breaking the silence.

He gave me a long, thoughtful look, his eyes clouding over as if haunted by a distant memory. "Yes, Ezekiel, I do know it," he finally said, his voice tinged with a hint of sorrow. "But it's a spell I've already used, a long time ago... to protect you and Elijah."

He paused, seemingly lost in the past, then shook his head slightly as if to clear it. "It was a desperate time, a moment that called for extreme measures. But-" he stopped mid-sentence, his gaze refocusing on the present, "that is a story for another time. Right now, our focus must be on the journey ahead and the tasks at hand."

I nodded, understanding the weight of his words. The revelation added another layer to the complex tapestry of our past, a reminder of the sacrifices made for our safety.

Suddenly, a large shadow passed under our boat, causing it to rock gently. Camila tensed, her hand going to the hilt of her sword. "What was that?" she asked, her voice barely above a whisper.

"Just a swamp creature," Papa Yamah reassured her. "They're more curious than dangerous, nothing to worry about."

Gaianor, seemed unusually tense, his gaze fixed on the dark water. "I've always preferred solid ground beneath my feet," he muttered, his voice betraying a hint of unease. "Water is... unpredictable."

Camila chuckled softly, trying to lighten the mood. "That's such an Earth Elemental thing to say," she teased, giving Gaianor a friendly nudge.

Before he could answer, the water erupted in a massive upheaval. A colossal swamp monster emerged, its eyes glowing with a malevolent light. It towered over our boat, its scales glistening in the dim light, water cascading off its massive body.

Camila was quick to react, drawing her sword with a fluid motion. "Looks like we've got company!" she exclaimed, her voice betraying no hint of fear.

Papa Yamah unsheathed his sword, the one I had grown up admiring. Its dragon-shaped hilt with ruby eyes seemed to come alive in his hands. "Remember, no dragon forms," he reminded us. "We can't risk Yrome sensing us."

The monster let out a deafening roar, sending a spray of swamp water over us. Its massive tail swung towards our boat, threatening to capsize us.

Gaianor, overcoming his initial hesitation, stood firm. His hands glowed with an earthen energy. "I may not like water, but I'll stand my ground," he declared, his voice steady.

Aria, her eyes wide with fear, steadied herself. "I can try to open a portal, but it'll take a moment," she said, her voice shaking.

"We don't have a moment," Camila replied, deflecting a swipe from one of the monster's massive claws. "We fight!"

The battle was intense, with each of us using our skills and powers to fend off the swamp monster. Camila's sword danced in her hands, a blur of steel and grace. Aria opened small portals, attempting to redirect the monster's powerful swipes and lunges. I joined the fray, every strike and dodge a culmination of the skills I had honed over the past months.

Gaianor, channeling his earth powers, attempted to ensnare the beast with tendrils of rock and soil that sprouted from the swamp bed. The monster, however, was relentless, breaking free from Gaianor's earthen restraints with brute force.

In a moment of quick thinking, Papa Yamah used his sword to deflect a powerful blow from the monster's tail, the sound of metal against scale ringing through the air. "Stay focused!" he yelled over the din of battle.

The battle with the swamp monster intensified as it unleashed a barrage of attacks, each more ferocious than the last. The boat rocked violently under the onslaught, and despite our best efforts, it capsized, throwing us into the murky waters.

Camila, quick to react, summoned her water powers. With a graceful motion of her hands, she manipulated the water around us, righting the boat and creating a temporary barrier to hold back the monster's advances. Her control over the element was a sight to behold, the water bending to her will as if it were an extension of herself.

We scrambled back onto the boat, soaked but undeterred. Papa Yamah, his sword gleaming in the dim light, parried the monster's attacks with skill and precision. His years of experience as a Dragon Slayer were evident in every move he made.

Gaianor attempted to ensnare the wild creature for a second time, but the monster let out a thunderous roar that echoed through the swamp. It thrashed violently, breaking free from Gaianor's earthen restraints. Its massive tail swung towards our boat again, threatening to send us into the murky waters once more.

I acted on instinct. Leaping into the air, I focused all my energy, feeling a surge of power coursing through me. For a brief moment, a wave of heat enveloped me, and I sensed something new, something different.

My sword, which I held tightly in my grasp, began to heat up, its blade glowing with an intense, fiery light.

With this newfound power, I struck at the beast. The heated blade sliced through the air, leaving a trail of flames in its wake. As the sword connected with the monster's hide, it seared the flesh, causing significant damage. The beast let out a pained roar, the sound reverberating through the swamp.

Startled and wounded, the swamp monster retreated, disappearing into the murky depths from which it had emerged. We watched in silence as the ripples on the water's surface slowly faded away, leaving us alone once again in the quiet of the swamp.

I landed back on the boat, my heart racing from the adrenaline and the shock of what I had just done. The others looked at me, their expressions a mix of awe and disbelief. I looked down at my sword, still warm to the touch, and realized that my journey as a Pure Elemental was taking a new, unexpected turn.

We took a moment to gather ourselves. Papa Yamah sheathed his sword, his gaze meeting each of ours. "Well done," he said, a hint of relief in his voice.

As we resumed our journey, the encounter with the swamp monster left us with a renewed sense of purpose and a reminder of the dangers that lay in our path. The Whispering Woods were still ahead, and our quest was far from over.

As we continue floating over the swampy waters, I couldn't help but ask Gaianor about his abilities. More specifically how he was able to control them while still in human form.

Gaianor, still catching his breath from the recent battle, turned to me with a thoughtful expression. "Using your draconic element in human form is about understanding and channeling your inner dragon," he began, his voice steady despite the recent exertion.

He picked up a small pebble from the boat's floor, holding it in his palm. "For me, it's about connecting with the earth, feeling its energy flow through me. It's not just a physical connection, but an emotional and spiritual one as well."

He closed his eyes for a moment, and the pebble began to glow with a faint, earthen light. "I imagine the energy of the earth moving up through my feet, into my core, and then out through my hands or whatever part of me is channeling the power."

Opening his eyes, he looked at me directly. "For you, it would be about connecting with your dragon's essence. Feel the dragon within you, its power, its spirit. Imagine that power flowing through you, just like your blood. It's a part of you, Ezekiel. You just need to learn how to tap into it, to let it flow naturally."

As Gaianor finished speaking, I turned to Camila, curious about her perspective as a Water Elemental. "Camila, what about you? How do you control your water element in human form?"

Camila, who had been quietly listening to our conversation, shifted her gaze to the swamp water surrounding us. "Like Gaianor said, it's about connection," she started, her voice reflecting a deep understanding of her element. "For me, it's about feeling the flow of water, its rhythm, and its energy. Water is adaptable, fluid, and ever-changing. When I tap into my elemental power, I try to embody those qualities."

She extended her hand over the side of the boat, and the water below responded, rising in a graceful swirl around her fingers. "I visualize the water's movement, its currents and waves, and I let that energy become a part of me. It's about harmony and balance, moving with the water, not against it."

She withdrew her hand, and the water gently returned to its natural state. "Your recent experience with the swamp monster... it's intriguing. It suggests that you, like Elijah, might have the potential to harness multiple elements."

Her words sparked a new curiosity within me. The idea of wielding multiple elements was both exciting and daunting. "Do you think I could learn to control other elements like you and Gaianor do?" I asked, eager to explore this newfound possibility.

Camila exchanged a glance with Gaianor before answering. "It's possible," she said thoughtfully. "Each elemental affinity has its unique way of connecting with the world. If you can tap into that, understand it, and respect it, you might be able to channel its power. But remember, it's not just about control; it's about understanding and harmony with the element."

"That's right," Gaianor added. "Think about what you told us about how Elijah infused his sword with elemental power, he wasn't just using a skill; he was expressing a part of his very being. It's the same for you. Start by feeling that connection to your dragon, then let that energy flow into your actions, your weapons, whatever you need it to. You are his twin brother after all."

I nodded, absorbing his words. It made sense, but I knew it would take practice and a deep understanding of my own dragon nature to truly master this skill. "I'll try," I said, determination settling in my voice. "Thank you, guys."

He smiled, a genuine expression of encouragement. "You'll get there. It's in your blood, after all."

Aria's words hung in the air, casting a shadow of unease over us. "Hopefully, you won't have to resort to extreme measures like your brother, taking others' abilities to harness different elements," she said, her tone laced with a hint of concern.

A brief, tense silence followed her statement, as the gravity of her words settled among us. The thought of resorting to such drastic actions was unsettling, and I felt a twinge of discomfort at the mere suggestion.

Our journey through the swamp continued, the boat gliding silently over the murky waters. The dense foliage on either side seemed to watch us, an audience of twisted trees and hanging vines. The air was thick with the scent of damp earth and stagnant water, occasionally pierced by the distant call of an unseen creature.

Papa Yamah navigated the boat with a practiced hand, his eyes scanning the surroundings with vigilance. "Keep your eyes open," he advised. "As we've seen, the swamp is full of surprises, some less pleasant than others."

Camila, sitting at the front of the boat, turned back to us. "How much further to the Whispering Woods?" she asked, her voice carrying a hint of impatience.

"Not far now," Papa Yamah replied. "Once we reach the end of this waterway, we'll dock the boat and continue on foot. The woods are dense, and the paths are narrow."

As we continued, the swamp began to give way to firmer ground, and the dense underbrush slowly transformed into towering trees, their leaves whispering in the gentle breeze. The light filtered through the canopy in dappled patterns, casting the woods in a serene, almost ethereal glow.

"We're here," Papa Yamah announced as he steered the boat to a small clearing. "The Whispering Woods."

We disembarked, stretching our legs after the long journey. The woods seemed to welcome us, the air fresh and filled with the sounds of nature. It was a clear distinction to the oppressive atmosphere of the swamp.

"Stay close," Papa Yamah warned as we ventured into the woods. "It's easy to get lost in here. The paths change, and the woods have a way of... playing tricks on your mind."

As we ventured deeper into the Whispering Woods, the atmosphere shifted subtly. The trees grew taller, their branches intertwining overhead, creating a natural cathedral that seemed to hum with ancient energy. The light that filtered through the leaves was tinged with green, casting everything in an otherworldly hue.

The path beneath our feet was a mosaic of roots and earth, winding and twisting like a serpent through the forest. Every step seemed to echo, as if the very ground was listening to our passage. The air was alive with the sound of rustling leaves, and occasionally, a soft whisper would reach our ears, though its source remained unseen.

Papa Yamah led the way, his sword drawn, its blade reflecting the dappled light. "Stay close," he said, his voice low.

As we continued, the whispers grew more pronounced, a chorus of ethereal voices that seemed to be speaking directly to us. I could almost make out words, but they slipped away like smoke in the wind.

Suddenly, Gaianor stopped, his hand raised for silence. "Do you hear that?" he whispered.

We all listened, and that's when I heard it—a faint melody, haunting and beautiful, floating through the air. It seemed to be coming from deeper within the woods, luring us forward.

"We should be cautious," Aria said, her eyes scanning the shadows between the trees. "This could be a trick of the woods, a way to lead us astray."

But there was something compelling about the melody, something that tugged at my very soul. "We need to find the source," I said, my decision firm. "I don't know why, but I think it might be a key to understanding these woods."

We hesitantly followed the melody, the path becoming more treacherous as we went. Roots snaked across the ground, grasping like fingers, and the trees seemed to lean in closer, their whispers growing louder.

Then, without warning, the ground beneath us gave way, and we found ourselves sliding down a steep embankment, tumbling into a hidden glade. We landed with a thud, disoriented but unharmed.

As we picked ourselves up, we realized we were not alone. In the center of the glade stood a figure, ethereal and shimmering, like a being made of light and shadow. It was the source of the melody, a song that now filled the air with a palpable magic.

"Who are you?" I asked, my voice echoing in the stillness of the glade.

The figure turned to face us, its features indistinct yet somehow familiar. "I am the Guardian of the Whispering Woods," it said, its voice a melody in itself. "You have entered a sacred place."

As the Guardian's words resonated through the glade, Papa Yamah stepped closer, his demeanor calm yet assertive. "Guardian, it's been many years since I last stood in your presence," he began, his voice steady. "I was the one who brought Yrome's Crown to you, to be placed within the Cavern of Echoes for its protection."

The Guardian's form flickered slightly, as if stirred by a breeze that we could not feel. "Yes, Yamah, I remember your visit well," it replied, its voice carrying a hint of ancient wisdom. "You brought the crown here, entrusting it to the woods and to me. But why have you returned to reclaim it? The crown harbors a great and dangerous power."

Papa Yamah nodded solemnly. "We have come because a grave threat has reawakened in our world. Yrome has returned. We fear that he may come seeking the crown, and if he finds it, the consequences could be dire for all."

At the mention of Yrome's name, the Guardian seemed to shimmer more intensely, its form wavering like a reflection on water. "Yrome..." it murmured, a note of concern in its melodic voice. "His ambition and thirst for power were well known to the woods. If he seeks the crown once more, the balance of the world itself could be at risk."

"We believe we can find a way to hide the crown from him permanently, to keep it out of his reach," Papa Yamah continued. "But to do so, we need to secure it first. We ask for your permission to enter the Cavern of Echoes and retrieve the crown."

The Guardian seemed to contemplate this request, its form glowing softly in the twilight of the glade. After a moment of silence, it spoke again. "Your intentions are noble, Yamah, and the threat you speak of is grave. I will grant you access to the Cavern of Echoes. But be warned, you and your friends must prove your worthiness and your resolve."

Papa Yamah bowed his head in gratitude. "Thank you. We are prepared to face whatever challenges lie ahead. The safety of our world depends on it."

As I stood there, a profound sense of wonder washed over me. I was confronted with a reality far beyond my previous understanding. The Guardian's presence was both mesmerizing and humbling. I found myself captivated by the realization that there were beings and forces in this world that defied all conventional understanding, a reminder of the vast and mysterious world that lay beyond the realm of dragons and humans.

The Guardian's gaze seemed to pierce through each of us, assessing our determination and our courage. "Very well," it said. "But be warned, the woods will test you, not just in strength, but in heart and mind. You must prove yourselves worthy."

With a wave of its hand, the Guardian conjured an image in the air, a map of sorts, made of light and shadow. It showed a winding path through the woods, leading to a location marked by a glowing symbol.

"This is the path to the Cavern of Echoes," the Guardian explained. "Follow it, and you may find what you seek. Stray from it, and you may be lost forever in the depths of the woods."

We studied the map intently, memorizing its twists and turns. The path was complex, weaving through the densest parts of the forest, across hidden streams and through groves.

As we prepared to set off, the Guardian offered one final piece of advice. "The Whispering Woods are alive, and they will communicate with you. Listen to their whispers, for they may guide you in times of doubt. If your hearts are true, you may find what you seek."

With that, the Guardian's form faded away, leaving us alone in the glade, the map etched in our minds.

"You guys ready?" I asked, seeking affirmation in their eyes.

One by one, they nodded, their expressions a mix of determination and anticipation.

We set off, following the path as it had been shown to us, the whispers of the woods our constant companion.

The journey was unlike any other. The forest seemed to change around us, the scenery shifting subtly as we progressed. One moment we were walking through a grove of ancient oaks, their branches heavy with moss, and the next we found ourselves in a clearing filled with wildflowers, their colors vibrant and otherworldly.

The whispers guided us, offering hints and warnings. At times, the path would seem to disappear, only to reappear when we listened to the guidance of the whispers.

We eventually made it into another clearing that was shrouded by the intertwining branches of towering trees, and in which stood a stone pedestal. Atop it rested a peculiar object: a sphere, divided into segments, each inscribed with intricate symbols and patterns. The sphere radiated a soft, pulsating light, beckoning us to engage with its mystery.

Papa Yamah approached it first, his eyes narrowing as he studied the sphere. He circled the pedestal slowly, his gaze never leaving the intricate patterns and symbols that adorned the sphere. "Interesting," he muttered under his breath, his fingers hovering just inches from the sphere's surface.

Camila leaned in, her fingers tracing the symbols. "These look like ancient runes," she observed. "But they're unlike any I've seen before."

Gaianor knelt beside the pedestal, his hand hovering above the sphere. "The earth here... it's alive with energy. This object is connected to the woods themselves."

Aria stepped forward, deep in thought. "Hmmm, it looks like we can move parts of the sphere. A puzzle perhaps?"

"Maybe we need to align the symbols in a certain way," I suggested, my voice tinged with uncertainty.

Despite our efforts, spinning the segments yielded nothing. Frustration began to bloom when the forest's gentle whispers seemed to nudge us towards patience.

Then, Camila stepped closer, a knowing look in her eyes. "Guys, check this out," she said, pointing to the symbols. "These symbols seem to represent elements of the forest—the wind, the water, the earth, and the life that thrives. I think they need to be in harmony."

We followed her lead, and after what felt like an eternity, the segments clicked into place, aligning in a pattern that mirrored the harmony of the forest. The sphere glowed brightly, then slowly opened, revealing a hollow center. Inside lay a small, carved stone, pulsing with the same ethereal light as the sphere.

Papa Yamah picked up the stone, his fingers tracing the intricate carvings. "Strange," he murmured, a note of intrigue. "There's more here than meets the eye."

Gaianor peered closely. "It doesn't look like any stone I've seen."

"Well, it's coming with us," Camila said. "I'm sure we'll need it later."

As we ventured further into the Whispering Woods, the path ahead split into five distinct trails, each veiled in a different ethereal glow. The glows—green, blue, violet, crimson, and a soft gold—painted the way forward in a kaleidoscope of ethereal light.

"It looks like we have to split up here," said Papa Yamah, his voice tinged with a reluctant firmness.

"I don't think that's a good idea," I said. "Shouldn't we stick together?"

"I agree with Ezekiel," Camila added.

"Of course, that would be best," said Papa Yamah. "But it looks like we don't have a choice."

A sense of foreboding filled the air, and it was clear that our next challenge would require us to face individual trials.

"Everyone please be careful," I urged, my voice tinged with a subtle tremor of concern.

I found myself drawn to the path bathed in the soft, golden light. The trail wound through the dense forest, the trees arching overhead like silent guardians. The air was thick with a sense of anticipation, and every step I took seemed to echo in the stillness.

After what felt like miles, the path opened into a clearing dominated by a towering stone figure. It stood motionless, its surface etched with ancient runes that glowed faintly and the word golem. At its feet lay a stone tablet, inscribed with a riddle:

> "In heart of stone and ancient might,
> To pass, you must prove your right.
> Show your strength, both mind and brawn,
> Only then, the barrier's gone."

I approached the figure cautiously, my sword drawn, eyes scanning for any sign of movement. Without warning, the golem lurched to life, its massive stone limbs moving with a surprising speed. I rolled to the side, feeling the ground shudder under the impact. Scrambling to my feet, I barely managed to parry the next blow, the force of it sending shockwaves up my arm.

I realized quickly that my usual tactics were futile against this behemoth. Each swing of my sword felt like striking solid rock, the blade barely leaving a scratch on its surface. The golem's relentless assault gave me little room to think, each dodge and weave draining my stamina.

I tried to find a rhythm in the golem's movements, looking for an opening, but it was like fighting a mountain. The golem's fists were relentless, and I found myself on the defensive, narrowly avoiding crushing blows that would have ended the fight instantly.

As the battle wore on, I felt my energy waning. The golem, undeterred by fatigue, seemed to grow more formidable with each passing moment. In a desperate attempt, I lunged forward, aiming for what I hoped was a weak spot, but the golem caught me mid-strike, its hand closing around me with crushing force.

Pinned against the golem's chest, I struggled to break free, but it was like being held in a vice. Panic set in as I gasped for air, my sword knocked out of reach. It was in this moment of desperation, with defeat looming, that I remembered my fight against the swamp monster. I also remembered Gaianor's and Camila's words about channeling my draconic element.

With every ounce of willpower, I focused inward, calling upon the dragon's fire that lay dormant within me. I could feel the heat rising, a burning energy coursing through my veins. My hands began to glow with a fiery aura, the heat intensifying until it was almost unbearable.

Summoning all my strength, I pushed against the golem's grip. The heat from my hands began to sear into the stone, creating cracks where there were none. The golem, sensing the change, hesitated for a moment, its grip loosening just enough for me to wriggle free.

I fell to the ground, gasping for air, but there was no time to rest. I scrambled to my feet, my hands still glowing with draconic fire. I picked up and focused the energy into my sword, watching as the blade ignited with a brilliant flame.

Now armed with a weapon that could finally do damage, I renewed my assault on the golem.

As I engaged the golem, my sword ablaze, I felt a surge of confidence.

With each swing of my sword, the air sizzled, and the heat intensified. The golem met my attacks with powerful, ground-shaking blows. But where once its strikes had seemed unstoppable, now they faltered against the onslaught of my fiery blade.

I moved with purpose, each step calculated, each strike precise. The golem's stone skin, impervious to ordinary weapons, could not withstand the searing heat of my sword. Chips and cracks appeared on its surface, glowing red as the heat penetrated its core.

The runes on the golem reacted to the intense heat. They glowed brighter, pulsating with an eerie light, as if protesting against their imminent destruction.

I saw my opportunity and took it. With a powerful leap, I soared into the air, my sword raised high. I descended upon the golem with all the fury of a dragon, my blade aimed at its heart, where the runes converged in a nexus of power.

The impact was monumental. My sword pierced the golem's chest, driving deep into its stone heart. A blinding explosion of light and heat erupted, engulfing us both. The golem's rumbling groan was almost a cry of defeat, its body unable to withstand the internal inferno.

As the light faded, the golem's form began to crack and crumble, its once mighty frame now succumbing to the ravages of fire. Stone and rune fell away, revealing the hollow core within. With a final, resounding crack, the golem collapsed, reduced to rubble at my feet.

Exhausted but triumphant, I stood amidst the remnants of the shattered golem, catching my breath. The air was thick with dust and the scent of scorched stone. My heart still raced from the battle, a mix of adrenaline and a newfound respect for the challenges the Whispering Woods presented.

I took a moment to gather myself, feeling the lingering warmth of my draconic power slowly fading from my hands. The realization of what I had just accomplished began to sink in. I had tapped into a part of myself that I barely understood, a part that Elijah had already tapped into. It was both exhilarating and terrifying.

Just as I was about to continue, a strange yet familiar sensation fell over me. The world around me blurred. Ytfen's memories began to consume me once more.

8
Limitless Power

As another wave of Ytfen's memories enveloped me, I found myself in the midst of a war camp, the air thick with tension and the distant sounds of battle. The ground beneath my feet was rough and uneven.

Around me, commanders and soldiers moved with urgency, their faces etched with concern. Maps and plans were spread across a large wooden table, illuminated by flickering torches. The atmosphere was charged with a sense of impending crisis.

Standing across from me was Tarn, his expression grave. His armor, adorned with symbols of mountains and stone, seemed to weigh heavily on him, mirroring the burden he carried.

"Your Majesty," Tarn began, his voice strained, "our forces are being overwhelmed. An army of golems, unlike anything we've seen before, is advancing towards Terra. They are relentless, and our defenses are faltering."

I leaned over the map, studying the terrain and the advancing enemy lines. "How did they amass such a force without our knowledge?" I asked, my mind racing through strategies and possibilities.

Tarn shook his head, frustration evident in his furrowed brow. "We don't know, my king. It's as if they appeared out of thin air. Our scouts reported no such gathering of forces until it was almost upon us."

I looked into Tarn's eyes, seeing the fear for his people and the desperation for a solution. "We must act swiftly. Terra cannot fall. It is not just a village; but a very important military outpost in our kingdom."

Tarn nodded, his resolve returning. "What do you propose, my king? Our traditional tactics seem futile against this tide of stone and magic."

I pondered for a moment, the weight of command heavy upon me. "I'll take care of it."

Tarn's expression shifted to one of apprehension. "My king, you should not be directly involved. We both know how immense your power is. The destruction you could cause..."

"I am aware," I interrupted, my tone firm yet tinged with regret. "But the safety of Terra and our people is paramount. I cannot stand by while our lands are threatened. Where are these golems?"

Tarn pointed to a location on the map, a narrow pass leading to the Earth Village. "They are here, advancing quickly. But, King Ytfen, please reconsider. There must be another way."

I shook my head, my decision unwavering. "There is no time, Tarn. Order your soldiers to retreat to a safe distance. I will confront the golems alone. It is the only way to ensure minimal collateral damage."

Tarn hesitated, the conflict evident in his eyes. Finally, he nodded, a gesture of trust and respect. "Very well, my king. I will relay your orders. Our soldiers will fall back and await your command."

As Tarn hurried away to execute my orders, I steeled myself for what was to come. The power I possessed was a double-edged sword, capable of both protection and devastation. As I prepared to face the golem army, I knew the responsibility that lay on my shoulders. I had to end this threat, but in doing so, I had to be mindful of the very lands and people I sought to protect.

With a deep breath, I focused my energy, feeling the familiar surge of power within me. I pushed off the ground. The ground beneath me cracked slightly from the force of my launch.

The world blurred as I propelled myself forward at an incredible speed, the landscape rushing past in a whirl of colors. The lush green of the forests, the rugged browns of the mountains, and the winding blues of the rivers all merged into a vibrant tapestry beneath me.

As I neared the site of the advancing golems, the serene beauty of nature gave way to a scene of impending conflict. The golem army, an array of stone and magic, moved with a relentless, methodical pace. From my vantage point, they looked like a dark tide, an unnatural force in stark contrast to the natural world around them.

Hovering above the site, I took in the scene below. The golems, towering and formidable, marched in unison. Their movements were synchronized, each step a demonstration to the dark magic that animated them. There looked to be thousands of golems marching on. It was a chilling sight – an army of soulless constructs, a threat to all that was living and breathing.

"How strange," I whispered to myself. "Golems never leave their territory. It's as if they are running away from something."

In that moment, I felt the weight of my responsibility. I was not just a king; I was a guardian, a protector of the land and its people. I had to do what had to be done.

I extended my hand, palm facing the sky. Drawing upon the deep well of power within me, I began to channel my energy, focusing it into a single point above my palm. The air around me crackled with electricity, the atmosphere charged with raw elemental force.

Slowly, a small orb of light began to form, growing steadily as I poured more of my energy into it. The orb expanded, pulsating with a brilliant radiance that illuminated the sky. It was a sphere of pure, concentrated energy.

The ground below trembled, the very air vibrating as the energy ball grew in size and intensity. The trees swayed, their leaves rustling in the tumultuous winds that my power had conjured. Even the golems, in their relentless march, seemed to pause, as if sensing the impending force.

I glanced around, ensuring that no soldiers or innocents were in the vicinity. It was crucial that this strike be precise, its impact confined to the golem army alone.

With a final surge of energy, I completed the charging of the energy ball. It was now a massive, swirling vortex of light and power, a miniature sun glowing with an intensity that was almost blinding.

Taking a deep breath, I steeled myself for the release. With a determined thrust of my hand, I unleashed the energy ball towards the golems. It hurtled down with incredible speed, a comet of destruction on a collision course with the army of stone.

The moment it made contact, a deafening explosion ripped through the air. A blinding flash of light enveloped the area, followed by a shockwave that radiated outwards with ferocious intensity. The ground shook as if in the throes of an earthquake, the very air seething with the unleashed power.

When the light finally receded, the scene below was one of devastation. The golem army had been decimated, reduced to rubble and dust. The landscape was scarred, a confirmation to the destructive power I had wielded.

I felt a mix of relief and sorrow. Relief that the threat had been neutralized, but sorrow for the necessity of such destruction. It was a stark reminder of the responsibility that came with my power, a burden I carried as both a king and a protector.

As the aftermath of the unleashed power settled below me, the memory of Ytfen began to wane, the vividness of the scene gradually fading. The once clear and sharp details of the devastated landscape started to blur, the sounds of the aftermath growing distant and muffled.

I felt myself being pulled back, the grip of the memory loosening.

9

Yrome's Crown

The experience of Ytfen's memory left me with a mix of awe and introspection. The power he wielded, the decisions he made, and the sacrifices he endured were now a part of my consciousness, a shared history that connected me to him in ways I was still trying to comprehend. With each memory, I was piecing together the legacy of Ytfen, understanding more about the dragon king.

After a few moments of regaining my composure, I continued forward. As I ventured deeper into the woods, the environment began to change. The trees grew taller, their branches intertwining above to form a canopy that barely let any light through. The air was cooler here.

The path ahead was less defined, often disappearing under a blanket of moss and roots. I had to rely on my instincts to guide me, the sense of direction that had been honed during my time in the wilderness. Every so often, I would catch a glimpse of a shadow flitting between the trees or hear the rustle of foliage that suggested I was not alone in these woods.

Eventually, I came upon yet another clearing, where the light filtered through in ethereal beams, illuminating the forest floor in patches of gold and green. In the center of the clearing stood what seemed to be an altar, its surface covered in runes like those on the golem.

I approached the altar cautiously, aware that this could be another test. The runes glowed faintly as I drew near, pulsating with an energy that resonated with the dragon power within me. I reached out, my fingers hovering over the stone, feeling the hum of magic beneath my touch.

Suddenly, the ground trembled, and from the shadows of the forest emerged my companions, each looking as weary and battle worn as I felt. Papa Yamah's eyes met mine, a mix of concern and pride in his gaze.

"Is everyone alright?" he asked, his voice steady despite the fatigue that lined his face.

Camila brushed a leaf from her hair, her laughter tinged with fatigue. "Yes, but these trials are no joke."

"I couldn't agree more," Gaianor added.

"Did everyone have to fight a golem?" I asked.

A puzzled hush fell over the group as they turned their attention toward me, their faces a mix of quizzical expressions.

"My trial was a test of leadership, of making decisions under pressure that could mean life or death," said Camila.

Gaianor, his hands still trembling slightly from the ordeal, added, "And for me, it was about overcoming my own limitations. The trial forced me to confront my fear of water, to find strength in vulnerability."

Aria, the quietest of us all, had a faraway look in her eyes. "My trial... it was about trust. Trusting in my own abilities and in the strength of those around me. It was a lesson in opening up, in letting others in."

As they spoke, I reflected on my own trial. It had been a harrowing experience, one that had forced me to confront my own doubts about my ability to protect those I cared about.

"What about you, Papa Yamah?" I inquired, my gaze steady and curious.

"I'd rather not discuss it," he replied, his tone tinged with a hint of reluctance.

A heavy silence hung in the air, the unspoken words echoing between us. Aria, sensing the tension, stepped up to the altar beside me.

"What's this?" She gestured toward the intricate runes etched into the altar, her voice breaking the oppressive stillness. "These runes bear a striking resemblance to the ones on the stone."

Papa Yamah, approached, the stone held gently in his weathered hands. "You're right."

As he got closer to the altar, the stone started to glow in sync with the altar. "They seem to be resonating with each other," he said, meticulously analyzing the altar. "Ah so that's it," he nestled the stone into a perfectly shaped hollow on the altar, the runes sprang to vibrant life, a symphony of light playing between them. "It's a key," Papa Yamah whispered, his eyes alight with the dance of ancient magic.

The light crescendoed around us, a warm, pulsing glow that seemed to hold the very essence of the forest. The earth trembled beneath our feet, and with a groan of stone on stone, the ground opened before us. A staircase, wrought of the same glowing runes, spiraled down into the earth's heart.

"Woah," I said, a mix of trepidation and awe in my voice.

We all looked at each other and simply nodded in silent agreement. Together, we took a collective step toward the yawning mouth of the staircase, each step a silent pact to protect one another against the unknown perils that lay ahead. The air grew colder as we descended, and the sound of running water echoed softly in the distance.

"There," Papa Yamah pointed ahead, where towering stone pillars stood, their surfaces covered in the same glowing runes we had seen in the woods. They pulsed gently, casting a dim, otherworldly light that illuminated our path.

We approached cautiously, aware that this place was steeped in magic. The air was thick with the scent of damp earth and moss, and a sense of ancient power permeated the atmosphere.

As we crossed the threshold of the cavern, a shiver ran down my spine. The interior was vast, the ceiling lost in shadows high above. Stalactites hung like jagged teeth, and the walls glistened with moisture. The sound of our footsteps echoed in the cavernous space, a reminder of how small we were in this grand, ancient place.

The path ahead was lit by a series of luminescent crystals embedded in the walls, casting a soft, ethereal glow that guided our way deeper into the cavern. The air was cool and still, as if the cavern itself was holding its breath, waiting for something momentous to occur.

We moved in silence, each lost in our own thoughts. The weight of our quest pressed heavily upon us, the knowledge that the fate of our world could hinge on what lay within these ancient walls.

As we delved deeper, the cavern began to open up into a larger chamber. In the center of this chamber stood a pedestal, upon which rested an object that immediately drew our attention. It was a crown, but unlike any crown I had ever seen. It was crafted from a material that seemed to absorb the light around it, giving it an otherworldly appearance. The crown was adorned with red jewels that pulsed with an inner light, and it seemed to throb with a life of its own.

"This is it," Papa Yamah whispered, his voice filled with a mix of awe and trepidation. "Yrome's Crown."

We gathered around the pedestal, each of us aware of the significance of the artifact before us. This crown was the source of the Dragon Slayers' abilities, and perhaps our only hope in stopping Yrome.

The chamber within the Cavern of Echoes seemed to hold its breath as we encircled the pedestal, our eyes fixed on the crown that lay upon it.

"It's... beautiful," Camila murmured, her voice tinged with a mix of awe and fear. "But in a way that's almost... terrifying."

Papa Yamah nodded, his gaze never leaving the crown. "This artifact has been the heart of the Dragon Slayers for generations," he began, his voice echoing softly in the chamber. "Passed down from one leader to the next, it's the source of our power, the means by which new Dragon Slayers are created."

Gaianor leaned in closer, his brow furrowed in thought. "But where does its power come from? How can something like this exist?"

Papa Yamah sighed, a look of contemplation crossing his face. "There are many theories, but the truth has been lost to time. Only Yrome knows the truth. As the crown is passed down, we are told not to question such things."

"But why?" I asked. "Why create something with so much power that has the potential to harm others?"

"That," Papa Yamah said, "is the greatest mystery of all. Perhaps it was meant as a balance, a way to ensure that dragons could not dominate the world. Or so we're told. Or maybe it was simply a tool, created for a purpose we can no longer comprehend."

We all stood in silence, contemplating the crown and the countless lives it had touched, shaped, and destroyed. It was a symbol of power, but also a reminder of the endless cycle of conflict between dragons and humans.

"We must be quick," Papa Yamah said, his eyes fixed on the crown.

We gathered around the pedestal, each of us aware of the significance of the artifact before us. This crown was likely the key to Yrome's power, the source of the Dragon Slayers' abilities, and perhaps our only hope in stopping him.

As we stood there, contemplating our next move, the air in the chamber shifted. A low hum began to resonate through the cavern, growing louder and more insistent. The crown's jewels glowed brighter, and a sense of urgency filled the air.

I turned to Papa Yamah, the crown's ominous glow reflecting in his eyes. "We should destroy it," I said firmly, feeling the danger it posed. "It's too powerful, too corrupting. It's what Yrome wants, and it's only brought pain and suffering."

Papa Yamah's expression darkened, a mix of sadness and resignation. "I understand your reasoning, Ezekiel," he began, his voice heavy with unspoken burdens. "But there's something you need to know."

I waited, sensing the gravity of his words.

"All Dragon Slayers are connected to the crown. Our bond to the crown is deep. To destroy the crown is to unravel the very essence of our being."

My heart sank. "So, destroying the crown..."

"Would mean the end of every Dragon Slayer's life," he finished, his gaze meeting mine.

The revelation hit me like a physical blow. The idea of losing Papa Yamah, the man who had been a father, a mentor, and a guide, was unthinkable. It wasn't just him; it was the looming specter of losing everyone in Serenity's Edge. The innocent lives, like flickering candles in the darkness, would be snuffed out. And then there was Aria, whose choice to no longer be a dragon slayer was a testament to the transformative power of friendship and understanding.

Yet, the threat the crown posed was undeniable.

"We have to find another way," I said, determination steeling my voice. "There has to be a solution that doesn't involve sacrificing anyone."

Papa Yamah nodded, a faint smile touching his lips.

The tension in the air was palpable as Gaianor stepped forward, his expression resolute. "We can't risk it," he said firmly, his gaze fixed on the crown. "The survival of the world outweighs the lives of a few. We have to destroy it, now."

I felt a surge of anger at his words. "No," I countered, my voice rising. "We can't just sacrifice people like that. It's genocide! There has to be another way."

Gaianor's eyes narrowed. "You're letting your emotions cloud your judgment, Ezekiel. This is bigger than us, bigger than any personal attachments. We're talking about the fate of the world here."

The argument escalated, our voices echoing off the cavern walls. "And what about the value of a life? What about the principles we stand for?" I shot back, my fists clenched. "We can't just throw away someone's life for convenience!"

Before I could react, Gaianor's hands glowed with an earthen light, his powers surging as he prepared to strike the crown. "I'm sorry, Ezekiel, but this is the only way."

Adrenaline pumping, I lunged forward, intercepting his attack. Our powers clashed, sending a shockwave through the cavern. "I won't let you do this, Gaianor!"

Camila stepped in, placing a hand on each of our shoulders. "Enough!" she bellowed, her voice commanding and powerful. "This is not the way. We don't sacrifice our own. We find solutions, together."

The tension broke, leaving us breathing heavily, the realization of our near-fatal impulse hanging heavily in the air. Gaianor stepped back, his expression conflicted but understanding.

"I... I'm sorry," he muttered, his gaze dropping. "Once again I let my fear of what might happen override my judgment."

I nodded, the anger dissipating as quickly as it had flared. "We're all scared, Gaianor. But we can't lose ourselves in that fear. We have to be better than that."

Papa Yamah looked at each of us, his eyes filled with a mix of pride and sorrow.

Camila, who had been watching the heated exchange with a troubled expression, finally stepped forward. "Enough," she said, her voice steady and clear. "Enough sacrifices have been made already. We've all lost too much to this war, to this endless cycle of power and destruction. It's time to break that cycle, not perpetuate it with more loss."

She turned to Aria, her eyes imploring. "Aria, can you open a portal back to Serenity's Edge? We need to regroup and think this through with the elders."

Aria nodded, a determined look on her face. "Yes, I can do that." She raised her hands, and the familiar swirl of a portal began to form, its edges shimmering with otherworldly light.

But just as the portal stabilized, ready for us to step through, the crown on its pedestal pulsed with a dark, ominous energy. The air in the cavern thickened, and a deep, resonating hum filled the space. I felt a strange pull, an irresistible force drawing me towards the crown.

Before I could react, the world around me blurred, and I was plunged into a different realm—a mindscape. The cavern and my companions faded away, replaced by an endless void. In this shadowy expanse, a sense of foreboding enveloped me, and I knew, instinctively, that I was not alone.

DRAGON'S FIRE

10

Awakened Fire

As the room plunged into darkness, I found myself in a vast, shadowy mindscape, standing before a throne upon which a hooded figure in a black cloak sat ominously. The air was thick with an unspoken menace, and a chill ran down my spine. This was the same figure from my nightmares. The figure looked like the same ones that emerged from Elijah and I before Yrome's appearance.

Without warning, the figure rose, its movements swift and predatory. In a blink, it charged towards me, its cloak billowing like the wings of a dark angel. I barely had time to react, my instincts kicking in as I braced for the attack.

The figure was relentless, its strikes precise and powerful, each one carrying the weight of a nightmare made real. I tried to speak, to ask who or what it was, but my words were lost in the din of our clashing wills. This was no time for questions; survival was all that mattered.

I dodged and weaved, trying to find an opening, but the figure anticipated my every move. Its strength was immense, its speed otherworldly. I felt like a novice, struggling to keep up with an unseen and unfathomable foe.

The figure's attacks were a blur, its hands and feet striking with the force of a tempest. I could feel the air crackle with dark energy every time it moved.

I managed to parry a particularly vicious strike, but the force of it sent me reeling back. I stumbled but regained my footing, my heart pounding in my chest.

As we fought, the landscape around us shifted and twisted, the mindscape reflecting the chaos of our battle.

In a desperate attempt, I feigned a move to the left and then quickly pivoted, swinging with all my might towards the figure. But it was as if it knew my intentions before I did, effortlessly dodging and countering with a blow that sent me crashing to the ground.

I lay there for a moment, dazed and breathless, the figure looming over me. Its presence was oppressive, a darkness that threatened to swallow me whole. But I couldn't give up. Not after coming so far. I had to fight.

The figure's movements were like shadows, fluid and unpredictable, making it nearly impossible to land a solid hit. I felt like I was fighting a ghost, a specter of darkness that defied the laws of the physical world.

I lunged forward, my fist aimed at the figure's midsection, but it sidestepped with an eerie grace, countering with a swift elbow strike that grazed my cheek. I staggered back, feeling a trickle of blood, the pain grounding me in the surreal reality of this mindscape.

Regaining my balance, I feinted to the right and then spun, delivering a roundhouse kick. The figure caught my leg effortlessly, twisting and throwing me to the ground. I rolled away, narrowly avoiding a stomp that would have crushed my ribs.

I sprang to my feet, my breathing heavy, my mind racing. In a flash of inspiration, I remembered where I was – in a mindscape, a realm of thought and spirit. Here, the usual constraints didn't apply. I could do something I dared not do in the physical world for fear of Yrome's detection.

With a deep breath, I focused inward, tapping into the core of my draconic essence. The air around me began to shimmer with dark energy, a visible manifestation of my transformation. My body started to change, growing larger, more powerful, dark scales forming on my skin, wings sprouting from my back.

The hooded figure paused, seemingly taken aback by my metamorphosis. I seized the moment, my newfound strength surging through me. I had become the Dark Dragon.

I roared, a sound that echoed through the mindscape, a declaration of my defiance and determination. The figure responded with a hiss, its own form seeming to waver and shift, as if unsettled by my transformation.

The figure moved with a sinister grace, its attacks precise and relentless. I countered with the full might of my draconic strength, my dark scales absorbing the brunt of its shadowy assaults.

Our fight was a whirlwind of destruction, each blow sending shockwaves through the mindscape. I unleashed torrents of dark energy, hoping to overwhelm the figure, but it deftly evaded my attacks, responding with swift, powerful strikes that seemed to drain my energy with every hit.

Despite my formidable size and strength, the figure's resilience was astounding. It seemed to feed off the darkness, growing stronger with each passing moment. I roared in frustration and defiance, refusing to back down, but I could feel the tide of battle turning against me.

As the figure landed a series of punishing blows, I found myself faltering, my movements becoming sluggish. What I was doing was not working. I needed to try something different. But what? Panic began to claw at my insides, a desperate scramble for something, anything that might turn the tide. "Think, think!" I urged myself, gasping for breath.

It was then, in the midst of my struggle, that I remembered my fight with the golem. The way I infused my sword with fire. "Could I...?" The thought was a wild spark, daring me to grasp it.

With a deep, guttural growl, I began to transform. My black scales, the armor of my past battles, shimmered with an emerging, fiery luster. One by one, they began to smolder, the black giving way to a vibrant, scorching red, the color of coals igniting under a bellows' breath. Flames erupted from my body, engulfing me in a fiery aura. The air around me crackled, superheated by the change; it was the herald of rebirth.

My talons grew sharper, like forged blades fresh from the forge, and from my maw, a heat distorted the air, promising conflagration. My wings, now vast and resplendent, were like sheets of living flame, each beat exuding waves of intense heat. My Dark Dragon form had now been infused with the element of fire.

I felt a surge of power. A fire that reminded me of David.

Now in my new form, I faced the hooded figure with renewed determination. The figure faltered before this blaze of newfound power. I seized the moment, unleashing a barrage of fireballs, each one exploding with intense heat upon impact.

The figure tried to counter, but the ferocity of my fire assault was relentless. I breathed a continuous stream of flames, turning the battlefield into an inferno. The figure's shadowy form wavered under the onslaught, its movements becoming erratic.

The battle between my Fire Dragon form and the mysterious figure reached a crescendo of epic proportions. Flames and shadows danced around us, creating a spectacle of light and darkness. My fiery breath clashed with the figure's dark energy, sending shockwaves through the mindscape.

I swooped and dived, my wings cutting through the air with precision. The figure countered with swift, shadowy strikes, its form blurring in and out of existence.

With each fiery breath, I unleashed a barrage of flames, seeking to engulf the figure. It dodged and weaved, its cloak billowing like a dark cloud. The figure retaliated with blasts of dark energy, each one narrowly missing me as I twisted and turned in the air.

The battle raged on, neither of us yielding. I felt the heat of my flames intensify, the fire within me burning brighter than ever. In a daring maneuver, I dove towards the figure, my jaws agape, ready to unleash a devastating blast of fire.

The figure quickly dodged and landed a powerful blow that sent a jolt through my entire being. As its strike connected, a sharp pain pierced my head, and for a moment, my vision blurred. In that split second, a vivid vision flashed before my eyes: a world engulfed in flames, a landscape consumed by fire and destruction.

Through the haze of this burning world, I saw a figure in the distance, unmistakably Yrome, his presence dominating the horizon. To my right, a shadowy silhouette emerged, its identity obscured, yet somehow familiar. Together, we charged towards Yrome, united in a common purpose.

But as quickly as the vision appeared, it vanished. The impact of the figure's strike had sent me reeling backward, and I found myself flying through the air. I landed with a heavy thud, the force of the blow momentarily stunning me.

As I lay there, trying to regain my senses, the realization dawned on me: what I had seen was not just a vision. It felt too real, too tangible. It was as if I had tapped into a memory, a fragment of a past that was somehow connected to me, to Yrome, and to the mysterious person I was battling alongside with.

Shaking off the disorientation, I prepared to reengage with the figure, my mind racing with questions about the vision.

The figure, with a swift and ominous motion, teleported high into the air, positioning itself above me. Suddenly, it extended its arms, and from its fingertips, a barrage of dark energy beams erupted, raining down upon me like a relentless storm.

Each beam struck with the force of a thunderbolt, sending waves of searing pain through my body. The onslaught was unyielding, a never-ending tempest of dark energy that pummeled me relentlessly. I tried to shield myself, to counterattack, but the sheer magnitude of the assault was overwhelming. My dragon form began to falter under the intensity of the attack, and I felt my strength waning.

As I struggled to maintain my dragon form, the figure raised its arms once more, and above it, a massive comet materialized out of the dark void. It was the same comet from my nightmares, the one that had haunted my dreamscape during my early attempts to control my Dark Dragon form. The figure swung its arm downward in a commanding gesture, and the comet began its descent, hurtling towards me with catastrophic force. It filled the entire sky, its fiery tail blazing a trail of destruction.

In that moment, as the comet bore down upon me, I braced for the impact, my mind racing with thoughts of my friends, my quest, and the uncertain fate that awaited us all. But just as the comet was about to collide with me, reality snapped back into focus.

11

Taming the Unseen Power

I was jolted back into the real world, the Cavern of Echoes coming into sharp relief around me. My friends were there, their faces etched with concern and determination. They had been working frantically to remove Yrome's Crown from my head, and as I regained my senses, I realized they had succeeded.

Papa Yamah was holding the crown, his hands trembling slightly from the effort. Camila was by my side, her expression a mix of relief and worry. Gaianor and Aria stood nearby, their eyes reflecting the intensity of the moment.

"You're back," Camila said, her voice filled with urgency. "What happened?"

Papa Yamah nodded solemnly, his gaze fixed on the crown in his hands. "We have to be careful. The power it holds – it reaches into the mind, into the soul."

I sat up, still feeling the remnants of the comet's impending impact in my mind. And then there was the vision, or memory, of Yrome and the shadowy figure battling alongside me. What did it all mean?

Gaianor stepped forward, his expression grave. "Are you alright?"

"Yes," I looked around at my companions, their faces a tapestry of concern and determination. "We can't let this crown fall into the wrong hands," I said, my voice steady despite the turmoil inside. "Whatever it takes, we have to keep it safe, and away from Yrome."

"I can't help but feel that there's more to this crown than just power," I said. "It's like it has a will of its own, a consciousness that's been guiding events for centuries."

Papa Yamah nodded in agreement, carefully wrapping the crown in a cloth. "We'll take it back to Serenity's Edge for now. We need to plan our next move carefully. Aria could you do us the honors?"

Aria, with a focused expression, conjured a swirling portal back to the village. Gaianor and Camila, without hesitation, stepped through the vortex of magic, disappearing from the cavern.

As the rest of us moved towards the portal, a deafening explosion echoed through the cavern, shaking the very ground beneath our feet. We turned in horror to see the Guardian of the Whispering Woods, plummeting from the cavern ceiling. Its massive body hit the ground with a thunderous crash, dust and debris clouding the air.

Before we could fully grasp the situation, a blinding flash, like a bolt of dark lightning, struck the fallen Guardian. The impact created a massive crater, the force of the blow reverberating through the cavern. Amidst the settling dust and the flickering shadows, a figure emerged, standing over the Guardian's lifeless form.

It was Yrome, his presence exuding an aura of malevolent power. In his hand, he wielded a katana, its blade pulsating with a sinister energy.

Papa Yamah's voice, filled with urgency and fear, broke through the shock that had momentarily paralyzed us. "Hurry, to the portal!" he screamed.

We snapped into action, the threat of Yrome's power propelling us towards the portal. Aria struggled to keep the portal open, her face etched with concentration and strain.

As we neared the portal, Yrome raised his katana, the dark energy around it crackling and growing more intense. He was preparing to unleash a devastating attack, one that could likely obliterate us in an instant.

"Go, now!" Papa Yamah yelled, pushing me towards the portal. We stumbled through the magical gateway, the world around me warping and twisting as the portal's magic surrounded me.

The portal snapped shut, cutting off the cavern from our view.

"Aria!" My voice broke through the labored breaths, a desperate plea as her name tore from my throat. "No!" The fear of her being left behind clawed at my chest.

Suddenly, another portal materialized before us, from which Aria emerged, sprinting full tilt, her face a mask of sheer panic.

I glimpsed Yrome in the fleeting connection of the closing portal, his figure desperate to reach us. But with a decisive, almost brutal, motion, Aria severed the link.

"Are you alright?" The words were barely a whisper, my concern mirroring in my eyes as I studied her.

Panting, terror still etched into her features, Aria nodded, the effort of speech seeming to elude her. "Yes, I think so," she managed, the words heavy with unspoken horror.

A hushed moment descended upon the group, like a heavy curtain dropping to shroud us in contemplative stillness.

Papa Yamah, clutching the crown tightly in his trembling hand, was the first to shatter the stifling silence that had gripped us all. His voice dripped with genuine concern as his gaze swept across our weary faces. "Is everyone else alright?"

Camila leaned heavily against a nearby wall, her chest heaving as she struggled to catch her breath. "I'm fine," she managed to utter, though the weariness etched in the lines of her eyes told a different story.

Gaianor, his shoulders still tense from the perilous escape, chimed in, his voice tinged with a touch of humor to alleviate the tension. "I'm unharmed, but that was a little too close for comfort."

Aria, visibly shaken, sank onto a nearby bench as if her legs could no longer bear the weight of her trembling emotions. "I didn't think we'd make it," she confessed, her voice a fragile whisper.

The weight of our recent ordeal pressed down on my shoulders, the realization of how narrowly we had escaped the clutches of danger weighing heavily upon me. "We were lucky to escape."

In the distance, I spotted the familiar figures of Nina and Gabriel hurrying toward us, their concern evident in their hurried pace.

Nina was the first to reach us, her eyes a mix of relief and anxiety. "Thank the stars you've arrived back safely," she exclaimed with genuine relief.

"What happened?" Gabriel asked.

With measured words, we recounted the harrowing tale.

Then, Papa Yamah stepped forward and revealed the crown, an undeniable sense of awe washing over them.

"What I don't understand," Nina mused, her brow furrowed in perplexity, "is how Yrome managed to locate you? Enchanted sanctuaries like the Whispering Woods are known for their uncanny ability to conceal their existence. This is how most of the world doesn't even know they exist."

The air was charged with curiosity and a touch of concern as everyone leaned in, eager for an explanation.

"The only thing I can think of," I began, my voice cautious as I pieced together the puzzle, "is that when the crown pulsated, maybe it somehow called out to Yrome. Maybe it acted as some kind of beacon."

"It's a good theory," added Papa Yamah. "Let's discuss in more detail somewhere more privately."

We nodded in agreement, recognizing the need for privacy as the villagers began to approach, their curiosity piqued by our intense discussion. With cautious glances exchanged, we retreated into the main hall.

As we gathered in the main hall, the question of how Yrome had located us hung heavily in the air. Our group formed a circle, the gravity of the situation reflected in each concerned glance.

Nina was the first to speak. "We have to assume that Yrome can track the crown's energy. We need to find a way to hide its presence from him."

Caius, known for his strategic prowess, entered the hall just in time to catch the tail end of our conversation. He furrowed his brow, deep in thought, before he spoke up, "Perhaps, we should consider a two-fold approach. First, we can conceal the crown with potent enchantments, burying it within layers of mystical protections. Then, we use our abilities to mask its energy, making it virtually undetectable."

The notion he put forth hovered in the air like a beacon of hope, and we turned to him with a mixture of intrigue and relief.

"It's possible," Papa Yamah added, his brows furrowed deep in thought. "But we must consider the monumental challenge ahead. How can we possibly accomplish such a feat? To conceal the crown and veil its energy signature would demand an extraordinary, unfathomable amount of power."

A heavy silence settled over the room, the implications of our task sinking in like an anchor dragging our hopes to deeper, uncharted waters. Nina, her gaze distant, nodded in somber agreement. "Indeed," she murmured, "the energy required would be monumental, surpassing anything we've ever dared to harness."

Papa Yamah's eyes bore into ours, emphasizing the gravity of his next words. "We must remember, Nina lost all of her powers in the act of casting forbidden magic to protect this village. We've seen the dire toll it exacts, and we can't afford to have anyone else sacrifice their powers. Every ounce of our strength and every fighter is vital in this dark hour."

Caius, however, interjected with a glint of optimism in his eyes, "Actually, that might work in our favor. We're forgetting that the crown would already be within the protective barriers of the village. We wouldn't need as much power to conceal it, thanks to the village's barrier."

The room fell into a contemplative silence as we considered Caius's proposal. Slowly, a spark of hope ignited within each of us, as we began to see a path forward. "Caius, you're a genius!" said Nina. "However, we'll need time to research and devise a strategy to accomplish this. It won't be an easy task, but I think we can manage."

The meeting continued as we discussed various strategies and contingencies. The air was thick with a sense of urgency, but also a collective resolve. We were united in our goal to safeguard the crown and thwart Yrome's plans.

As the meeting drew to a close, we all felt the weight of the task ahead. The elders assured us they would begin preparations immediately, rallying the village's resources and knowledge to devise a viable plan.

Exhausted but focused, we made our way to our respective quarters where we had stayed the night before. The night had deepened, casting a serene blanket over Serenity's Edge. Despite the tranquility of the village, my mind raced with thoughts of the challenges ahead. The responsibility we bore was immense, but I felt a sense of camaraderie and purpose that bolstered my resolve.

As sleep finally began to claim me, I clung to the hope that tomorrow would bring us closer to our goal. With that, the tendrils of sleep began to weave their nightly spell, the world around me softening, blurring at the edges as consciousness prepared to depart. In this twilight of awareness, however, a flicker of something else sparked—a whisper of Ytfen's memories.

12
Limitless Possibilities

I found myself in the bustling heart of a village, walking among the people. The sun shone brightly in the clear blue sky, casting a warm glow over the lively market square.

As I moved through the crowd, my guards flanking me, the people greeted me with smiles and bows. I made it a point to stop and talk with them, asking about their families, their work, and their well-being. Their faces lit up as they spoke, happy to share their stories with their king.

Near a stall, an elderly vendor struggled to lift a heavy crate of fruits. Without hesitation, I stepped forward to help, lifting the crate with ease and placing it on the stall. The vendor, surprised and grateful, thanked me profusely. "It's my duty to serve my people, just as it is yours to serve the kingdom with your hard work," I said, smiling.

Continuing my walk, I spotted a group of children playing. They ran up to me, their laughter filling the air. I knelt down to speak with them, their eyes wide with excitement. "Remember, you are the future of this kingdom," I told them. "Be brave, kind, and always seek knowledge." The children nodded eagerly, their faces beaming with pride and joy.

As I rose, my mother, Sonia, joined me, her presence always a source of wisdom and comfort. "My son, your connection with the people is what truly makes you a great king," she said, her eyes reflecting pride.

"I learned from the best," I replied, smiling at her. "You taught me that a ruler's strength lies not just in leading, but in listening and caring."

We continued our walk, and soon, Denise joined us, her grace and compassion equally known throughout the kingdom. She carried with her a basket of bread, which she had baked herself to distribute among the people. Together, we handed out the bread, sharing warm conversations with the citizens.

At one point, a young boy approached, his clothes worn and tattered. Denise knelt down, offering him a particularly large piece of bread. "What's your name, young man?" she asked gently.

"I'm Milo," he replied shyly, taking the bread with a small, grateful smile.

"Remember, Milo, you are valued and loved in this kingdom," Denise said, her voice full of kindness.

We watched him go, his step lighter, his back a little straighter.

A woman, her face lined with the story of her years, approached us hesitantly. "Your Majesty," she began, her voice quivering with unspoken need.

Sonia, with a gentle hand, guided her forward. "Speak, dear one," she encouraged. "Your king hears you."

The woman's eyes met mine, and in them, I saw the strength of our kingdom. "My lord, it's my son. He wishes to learn, to read and write, but we lack the means."

I knelt to her level, taking her work-worn hand in mine. "Your son's thirst for knowledge shall not go unquenched. We will see to his education," I promised, the words not just a decree but a vow.

"And I shall visit with books and help him begin his journey," Denise added, her smile as warming as the sun above.

Suddenly, without warning, the world around me blurred, as if Ytfen's memory struggled to contain itself.

I suddenly found myself in the training grounds where the guards practiced. Watching them, I noticed one young guard struggling with his technique. I approached him, offering guidance and encouragement. Together, we worked on his stance and swordplay, and soon he was moving with greater confidence. His grateful smile was a reminder of the impact a simple act of kindness could have.

As the day turned to evening, and the square began to empty, I reflected on the interactions of the day. These moments with my people, my mother, and my queen were what truly defined my reign. It wasn't just about ruling; it was about connecting, understanding, and caring for the people who made the kingdom what it was.

The world around me blurred once again and I suddenly found myself walking through the lush gardens of Ash Village with Denise. The gardens were a tranquil oasis, alive with the vibrant colors of blooming flowers and the soothing sounds of nature. Sunlight filtered through the leaves, casting dappled patterns on the winding paths.

Denise walked beside me, her hand gently resting in mine. There was a nervous energy about her, a sense of anticipation that was almost palpable. The air was fragrant with the scent of jasmine and roses, adding to the serene beauty of the moment.

As we strolled, I noticed her stealing glances at me, a hint of something unspoken in her eyes. "Denise, my love, what's on your mind?" I asked, sensing her hesitance.

She took a deep breath, her eyes shining with a mixture of joy and apprehension. "Ytfen, there is something I need to tell you," She began, her voice trembling slightly with emotion.

I stopped, turning to face her, my full attention on her words. "Anything, my queen," I replied, my heart beating with a mix of curiosity and concern.

Denise's smile was radiant, her happiness infectious. "My love, we are going to have a child. I'm pregnant," she announced, her voice filled with wonder and love.

The news struck me like a gentle wave, overwhelming and beautiful. Joy surged through me, a profound happiness that enveloped my entire being. "A child," I whispered, the words a mixture of awe and delight. "We are going to be parents."

I took Denise in my arms, holding her close. The world around us seemed to pause, the garden becoming a private sanctuary for our shared joy. "This is the most wonderful news,"

I said, my voice thick with emotion. "You have given me the greatest gift, Denise. Our love, now growing into new life."

Denise rested her head against my chest, her laughter light and melodious. "I knew you would be happy, my love. This child will be a symbol of our love, a new chapter in our lives."

We stood there, embraced in the heart of the garden, surrounded by the beauty of nature. It was a moment of pure bliss, a celebration of our love and the future we were going to build together.

The world around me blurred and I felt the pull back to reality.

13

Reunion

As the memory slowly faded, bringing me back to the present as Ezekiel, I was left with a sense of profound happiness and warmth. Ytfen's love for Denise and the joy of their impending parenthood was a testament to the depth of their bond, a reminder of the enduring power of love. I was left with a profound sense of the kind of ruler Ytfen was – fair, generous, and deeply connected to his people.

The morning in Serenity's Edge greeted me with a gentle warmth, the sun casting a golden hue over the quaint village. As we gathered in the central square, a sense of purpose filled the air, mingled with the faint aroma of freshly baked bread from nearby cottages.

Papa Yamah, stood with a map unfurled in his hands, his brow furrowed in concentration. Camila and Gaianor joined him, peering over his shoulder with equal intensity.

"We should head north, through the Whispering Woods, then veer east towards..." Papa Yamah's voice trailed off as he squinted at the map.

Gaianor leaned in closer. "Are you sure? It looks more like we should head south first, then..."

Camila, ever the pragmatist, interjected. "Does anyone actually know where we're going?"

A moment of awkward silence followed, punctuated by the distant chirping of birds. I couldn't help but chuckle at the scene – two seasoned warriors and a legendary Dragon Slayer, all befuddled by a map.

It was Aria who broke the silence, her voice laced with amusement. "Why are we doing this the old-fashioned way? I can just open a portal.

Papa Yamah looked up, a sheepish grin spreading across his face. "Ah, right. The wonders of portal magic," he said, rolling up the map with a chuckle.

Gaianor, not one to show much emotion, let out a rare, soft laugh. "I suppose that's why we have Aria with us."

Camila shook her head, smiling. "And here I was, ready for a grand adventure through uncharted lands."

The group laughed.

"What's going on?" I asked, feeling a bit left out.

"The elders said that the barrier will take some time so we thought it best head back to our villages to check in on them," said Camila.

"That's a wonderful idea," I said. "I suppose now would be a good time to check in on Oliver and Sombra."

Papa Yamah nodded in agreement. "It's important to keep in touch with our allies. Oliver and Sombra have been invaluable in their support. They might have new information or insights that could help us."

Aria stepped forward, her expression focused. "I can open a portal to Ash Village. From there, it's a shorter journey to Furki Village. It will save us time and energy."

The idea of returning to Ash Village, even briefly, stirred a mix of emotions within me. The village, once a symbol of peace and coexistence, now stood as a reminder of the destruction wrought by Yrome.

"Let's do that," I said.

With that, Aria weaved her hands and created a portal. "One at a time, please," she said, gesturing towards the portal with a flourish.

The portal opened with a soft whoosh, revealing the charred and desolate landscape of Ash Village. The once vibrant village, now a haunting testimony to the devastation wrought by Yrome's wrath, lay before us in ruins.

Aria stepped through first, her face etched with sorrow. "I'm sorry, Ezekiel" she whispered, her voice barely audible. "This was the only place I could think of."

One by one, we stepped through the portal, each of us pausing to take in the grim scene. The air was thick with the scent of burnt wood and ash, a stark contrast to the fresh, earthy aroma of Serenity's Edge.

Camila's eyes scanned the horizon, her expression hardening. "Let's take a moment to pay our respects," she suggested.

We walked through the remnants of the village, our footsteps echoing amidst the silence. The skeletal frames of houses stood like ghosts, their walls and roofs long since consumed by fire. Here and there, we saw remnants of life – a charred toy, a half-burnt book, a scorched piece of clothing – each a poignant reminder of the lives that were lost.

Gaianor knelt by a small, blackened tree, its branches reaching towards the sky like desperate fingers. "Even in destruction, there's a stark beauty," he murmured, his earth elemental nature finding solace in the resilience of nature.

I wandered through the ruins, each step heavy with the weight of what had happened here. Memories of Gloria and Junito. Memories of laughter and warmth in Ash Village clashed with the present reality, creating a dissonance in my heart.

After a while, we regrouped, our faces somber but determined. "We should move on," I said, breaking the silence. "We have other villages to protect, and we can't let this happen again."

Papa Yamah gathered us together for one final word before we parted ways.

"Remember," he said, his voice firm yet tinged with concern, "do not transform into your dragon forms. We cannot risk Yrome sensing our locations. Our strength lies not only in our powers but also in our discretion."

We nodded in understanding, each of us aware of the gravity of his words. The threat of Yrome loomed over us, a shadow that we could neither ignore nor underestimate.

Aria glanced at Camila and Gaianor, a determined look in her eyes. "I think it's best if I accompany you both to your villages," she said. "This way, I can familiarize myself with the locations. It'll be easier to open portals there in case of emergencies."

Camila nodded, understanding the strategic advantage of Aria's plan. "That's a wise decision. Having a quick way to reach each other could be crucial in the days to come."

Gaianor agreed, his expression serious. "And it'll give us a chance to strengthen our defenses, knowing we have a direct line to each other."

Papa Yamah gave Aria an approving nod.

Before we embarked on our journey to Furki Village, Aria approached me with a small, intricately designed ring. She held it out, a serious yet hopeful expression on her face.

"Before we part ways, Ezekiel, I've endowed this ring with a fragment of my portal powers," she explained. "It's not strong enough to transport you, but it will allow you to open a very small portal to communicate with me, no matter where you are."

I took the ring, examining its fine craftsmanship. The idea of having such a direct line of communication was both reassuring and impressive. "Thank you, Aria. This could make a huge difference," I said, slipping the ring onto my finger. It was a perfect fit, almost as if it was made just for me.

"Just focus on the ring and think of me when you need to send a message," Aria instructed. "I'll do my best to respond as quickly as possible."

With a nod of understanding, I thanked her again. This small piece of magic could be a lifeline in the times to come.

"If you have any issues with it, ask Yamah," she said. "I gave him one earlier today. He's the one that came up with the idea many years ago. It was a way for Dragon Slayers to communicate with each other at a moment's notice."

Papa Yamah, wearing a twinkle of pride in his eyes, chimed in with a touch of modesty, "Well, it was a rather good idea, if I may say so myself."

After our farewells, Papa Yamah and I set off for Furki Village, the ring a comforting weight on my finger, a symbol of our growing alliance.

As we walked, the silence between us was comfortable, each lost in our own thoughts about the journey ahead.

As the village came into view, I couldn't help but feel a surge of protectiveness. This was more than just a destination; it was a symbol of what we were fighting to preserve – peace, community, and a future free from the shadow of Yrome's tyranny.

As we approached the gates of Furki Village, our arrival was met with unexpected hostility. The guards, with weapons drawn, eyed us warily, their suspicion evident in their tense postures.

"Wait, we come in peace!" I exclaimed, trying to diffuse the situation. But my words seemed to fall on deaf ears as the guards began to advance, their weapons ready.

Just as the tension reached its peak, a familiar voice cut through the air. "Stop! They are friends, not foes!" Sombra emerged from the crowd, her presence commanding and authoritative. The guards immediately halted, though their suspicion remained.

"Sombra, it's so good to see you," I greeted her, my voice carrying a mix of emotions. The sight of her brought a sense of familiarity and comfort amidst the chaos that had become our lives.

She quickly closed the distance between us, embracing me tightly. "Ezekiel, I've been so worried," she said, her voice muffled against my shoulder. "The news about Ash Village... it's heartbreaking."

I returned her hug, feeling the weight of recent events in her embrace. "It's been tough, Sombra. We're all feeling the strain of this endless conflict."

She stepped back, her eyes searching mine. "You look exhausted, Ezekiel. This war... it's taking its toll on all of us."

I nodded, the fatigue evident in my voice. "It's a never-ending cycle of violence and loss. I just want it to end. But we can't give up, not now."

Sombra's expression hardened with steadfastness. "We won't give up. Oliver and I, we've been doing everything we can here. The village is holding up, but it's not easy. Oliver's been a rock through all of this."

I smiled faintly, grateful for their resilience. "How is he? And the villagers?"

"They're managing, but it's a daily struggle," she replied. "The village has been in disarray ever since we lost Chief Paco and the Warrior Leaders. Oliver's been coordinating our defenses and keeping everyone's spirits up. He's become quite the leader."

Her words brought a sense of pride, but also a reminder of the heavy burden we all carried. "I'm glad to hear that. We need all the strength and leadership we can get right now."

She gestured for us to follow her, leading us away from the gates and into the village, where the true extent of the changes would become apparent.

As we followed Sombra through the village, the changes were evident. The once vibrant and bustling Furki Village now carried a somber air, the laughter and chatter that used to fill the streets replaced by a quiet, almost mournful atmosphere.

We arrived at the cabin that once belonged to Elder Paco. The cabin, a symbol of wisdom and guidance in the village, now served as Sombra's residence and the new center of leadership. The weight of her new role was visible in her demeanor, a mix of determination and the burden of responsibility.

Sombra invited us inside, and we settled into the familiar space, now transformed by its new occupant. Weapons and maps were displayed on the well, reflecting the village's shift from peace to a state of readiness.

"The village was in chaos when I returned," Sombra began, her voice tinged with a hint of sadness. "There was a void in leadership."

She paused, collecting her thoughts. "The villagers needed someone to guide them, to bring order. I couldn't just stand by. So, I stepped up, took on the role of chief. It hasn't been easy, but we're surviving, rebuilding."

As we absorbed Sombra's words, Oliver burst into the cabin, his arrival breaking the heavy atmosphere. His youthful energy was a marked difference to the somber mood.

"Mate!" Oliver exclaimed, his face lighting up with a smile. "You're alive! Come 'ere and give me a hug!"

Before I could respond, I was wrapped in a fierce and brotherly embrace. "It's good to see you too, Oliver," I managed, the comfort of friendship infusing the simple words.

Papa Yamah chuckled softly, a rare moment of lightness in the serious discussion.

Oliver's smile faded slightly, replaced by a more serious expression. "It's been tough, but I'm learning a lot from Sombra. She's an amazing leader."

I felt a quiet respect thread through me. "I can only imagine," I said, my voice low with acknowledgment.

"You are too kind, Oliver," Sombra said. "Now, Ezekiel, could you share with us all that has happened so far?"

The conversation shifted as we shared our recent experiences and discussed the current situation. We took the time to bring Sombra and Oliver up to speed on our recent adventures. We recounted the events in detail, from what happened in Ash Village, Aria joining us, our journey to the Whispering Woods, the discovery of Yrome's Crown in the Cavern of Echoes, our harrowing escape from Yrome himself, to our plan to conceal the crown.

When we finished, there was a moment of silence as Sombra processed everything we had shared. Finally, she spoke, her voice firm yet filled with a sense of wonder. "I had no idea the stakes were this high. How can I help? What can Furki Village do to support you in this?"

We exchanged glances, appreciating her willingness to help, but also mindful of the sacrifices the village had already made. "Thank you, Sombra," I said, "but Furki Village has endured enough loss and hardship. Your place is here, leading and protecting your people. I just wanted to check in, make sure you're all doing okay."

Sombra nodded, understanding our position but still eager to offer support in any way she could. "Well, if you need anything, you know where to find us. We're stronger than we look, and we're here for you."

Our visit to Furki Village, though brief, was a poignant reminder of the resilience and strength found in communities like Sombra's. It reinforced our resolve to find a way to protect not just the crown, but all those who stood in the shadow of the looming threat.

As we prepared to leave, Sombra and Oliver expressed their determination to contribute to our cause in their own way. Despite our insistence that they focus on rebuilding Furki Village, they were adamant about playing a part in our quest.

"We'll do some research," Sombra declared with a resolute tone. "There might be something in the village archives or the old texts that could shed light on the crown and its origins."

Oliver nodded in agreement, his eyes reflecting a similar steadfastness. "Yeah mate, I'll reach out to some contacts I have in other villages. There are stories, legends that might have been overlooked. Anything that can give us an edge against Yrome and help us understand the crown better."

Their initiative was heartening. We thanked them for their willingness to help and promised to stay in touch, sharing any new information we might uncover on our journey.

"We just wish we could do more," Oliver added, his voice tinged with concern.

Papa Yamah nodded, appreciating their willingness to help. "Your research could be invaluable. We'll stay in touch."

Sombra looked thoughtful for a moment before speaking up. "What's the best way to reach you? Just in case we find something that requires your immediate attention."

I exchanged a glance with Papa Yamah, who nodded slightly. He reached out into his bag and pulled out a small ring, identical to the one Aria had given me.

"This is a portal device of sorts," he explained, handing it over to them. "Aria has attuned it to her magic. You can use it to send us messages or any findings you come across. Just be mindful, it's only for small items and brief notes."

"I still cannot believe Aria is on our side now…" Sombra remarked.

"You tellin' me, mate, I still can't wrap my head around it."

Sombra and Oliver examined the artifact with a mix of awe and curiosity. "We'll use it wisely," Sombra promised.

With heartfelt goodbyes and promises to stay safe, we left Furki Village, feeling a little more hopeful knowing that Sombra and Oliver were contributing to our cause in their own way.

Papa Yamah and I stood outside the gates of the village.

"Where to now?" I asked.

He looked at me thoughtfully before speaking. "Do you want to visit Bryson Village? It might help bring some closure."

I hesitated, feeling a tightness in my chest at the mention of Bryson Village. "Papa, I... I'm not ready yet," I admitted, my voice barely above a whisper. "There's so much trauma tied to that place, so many memories. I don't think I have the courage to face it all just yet."

Papa Yamah nodded, understanding and compassion in his eyes. "I understand, Ezekiel. We all have our own paths to healing. Take your time."

After a pause, he suggested a new direction for us. "How about we focus on your training? It seems you might have the potential to control other elements. It could be crucial for what lies ahead."

I felt a spark of determination ignite within me. "Yes, let's do that. I want to understand my abilities better, to see if I can really harness other elements."

"There's a place I know, not too far from here," he said, his voice tinged with nostalgia. "It's secluded, surrounded by nature. A waterfall cascades down a series of rocky cliffs, and there are mountains nearby. It's peaceful, perfect for training and reflection."

As we walked, I couldn't help but remember what Papa Yamah said in Serenity's Edge. "Papa Yamah," I said gently, "What exactly happened when you lost your powers?"

He sighed, a deep, weary sound. "It was during a fierce battle, many years ago. I was protecting you and Elijah. We had just left Serenity's Edge and we were on our way to Bryson Village. We were ambushed by a group of Dragon Slayers who had managed to track us. The fight was brutal. They were skilled, relentless. But I had something worth fighting for, something worth protecting at all costs." His voice grew heavy with emotion. "As the battle reached its peak, I realized that there were just too many. I was outmatched. I had to make a choice, a sacrifice."

His voice faltered, and for a moment, he seemed lost in the past. "The energy wave obliterated the attackers, but it left me... changed. Weakened. Not just in body, but in my very essence. My ability to harness my full power was diminished from that day forth."

I listened, a newfound respect growing within me. Papa Yamah had sacrificed so much, yet he carried his burden with such dignity.

After a few hours, the landscape gradually changed. The forest gave way to a more rugged terrain. The air grew crisper, the scent of pine and earth mingling together. Then the sound of rushing water reached our ears, growing louder with each step.

Finally, we arrived at the spot Papa Yamah had described. It was breathtaking. A majestic waterfall plummeted down from a great height, its waters crashing into a crystal-clear pool below. Towering mountains stood sentinel in the distance, their peaks touching the sky.

"This is incredible," I said, my eyes wide with awe. The power and beauty of nature here were overwhelming, yet there was a sense of tranquility that settled over the area.

Papa Yamah smiled, pleased by my reaction. "This place has always been special to me. I used to come here to think, to train, to be alone with my thoughts. Now, it's your turn to find what you need here."

I nodded, feeling a sense of purpose and determination. "I'll do my best."

We set up a small camp near the waterfall, the sound of the water a constant companion. Here, amidst the beauty and solitude of nature, I would embark on a new phase of my journey, pushing my limits and discovering the true extent of my powers.

As we finished setting up our modest camp near the waterfall, the sun began to dip below the horizon, painting the sky in hues of orange and purple. The tranquil sound of the waterfall provided a soothing backdrop to our conversation. I took a deep breath, feeling the weight of the revelation I was about to share with Papa Yamah.

"Papa, there's something important I need to tell you," I began, my voice slightly hesitant. "I've been experiencing Ytfen's memories. They've been coming to me in fragments, revealing the truth behind the war between dragons and humans."

Papa Yamah's expression shifted from one of calm to surprise, his eyes widening slightly. He sat down on a fallen log, gesturing for me to join him. "Ytfen's memories? That's... that's extraordinary, Ezekiel. How is this possible?"

I explained as best as I could, detailing my last moments with Gloria and the moments when the memories surfaced, each one providing a piece of a larger, more complex puzzle. "It's like I'm living through his experiences, seeing the world through his eyes. It's helping me understand the origins of this conflict, the pain, and the betrayals that fueled it."

Papa Yamah listened intently, his face a mask of concentration. When I finished, he remained silent for a moment, lost in thought. "This is a significant revelation," he finally said. "Ytfen's perspective could change everything we know about the war. It could even help us find a way to end it."

His gaze met mine, filled with a mixture of concern and determination. "But this must be overwhelming for you, to carry such memories, such a burden."

I nodded, feeling a mix of responsibility and resolve. "It is, but I believe it's necessary. These memories might hold the key to understanding Yrome's motives and finding a way to stop him."

Papa Yamah placed a reassuring hand on my shoulder. "You're not alone in this, Ezekiel. We'll face whatever comes together. And with this new knowledge, we stand a better chance of bringing peace to our world."

As the night deepened, the comforting sounds of the waterfall and the distant calls of nocturnal creatures filled the air. Papa Yamah and I exchanged a final few words, acknowledging the long day of training that awaited us. "Goodnight, Ezekiel. Rest well," he said, his voice carrying a fatherly warmth.

"Goodnight, Papa," I replied, feeling a sense of comfort in his presence. I settled into my makeshift bed, the soft rustling of leaves and the gentle flow of the waterfall lulling me into a state of relaxation.

Just as I was drifting off to sleep, a familiar sensation began to take hold. It was as if the world around me was fading away, replaced by a different reality. I could feel myself being drawn into Ytfen's memories once again, the boundary between his past and my present blurring.

As the sounds of the forest faded into silence, the vivid scenes of Ytfen's life began to unfold in my mind. I braced myself for the journey through his memories, ready to uncover more truths hidden in the depths of the past. With each memory, I hoped to piece together the puzzle of the war and find the key to ending the conflict that had shaped our world for so long.

14
The Gift of the Dragons

I found myself in the grand council chamber, a room adorned with symbols representing each elemental kingdom. The atmosphere was charged with anticipation and a hint of apprehension. Seated around the large, circular table were my Pure Elemental generals.

Denise, my queen and confidant, stood beside me, her presence a source of strength and wisdom. Her insight had always been invaluable, especially in matters that required a delicate balance of power and diplomacy.

"I have called you all here to discuss a matter of great importance," I began, addressing the council. "Our relations with the humans have been strained, to say the least. Their fear of our power has been a barrier to peace for too long."

The generals shifted in their seats, their expressions a mix of curiosity and concern. Zephyra was the first to speak.

"You have always sought harmony, my king. What do you propose?"

I took a deep breath, knowing my next words would be met with surprise. "I believe that if we share some of our power with the humans, specifically with King Yrome, it could serve as a gesture of trust and goodwill."

The tension in the room was intense as I laid out my proposal. The idea of sharing our elemental powers with humans, with King Yrome no less, was unprecedented. I could see the wheels turning in the minds of my most trusted generals, each grappling with the implications of such an act.

"Your Majesty," Tarn spoke up, his voice echoing the unease that filled the room, "our powers have been safeguarded for centuries, passed down through generations. To share even a fraction of that power with humans... it's unheard of."

I nodded, acknowledging his concern. "I understand the weight of what I'm proposing. Our powers are sacred, a bond between us and the elements we command. But consider this—our isolation, our refusal to share, has only fueled human fears and misconceptions. They see us as threats, as monsters to be vanquished, not as allies or equals."

"And what of the risk?" Zephyra asked. "To bestow power on those who have not been born to it, who have not trained their entire lives to wield it responsibly... it could lead to disaster."

I turned to face her, my resolution firm. "That is why we must be selective, why King Yrome himself must be the recipient. He is a leader, one with the influence and the wisdom to use this power as a beacon of unity, not as a weapon of war."

Denise stepped beside me. "Fear breeds in the unknown. By sharing our power, we make the unknown known. We show that our strength can be shared, that it can be a source of healing and growth, not just destruction."

The room fell silent as her words sank in. It was a gamble, to be sure, but one that held the promise of a new era. An era where dragons and humans could stand side by side, united by the very powers that had once driven them apart.

Finally, it was Joaquin who broke the silence, his voice resonant and clear. "If there is even a chance that this could lead to peace, to a better understanding between our peoples, then it is a chance worth taking. Your vis-"

"That is a rather risky proposition," Pyrus interrupted, his voice a blend of caution and curiosity. "How can we ensure it will be used for good?"

I met his gaze squarely, understanding the depth of the responsibility I was proposing to undertake. "Pyrus, your concern is valid and one I share deeply. The risk of misuse is not lost on me. However, I believe that with the right guidance and oversight, we can mitigate these risks."

I paused for a moment, gathering my thoughts before continuing. "I will personally take on the responsibility of training King Yrome. I will teach him not just the mechanics of wielding elemental power, but the ethos that governs its use. He will learn that this power is a gift, one that comes with a heavy burden of responsibility."

The room listened intently, the weight of my commitment silencing any immediate objections. "This training will not be a simple transfer of power. It will be a comprehensive mentorship, covering the ethical, moral, and practical aspects of elemental control. I will ensure that King Yrome understands that this power is to be used for the betterment of all, to protect and to heal, not to dominate or destroy."

Pyrus nodded slowly, the skepticism in his eyes giving way to a cautious optimism. "And if he fails to uphold these principles?" he asked, the question not a challenge but a necessary consideration.

I nodded, acknowledging the gravity of his question. "If he fails, then I will take full responsibility for the consequences. I will do everything in my power to rectify the situation. But all I can do is have faith in King Yrome's character and in our ability to guide him towards a path of righteousness."

The room erupted in murmurs.

Denise stepped forward, her voice calm yet firm. "It's a gesture that could change the course of our relationship with the humans. By showing them that our power can be a force for good, we might dispel their fears and build a foundation of trust."

Glacius nodded thoughtfully. "It is a bold move, but it could be the bridge we need."

Joaquin leaned in. "It's a gamble, but one that might pay off. We stand with you, Your Majesty, in whatever decision you make."

I looked around the table, meeting each of their gazes. "This decision is not made lightly. But I believe it is a step towards a future where humans and dragons can coexist in peace and mutual respect."

Denise placed a hand on my shoulder, a silent show of support. "Together, we can turn fear into understanding, and enemies into allies."

The world suddenly blurred around me and I suddenly found myself standing in the grand throne room of the human kingdom, a vast and opulent space adorned with banners and tapestries depicting human history and achievements. The air was thick with anticipation, and the room was filled with an array of human dignitaries, nobles, and scholars, all gathered to witness a historic event.

Beside me stood Denise and my generals. Each general bore the insignia of their element, a symbol of the power they wielded and the deep connection they shared with the natural world. A symbol that also served as a reminder of the diversity of our dragon kingdom.

Their presence was a sign of unity and support for the decision I was about to make.

At the far end of the room, on an elevated dais, sat the king of the human kingdom, Yrome, his expression a mix of curiosity and cautious optimism. His eyes, sharp and discerning, watched our approach with keen interest.

As we reached the center of the throne room, I addressed the assembly. "Today marks a new chapter in the history of our two great kingdoms," I began, my voice echoing through the hall. "For too long, fear and misunderstanding have kept us apart. But today, we take a step towards a future built on trust and cooperation."

Yrome nodded, acknowledging my words. "We welcome you, King Ytfen, and your esteemed generals. Your presence here is evidence to the possibility of peace and understanding between our peoples."

I turned to face Yrome directly. "King Yrome, in the spirit of this newfound alliance, I wish to offer a gift. A gift that symbolizes our commitment to peace and our trust in your leadership."

Yrome watched us with a discerning eye. His posture was regal, yet there was an openness to his demeanor, a willingness to embrace this unprecedented gesture of trust.

I raised my hand, and the air seemed to still. A small orb of light began to form above my palm, glowing with an inner radiance. It was a concentrated essence of dragon power, a tangible representation of our strength and our willingness to share it for the greater good.

"This orb," I began, my voice resonating with a calm authority, "contains a fraction of the elemental power that flows through our veins. It is a power that can be used for protection, for healing, and for the betterment of your kingdom."

A murmur ran through the assembly as the orb grew brighter, its light casting ethereal shadows across the room. Yrome rose from his throne, his eyes never leaving the orb. "This is a generous offer, King Ytfen," he said, his voice steady. "One that I accept with the utmost respect and gratitude."

I stepped forward, the orb floating gently towards Yrome. The room held its breath as he reached out to receive it. As his hand touched the orb, it dissolved into a shower of light, infusing him with a trace of dragon power.

The human audience erupted in a mix of gasps and murmurs, the display of magic both awe-inspiring and unsettling. The symbol of our trust had been given physical form, and its implications were profound.

Denise spoke softly, yet her words carried through the throne room. "Let this moment mark the beginning of a new era.

An era where our strengths are shared, and our differences are not just accepted, but celebrated."

Yrome, standing tall and imbued with the newly acquired dragon power, addressed the gathered crowd with a sense of gravitas and purpose. The throne room, filled with representatives from both human and dragon realms, fell silent as his voice resonated through the hall.

"Today, we stand at the threshold of a new alliance," Yrome began, his voice steady and commanding. "An alliance born not out of necessity, but out of a shared vision for a future where our two great peoples can coexist in harmony and mutual respect."

He paused, allowing his words to sink in, his gaze sweeping across the room. "For too long, our histories have been marked by fear and misunderstanding, by conflicts that have brought untold suffering to both our worlds. But today, we choose a different path."

Yrome's eyes met mine, a glimmer of something deeper behind his gaze. "King Ytfen, your generous gift is not merely a transfer of power; it is a symbol of trust, a bridge between our cultures. It represents a hope that together, we can achieve more than we ever could apart."

The room remained captivated by his words, a sense of hope and anticipation hanging in the air. "This power will be used not for conquest, but for the protection of our people, for the betterment of our lands, and for the forging of a lasting peace that will be remembered for generations to come."

Yrome's voice grew more passionate. "Let this day be remembered as the beginning of a new era—an era where the dragon's strength and the human's resolve unite to create a world where our children, and their children, can grow up without the shadow of war looming over them."

He raised his hand, the dragon power within him subtly manifesting as a soft glow. "Together, we will build a future based on understanding and cooperation. Together, we will show that unity is not just a dream, but a reality we can achieve."

As he concluded his speech, the room erupted in applause, a chorus of approval and hope echoing off the walls of the throne room.

As the memory began to fade, pulling me back to the present as Ezekiel, I was left with a sense of the monumental nature of Ytfen's decision. His bold move to share dragon power with a human ruler was a gamble, but one driven by a vision of unity and peace. It was a legacy of courage and hope, a reminder of the possibilities that arise when we dare to trust and share our strengths.

It stood as his greatest mistake, casting a long, dark shadow over his legacy.

A lone tear welled in my eye. I knew how this tragic tale would inevitably end.

15
Tides of Training

I awoke to the gentle sounds of the forest and the soothing rush of the waterfall nearby. The sun was just beginning to peek through the trees, casting a warm, golden light over our camp. Papa Yamah was already up, tending to a small fire where he had prepared breakfast.

"Good morning, Ezekiel," he greeted me with a smile. "I hope you slept well."

"Morning, Papa," I replied, still feeling the remnants of Ytfen's memories lingering in my mind. "I did, thank you."

As we ate, Papa Yamah brought up the day's training. "I've been thinking about your training," he said thoughtfully. "Since you've already shown an affinity for both the fire and wind elements, perhaps we should start with something different. The waterfall here could be perfect for practicing control over the water element."

I nodded, intrigued by the idea. "That sounds like a good plan. I'm ready to give it a try."

After breakfast, we made our way to the base of the waterfall. The water cascaded down with a powerful yet graceful force, creating a mist that hung in the air like a fine veil.

"You know, Ezekiel, when I was a Dragon Slayer, part of my role was to train the younger ones," he began, his voice tinged with a hint of nostalgia. "I taught them how to harness their powers, to control their elements. It was a crucial part of their development."

I looked at him, curious and eager to learn. "How did you train them, Papa?"

He smiled, a distant look in his eyes as if recalling a long-forgotten memory. "It was about more than just physical strength or technique. It was about understanding the essence of their power, the very nature of the element they were connected to."

He picked up a small stone, rolling it between his fingers. "For instance, those with an affinity for earth had to learn to feel the world beneath their feet, to understand its stability, its endurance. They had to become one with the earth, to draw strength from its depths."

He then glanced at the waterfall, its water cascading down gracefully. "For water, it was about adaptability, flow, the ability to change course yet retain your essence. Water can be gentle, nurturing, but also powerful and unstoppable. It's about finding that balance, that harmony."

I listened intently, absorbing every word. "And fire?" I asked, curious about the element I had already shown an affinity for.

"Fire is about passion, energy. It's a force of creation and destruction," he explained. "To control fire, one must understand its dual nature, to harness its warmth without being consumed by its flames. It's a delicate balance, requiring focus and discipline."

I nodded, understanding the depth of his words. "And now, you'll train me in the same way?"

"Yes, Ezekiel," he replied, his gaze meeting mine. "I'll guide you as I did them. But remember, your journey is unique. You're not a Dragon Slayer; you're a full-blown dragon. We'll take what I know and adapt it to your needs, to your nature."

I nodded.

"Let's start with the basics," he said. "Controlling an element is about more than just wielding its power. It's about understanding it, feeling it as a part of you. You've already mastered the wind element during your travels, so let's go ahead and try water, using the waterfall as your guide."

He led me closer to the water, where the mist from the falls gently sprayed our faces. "Close your eyes, Ezekiel. Listen to the water, feel its flow, its energy. Water is adaptable, ever-changing, yet always true to its nature."

I closed my eyes, focusing on the sound of the waterfall. At first, all I could hear was the roar of the water, but gradually, I began to discern the subtle nuances in its movement, the way it danced and played on the rocks.

"Now, reach out with your senses," Papa Yamah continued. "Imagine the water's journey, from the sky to the earth, through rivers and streams, until it reaches this waterfall. Feel its cycle, its eternal flow."

I extended my hand towards the waterfall, trying to connect with the water's essence. At first, nothing happened, but as I concentrated, I began to feel a faint tingling in my palm, a connection forming between me and the water.

"Good," Papa Yamah said, sensing my progress. "Now, let's try to shape it. Water can be guided, directed. Try to pull a stream of water from the fall, bend it to your will."

I focused harder, envisioning the water leaving its natural path and coming towards me. Slowly, a thin stream of water broke away from the waterfall, hovering in the air before me. It was a small achievement, but it filled me with a sense of wonder and possibility.

"Excellent," Papa Yamah praised. "You're starting to understand. Remember, it's not about forcing your will upon the element. It's about harmony, working together with it."

We spent the rest of the day practicing, with Papa Yamah guiding me through various exercises. He taught me how to sense the water in the air, in the plants around us, even in the moisture in the soil. Each lesson brought a deeper understanding, a stronger connection to the element of water.

As the sun began to set, casting a golden light over the training area, I realized how much I had learned in just one day. Papa Yamah's teachings were more than just techniques; they were lessons in balance, harmony, and respect for the natural world.

Exhausted but exhilarated, I knew this was just the beginning of my journey to master the elements. With Papa Yamah's guidance, I felt ready to face the challenges ahead, to grow stronger not just in power, but in spirit and understanding.

As our training progressed, I encountered moments where my connection to the water element wavered. Frustration began to set in, and I found myself struggling to maintain the delicate balance I had started to understand.

One afternoon, after several failed attempts to manipulate a larger volume of water, I let out a sigh of exasperation. "I don't understand," I said, turning to Papa Yamah. "I was doing so well, and now it's like I've taken two steps back."

Papa Yamah watched me with a patient gaze. "Ezekiel, mastering an element isn't a straight path. It's normal to have setbacks. The key is not to force it. You need to let the element flow naturally, become a part of you."

I nodded, trying to absorb his words. "But how do I get past this block? It feels like I'm missing something."

He walked over and placed a reassuring hand on my shoulder. "Remember, each element has its own nature. Water is adaptable, but it also follows the path of least resistance. It's about harmony, not control. You need to be patient, let the water guide you as much as you guide it."

His words struck a chord in me. I realized I had been trying to impose my will on the water, rather than working with it. I took a deep breath and closed my eyes, focusing on the sensation of the water around me, its gentle ebb and flow.

"Try again," Papa Yamah encouraged. "But this time, don't think about what you want the water to do. Feel what it wants to do, and work with that."

I opened my eyes and reached out to the water again. This time, I let go of my expectations, my frustrations. I felt the water's natural course and gently nudged it, guiding it without forcing it. To my amazement, the water responded, swirling around my hand in a graceful dance.

A smile spread across my face, and I looked at Papa Yamah. "I think I understand now," I said. "It's not just about power. It's about understanding and respect."

Papa Yamah nodded, a look of pride in his eyes. "Exactly. And that understanding will make you not just a powerful dragon, but a wise one."

We continued our training into the evening, and with each passing day, my connection to the water element grew stronger. Papa Yamah's guidance was invaluable, teaching me not just the mechanics of elemental control, but the philosophy behind it.

As we continued our rigorous training regimen, Papa Yamah and I made sure to take occasional breaks to rest and refuel. During these moments of respite, Papa Yamah would venture into the surrounding wilderness to hunt. With his keen instincts and years of experience living off the land, he always managed to find something to sustain us.

Each time he returned, he brought with him an assortment of game – sometimes fish from the nearby stream, other times small game like rabbits or birds. He prepared the food with the skill of a seasoned outdoorsman, cooking over a makeshift fire, seasoning with herbs he found in the wild. The meals were simple, but they were nourishing and surprisingly flavorful.

Sitting by the fire, eating the food Papa Yamah had hunted and cooked, I felt a deep sense of gratitude. These moments, though brief, were a comforting reminder of the bond we shared. They were a chance to relax, to talk about things other than training and the looming threats we faced. It was during these times that I felt the closest to the man who had raised me, the man who had sacrificed so much for my brother and me.

As we ate, we would often share stories – he would recount tales of his past adventures, and I would tell him about my experiences since leaving Bryson Village.

It's funny how the world works. I remember those days when I would incessantly pester Papa Yamah to teach me hunting. Back then, it seemed like the most important skill I could ever acquire, a crucial step towards self-sufficiency and survival. But now, as I reflect on those moments, they seem like distant memories from another life. The scale of what's at stake has changed everything. The responsibility of saving the world, of preventing the spread of darkness and despair, overshadows all else.

One night, the fire crackled and the night deepened, the warmth of the flames and the comfort of our conversation gradually lulled me into a state of relaxation. The stars above twinkled in the clear sky, a silent audience to our shared moments. Papa Yamah's stories, filled with adventure and wisdom, were a balm to my soul, reminding me of the depth of life beyond our current struggles.

But as I dozed off to sleep, nestled in the safety of our camp, I felt a familiar tug at the edges of my consciousness. It was a sensation I had come to recognize – the onset of another of Ytfen's memories. The world around me began to blur, the sounds of the night fading into a distant echo. I was being pulled back into the past, into another time and place, to witness yet another chapter of the story that had shaped the world as I knew it.

16

Whispers of Ambition

As I stood amidst the serene mountains, the crisp air filling my lungs, I faced Yrome, ready to guide him through his newfound powers. "Yrome, the power you now possess is both a gift and a responsibility," I began, my voice steady and reassuring. "It's not merely about wielding it; it's about understanding and respecting its nature."

Yrome, his eyes reflecting a mix of eagerness and uncertainty, nodded in agreement. "I understand, King Ytfen. I am grateful for your guidance and the opportunity you've given me."

I smiled, encouraged by his attitude. "Let's start with the fundamentals. Focus on the energy within you. Feel it as an integral part of your being, flowing through your veins. It's not an external force to be controlled, but an extension of your own essence."

Closing his eyes, Yrome took a deep, focused breath. Moments later, a soft glow began to radiate from his hands, signaling the awakening of his power.

"Good," I commended him. "Now, try to direct that energy. Imagine it as a stream of water that you can guide. Start with something simple. Light a flame or move a small stone."

With concentration, Yrome managed to ignite a small flame in his palm. His eyes opened, shining with a mix of excitement and awe.

"Well done! Remember, control is crucial. Power without control is a path to destruction. Let's continue practicing until you feel at ease with it."

As the session progressed, Yrome's confidence visibly grew. He started manipulating small stones, creating gentle breezes, and even shaping water from a nearby stream.

I offered gentle guidance and encouragement throughout. "You're adapting well, Yrome. With practice, these elements will respond to you more naturally. Remember, it's not about dominating them, but harmonizing with them."

Drenched in sweat from his efforts, Yrome acknowledged my advice. "I'm beginning to understand, King Ytfen. This power... it's deeper than I ever imagined. It's about balance, isn't it?"

"Exactly," I replied, pleased with his insight. "Balance is the core of all existence. In harmony, there is strength, and in understanding, there is wisdom."

We continued our training sessions over the span of several days. Each day, as the sun rose, casting its first light upon us, we would begin anew, delving deeper into the essence of the elemental powers. However, I began to notice a subtle shift in

Yrome's demeanor. His initial awe and respect for the powers he wielded gradually gave way to a more reckless enthusiasm. The once cautious and measured use of his abilities started to become more extravagant and unrestrained.

On one particular afternoon, as the sun hung low in the sky, bathing the landscape in a golden hue, I watched Yrome from a distance. He stood at the center of a clearing, his figure silhouetted against the light, his hands raised as he summoned a whirlwind.

"Yrome, remember the importance of control," I cautioned, observing him as he enthusiastically manipulated the whirlwind, his long black hair shifting wildly in the wind. "Your connection with these elements must be grounded in respect, not just excitement."

He paused, the whirlwind dissipating as he turned to me, a glint of something unrecognizable in his eyes. "But King Ytfen, isn't this power meant to be embraced? To be celebrated?" His voice carried an edge, a hint of defiance that hadn't been there before.

I sighed, sensing the dangerous path his thoughts were treading. "Embraced, yes, but with wisdom and humility. Power for its own sake leads to arrogance and, ultimately, to ruin. You must learn to temper your abilities with discernment."

For a moment, Yrome's expression hardened, and I saw a flicker of something darker in his gaze. It was as if the power he now held was igniting a part of him that craved more, a part that reveled in the sheer force at his command.

"Yrome," I said firmly, stepping closer to him, "you must understand that this power is a tool, a means to protect and serve, not to dominate or intimidate. The moment you lose sight of that, you lose yourself."

He looked away, his expression a mix of frustration and contemplation. After a moment of silence, he nodded slowly. "I understand, King Ytfen. I will try to remember your words."

But as we resumed our training, a nagging doubt lingered in my mind. Had I awakened a thirst in Yrome that could not be easily quenched? The thought troubled me, and I resolved to keep a closer eye on his progress, hoping that my guidance would steer him towards a path of wisdom rather than one of unchecked ambition.

Unfortunately, that was not the case.

Our training session progressed, but the subtle undercurrents of Yrome's growing fascination with his newfound powers became increasingly apparent. Each display of elemental control, while impressive, seemed tinged with an underlying hunger for more.

As we moved to a more challenging exercise, I demonstrated how to harness the elemental energy to create a protective barrier. "Concentrate on the essence of the element, feel its flow, and direct it with purpose," I instructed, my own barrier shimmering with a gentle light.

Yrome followed suit, his barrier initially flickering into existence. But then, with a determined look, he pushed more energy into it. The barrier expanded rapidly, crackling with raw power, far more forceful than necessary.

"Yrome, restrain your power. The goal is protection, not intimidation," I reminded him, watching as his barrier pulsed with an intensity that bordered on aggressive.

He seemed to struggle for a moment, caught between the thrill of his power and the discipline I was trying to instill. Finally, with a visible effort, he reined in the energy, and the barrier returned to a more controlled state.

"Good," I acknowledged, "but remember, power must be balanced with responsibility. It's not just about what you can do, but what you should do."

Our training continued, shifting focus to the element of fire. I demonstrated the art of conjuring flames, emphasizing control and precision. "Fire is a living element," I explained. "It breathes, it consumes, but it must never be allowed to rage unchecked."

Yrome watched intently as I summoned a small flame in my palm, manipulating its size and intensity with careful concentration. "Your turn," I prompted, extinguishing the flame.

He extended his hand, and a flame burst to life, larger and more fierce than necessary. I could see the exhilaration in his eyes as he watched the fire dance at his command. "Control it, Yrome. Smaller, more focused," I urged.

He struggled momentarily, the flame flickering wildly before he managed to reduce its size. But even then, it seemed to crackle with an excess of energy, as if mirroring Yrome's own internal fire.

After several days of training, we moved on to earth manipulation, shaping the very ground beneath our feet.

"Feel the earth, its stability, its strength," I guided. "Channel that essence."

Yrome's hands moved, and the earth responded, rising and falling at his command. Yet, there was an aggression to his movements, a forcefulness that went beyond the exercise's intent.

Finally, we practiced with lightning, an element that required utmost precision and restraint. As Yrome summoned a bolt of lightning, it struck with a ferocity that left a scorched mark on the ground.

"Yrome, you must temper your power with wisdom," I cautioned, a note of sternness in my voice. "These elements are not just tools; they are a part of the natural world. Respect them."

He nodded, but there was a flicker of something unspoken in his gaze. A desire, a yearning for the raw power he now wielded.

As the days turned into nights, and the nights back into days, this pattern continued. I couldn't shake the feeling of unease. Yrome's quick mastery of the elements was undeniable, but so was the growing gleam of ambition in his eyes. It was as if each new display of power fed a part of him that yearned for more than just the ability to protect and serve.

On the last day of training, I found myself deep in thought, pondering the implications of what I had set in motion. The power I had shared with Yrome was meant to bridge our worlds, to foster trust and cooperation. But had I inadvertently sown the seeds of something far more dangerous? The question lingered in my mind, a silent warning of potential perils yet unseen.

As we gathered our belongings, preparing to conclude our training session, Yrome hesitated, a contemplative look crossing his face. "Ytfen, may I try one last thing?" he asked, his voice laced with a hint of something I couldn't quite place.

He walked over to where his katana lay, picking it up with a reverence that spoke of a warrior's bond to his weapon. Turning towards the distant mountains, he stood in silence for a moment, as if communing with some unseen force.

Then, with a deep inhale, Yrome began to channel his power into the katana. The air around us grew tense, charged with energy. The blade of the katana started to glow, first a faint shimmer, then brighter and brighter, until it was like a beacon of concentrated power.

I watched, a sense of unease growing within me. This was more than a simple display of skill; it was a test of the limits of his newfound abilities.

With a sudden, explosive movement, Yrome swung the katana. The air itself seemed to split, a visible shockwave emanating from the blade. It raced across the landscape, a roaring force of destruction.

As the shockwave hit the mountains, it was as if the world itself shuddered. Rocks and earth were torn asunder, trees uprooted, and the very mountains seemed to crumble under the sheer force. A cloud of dust and debris billowed into the sky, obscuring the sun for a moment, casting a shadow over the land.

The aftermath was a scene of devastation. Where once stood a majestic range, now lay a scarred and fractured landscape.

I stood there, speechless, the sight before me a reminder of the fine line between mastery and recklessness. Yrome turned to face me, his expression one of triumph mixed with an unsettling hunger for more.

In that moment, I realized the gravity of what I had set in motion. The power I had helped awaken in Yrome was not just a tool for peace; it was a weapon, one that, in the wrong hands, could bring untold destruction.

A chill ran down my spine as I pondered the future. Had I nurtured a protector of peace, or had I unwittingly unleashed a force that could threaten the very world we sought to unite?

The world around me began to blur and I could feel myself being pulled back to the present.

17
A Brother's Ruse

Today was the final day of my water training, I stood before the cascading waterfall, feeling a deep connection with the element I had been working so hard to understand. Over the past few days, my control and affinity with water had grown exponentially, and I felt ready to test the limits of my newfound abilities.

Papa Yamah watched from a distance, his eyes reflecting a mix of curiosity and anticipation. I took a deep breath, focusing on the waterfall, feeling its powerful flow, its relentless energy. I raised my hands, and slowly, the waterfall began to respond to my command.

At first, the water's movement was subtle, a slight deviation from its natural path. But as I concentrated, the entire waterfall began to shift, the water bending and twisting in the air, defying gravity. I could feel every droplet, every ripple, and with a mere thought, I directed them, creating intricate patterns and shapes in the air.

The water spiraled around me, forming a towering column that shimmered in the sunlight, casting rainbows in all directions. Then, with a flick of my wrist, I sent the water shooting upwards, creating a geyser that soared high into the sky before gently raining down like a like a soft spring shower. The droplets danced in the light, a liquid ballet at my behest. I could sense Papa Yamah's gaze on me, intense and calculating, as I pushed the boundaries of my mastery.

The water then gathered into a swirling vortex, a cyclone suspended in mid-air, a display of power and grace. I stood at its eye, the master of the storm I had summoned, every motion of my body an extension of my will upon the water.

Yet, as I commanded the elements, a voice within whispered caution, a reminder that power, while exhilarating, required respect and restraint. I let the waters gently fall back into their natural course, the river once again following the path laid out by the earth, not by man.

I turned to Papa Yamah, a question unspoken between us. His nod was subtle but approving. "You have learned well," he said, his voice carrying over the sound of the returned waterfall. "I think you're ready for the next phase of your training."

For the rest of the day, we relaxed, sharing stories and laughter, recalling the days of when it was just Papa, me, and Elijah.

The following day marked the beginning of a new challenge: learning to harness the earth element. As the sun rose, casting its first light on the mountains, Papa Yamah and I set out for the rocky terrain that would serve as our training ground.

The mountain, with its rugged cliffs and ancient boulders, was a stark contrast to the serene waterfall where I had practiced water manipulation. The air was cooler here, the ground firm and unyielding beneath our feet. Papa Yamah led the way, his steps sure and steady, as we climbed to a plateau that offered a panoramic view of the surrounding landscape.

"Earth is the element of stability, endurance, and strength," Papa Yamah began, his voice echoing slightly in the open space. "To control it, you must connect with these qualities within yourself. Feel the weight and solidity of the earth, its ageless presence, and unbreakable will."

I nodded.

"Try it," he gestured towards a large rock.

I approached the rock, placing my hand on its rough surface. I closed my eyes, trying to sense the earth's energy, but the rock remained inert, unresponsive to my efforts.

Throughout the day, I struggled. The earth element felt alien, its dense nature contrasting sharply with the fluidity of water. Frustration crept in with each unsuccessful attempt.

Papa Yamah, observing my growing frustration, offered guidance. "Earth requires a deep connection, a sense of unity with the land. It's not just about physical strength but an inner resilience. Be patient with yourself."

Despite his advice, I felt a sense of defeat as the sun dipped below the horizon. We decided to end the day's training, leaving me with much to ponder.

The following day, under the watchful gaze of the mountains, Papa Yamah and I resumed the earth training.

Despite his patient guidance, the connection to the earth element continued to elude me. My attempts to draw energy from the earth felt like reaching into an abyss, with no response or resonance.

As I grappled with my frustration, a sudden pulsing sensation interrupted my focus. It was the ring Aria had given me, vibrating with an urgent rhythm. I glanced at Papa Yamah, who noticed the change immediately.

"It seems Aria is trying to reach you," he said, his tone laced with concern.

I concentrated on the ring, and a small portal materialized before us. Aria's voice, tense and anxious, echoed from the portal. "Ezekiel, Yamah, there's an emergency. You need to come back to Serenity's Edge immediately. The crown... it's gone."

The words struck like a thunderbolt, shattering the calm of our training session.

"Meet me in Ash Village as soon as you can," Aria instructed, her tone underscored with seriousness. "I'll open a portal there to bring you straight to Serenity's Edge. We must act quickly."

Papa Yamah nodded in agreement, his expression grave. "We'll be there as fast as we can, Aria. Stay safe until we arrive."

I felt a surge of anxiety mixed with determination. "We're on our way," I assured her, the ring's portal closing as the communication ended.

Without hesitation, Papa Yamah and I gathered our belongings, preparing to leave. The urgency of Aria's message propelled us forward, each step fueled by a mix of apprehension and determination.

As we journeyed towards Ash Village, the silence between us was filled with unspoken concerns. The disappearance of the crown was a critical issue, one that could have far-reaching implications.

"I can't believe the crown is gone," I said, breaking the silence. "After all the efforts to keep it safe..."

Papa Yamah's gaze was fixed on the path ahead. "We don't know the full situation yet, Ezekiel. Let's not jump to conclusions. Our priority is to get there and assess what happened."

His words were a reminder to stay focused, but my mind raced with possibilities and potential threats. The crown's power, in the wrong hands, could be catastrophic.

The journey to Ash Village felt longer than usual, each step heavy with the burden of the unknown. But we pushed on, driven by the need to confront whatever awaited us at Serenity's Edge.

As Papa Yamah and I approached Ash Village, the familiar figures of Aria, Camila, and Gaianor came into view, waiting for us at the village's outskirts.

"Looks like you made good time," I said, relieved to see them.

Aria nodded, a hint of worry in her eyes. "I went to pick them up. Having access to their villages is already proving useful."

Camila and Gaianor exchanged glances, their expressions mirroring the gravity of the situation.

"Let's hope we can resolve this quickly," Gaianor remarked.

Without further delay, Aria activated her portal, and in a swirl of energy, we were transported to Serenity's Edge. The sudden shift in surroundings was disorienting, but we quickly regained our bearings, finding ourselves in the village's meeting room.

Nina, Joren, Gabriel, and Caius stood around a large table, maps and documents scattered across its surface.

"We've been waiting for you," Nina said, her voice tense. "The situation is dire."

Papa Yamah stepped forward, his posture authoritative yet respectful. "What happened?"

"We thought we were giving you the crown, Ezekiel," said Joren, his voice laced with disbelief. "Little did we know it was someone claiming to be you. He told us that you had discovered a way to destroy the crown and that it needed to be done immediately, before Yrome could find it."

As they spoke, a sinking feeling grew within me. "Elijah," I murmured, the pieces falling into place. The realization hit me like a wave – my brother had deceived them all.

"It was so convincing," Nina added, her voice heavy with regret. "We didn't question it. We thought we were aiding you in protecting the world."

Papa Yamah's expression darkened, a mix of anger and concern etched on his face. "Elijah has the crown," he said, his voice low and steady. "This is a dangerous turn of events."

I felt a surge of frustration and worry. Elijah, consumed by his quest for vengeance, now possessed an artifact of immense power. The implications were alarming.

Aria stepped forward, her expression serious. "As soon as they told me what happened, I knew it couldn't have been you, Ezekiel. You were still taking care of things with Yamah. Not only that but you have no way of knowing how to get here."

The urgency of the situation was palpable. Elijah, now in possession of the crown, posed a threat we couldn't ignore.

"I don't understand," I said, frustration evident in my voice. "The village's barriers should have made it impossible for anyone to find it."

Papa Yamah rubbed his chin thoughtfully. "It's perplexing. In addition to the barriers, the village is nestled deep within the heart of an impenetrable swamp. It just doesn't make any sense."

Camila interjected, her brow furrowed in concentration. "Could it be possible that Elijah has developed a way to bypass such magic?"

"Perhaps," countered Papa Yamah. "But it still doesn't explain how he would know the exact location of the village."

Gaianor shook his head, clearly troubled. "We're clearly dealing with an unknown variable here."

Aria looked around the room, her eyes reflecting the gravity of the situation. "Whatever the means, the fact remains that Elijah has the crown. We need to focus on finding him before he can use it."

"Joren," I pressed, my tone filled with anticipation. "Did he share anything else?"

The group exchanged glances, their expressions a mix of regret and concern. Nina spoke up, her voice tinged with unease. "When we asked him about his plan to destroy the crown, he was vague. All he said was that he needed to go back to where everything began. We didn't understand what he meant, but we trusted him, thinking it was you."

I felt a chill run down my spine as the implications of Elijah's words sank in. "Back to where everything began..." I murmured, the realization dawning on me. "He's talking about Bryson Village."

Papa Yamah's eyes widened in recognition. "Of course, Bryson Village... the place where your paths diverged, where everything changed for both of you."

Camila nodded, her expression grave. "It makes sense. Bryson Village holds significant meaning for both of you."

Gaianor clenched his fists, his frustration evident. "We need to act quickly."

Aria stepped forward, determination in her eyes. "Let's go to Bryson Village then. I can open a portal to get us close."

I took a deep breath, steeling myself for what lay ahead. Returning to Bryson Village wouldn't be easy, but it was necessary. "Let's do it," I said. "We need to stop Elijah before it's too late."

As Aria's portal shimmered into existence, casting a radiant glow in the meeting room, the village leaders stood up, their faces set with determination. Joren, his voice firm and resolute, addressed us. "We may have left our Dragon Slayer lives behind, but we haven't forgotten how to fight. This village is full of skilled warriors who once wielded great power. We'll gather as many as we can and join you in this battle. For the sake of our world, for peace, we'll stand together one more time."

Nina nodded in agreement, her eyes reflecting the fire of a leader ready to defend her people. "We'll rally the villagers.

Many here still remember the call to arms. They'll be ready to fight for a cause that's just and true."

Gabriel added, his voice echoing the sentiment of unity, "This is our fight too. Yrome's threat endangers us all. We'll stand with you, shoulder to shoulder, to protect our world from his tyranny."

I looked around at the determined faces of the village leaders and felt a surge of gratitude and solidarity. "Thank you," I said, my voice thick with emotion.

With a final nod to the leaders, we stepped into Aria's portal.

As we stepped through the portal, Papa Yamah's voice carried a note of reflection and hope. "You know, Ezekiel," he began, his gaze fixed on the swirling vortex of the portal, "seeing dragons and Dragon Slayers working together towards a common cause... it's the future I always dreamed of. It's not under the circumstances I would have wished for, but it's a start—a step towards the world I envisioned when I first took you and Elijah under my wing."

He paused, his eyes distant yet filled with a quiet determination. "This alliance, born out of necessity, might just be the foundation we need to build a new era. An era where fear and hatred give way to understanding and cooperation. It's a tough battle ahead, but it's also a chance to show that dragons and humans can stand side by side, united against a common enemy."

I nodded, feeling the weight of his words. "It's a powerful vision, Papa. And I believe we can make it a reality. This battle... it's more than just a fight against Yrome. It's a chance to change the course of history, to heal old wounds and forge a new path."

Papa Yamah smiled, a glimmer of hope shining in his eyes. "Exactly. And it starts with us, here and now. Let's make this count, for the future we all deserve."

The portal left us in front of the gates of a ruined Bryson Village. A wave of emotion washed over me.

The sight of the once vibrant village, now reduced to ruins, was a harsh reminder of the pain and loss we had endured. The memories of laughter, joy, and simpler times seemed to echo through the desolate streets.

Papa Yamah and I exchanged a look, a silent understanding passing between us. This place held a special significance for both of us—it was more than just a home; it was a part of who we were.

"Papa," I began, my voice thick with emotion, "seeing Bryson Village like this... it's hard. This place was full of life, full of memories."

He nodded solemnly, his eyes reflecting the sorrow of the scene before us. "I know, Ezekiel. This village was a sanctuary, a place where we found peace and purpose. It's heartbreaking to see it in ruins."

I took a deep breath, trying to steady my voice. "But we can't let this be the end of its story. We have to fight, not just for what Bryson Village was, but for what it can be again."

Papa Yamah placed a reassuring hand on my shoulder. "We will, Ezekiel. We'll rebuild, not just the buildings, but the spirit of this place. Bryson Village will live again, through our memories and our efforts. Right now, though, we have a more immediate battle to face."

Papa Yamah reached into his cloak and pulled out two necklaces, their chains glinting in the dim light. He held them out to me, and I saw that each bore a name: one inscribed with "Ezekiel" and the other with "Elijah."

"These," he said, his voice laden with a mix of sorrow and resolve, "were the necklaces I told you about. The ones you and your brother had on when I found you in that cave all those years ago. They are a part of your heritage, a connection to who you are and where you come from. I want you to have them."

I took the necklaces from him, the weight of their significance heavy in my hands. The names etched into the metal were more than just identifiers; they were a link to a past I was only beginning to understand.

"Thank you, Papa," I whispered, clutching the necklaces tightly. "These mean more to me than you can imagine. They're not just reminders of where we've been; they're symbols of where we're going. Together, we'll honor the memory of this place and fight for its future."

Papa Yamah nodded, a determined glint in his eyes. "Together," he echoed, and in that moment, I felt the strength of our bond, forged through trials and tribulations, ready to face whatever lay ahead.

With the necklaces securely around my neck, serving as a tangible reminder of my roots and my purpose, I turned to face my companions once more. I nodded, feeling a renewed sense of determination. "Let's do this, for Bryson Village, for all the villages, and for the future we believe in."

The air was thick with tension, a palpable sense of urgency enveloping us as we stood at the threshold of what was once Bryson Village.

"Are you guys ready?" I asked, my voice steady yet charged with the weight of the moment. My eyes met each of theirs, seeking affirmation, solidarity.

Camila nodded, her expression resolute. "We've come this far together. We're ready for whatever lies ahead."

Gaianor clenched his fists. "We stand with you, Ezekiel. Let's see this through to the end."

"I'm with you," said Aria. "We'll face whatever comes, together."

Their words bolstered my resolve. We were more than just a group of individuals; we were a united front, ready to confront whatever challenges awaited us in the ruins of my once-beloved home.

With a deep breath, I stepped forward, leading the way into the ruined village. The air was still, the silence of the ruins speaking volumes of the tragedy that had befallen this place. But we were here now, ready to face whatever Elijah, or fate, had in store for us.

Then, without warning, a familiar sensation began to take hold. The world around me blurred and I felt myself being drawn to Ytfen's memories.

18
A Kingdom's Unease

I found myself in a somber council meeting with my Pure Elementals. The atmosphere was heavy with concern, a sharp divergence to the usual unity and strength that characterized our gatherings.

We were in the war room, a place usually reserved for discussions of defense and strategy. The walls were lined with maps of our kingdom and the surrounding lands, including the human territories. The recent actions of King Yrome had cast a shadow of doubt over our once hopeful alliance.

Tarn was the first to speak. "My king, there are troubling reports from the borderlands. Yrome's expansion has been swift and aggressive. He's annexed several neighboring human kingdoms under the guise of unification."

I leaned forward, my hands clasped tightly. "This is not what we envisioned when I shared my power with him. It was meant to be a symbol of trust, a tool for peace."

"The winds carry whispers of dissent and fear. Yrome's actions are causing unrest, not just among his people, but ours as well," Zephyra added.

"It seems he's become intoxicated with the power that was bestowed upon him," Pyrus said, his voice tinged with anger. "What was intended as a bridge to peace might have turned into a weapon of conquest."

Joaquin, spoke up, his tone measured yet firm. "We must consider the possibility that Yrome is not the ally we hoped for. His actions are endangering the balance we've strived to maintain."

I nodded gravely. "We cannot ignore these signs. If Yrome is using the power we gave him for personal gain, we must be prepared to act."

Denise, who had joined the meeting, said softly, "We must tread carefully. Accusations and hasty actions could lead to open conflict. Perhaps a diplomatic approach, a meeting to understand his intentions?"

As Denise offered her perspective on the situation with Yrome, her wisdom and insight bringing a calming influence to the tense council meeting, Tarn expressed his concern for her well-being.

"My lady, you must consider your health," he said, his voice laced with respect and concern. "The birth of your child is near, and you should be resting."

Denise offered a gentle smile in response. "Thank you, Tarn, for your concern. But I cannot simply stand aside when the future of our kingdom, and our child's future, is at stake."

I watched her, admiration and love filling my heart. Her strength and commitment were unwavering, even in the face of personal challenges. However, I knew the importance of her well-being, especially now.

"Denise, my love," I interjected softly, "while your counsel is invaluable, Tarn is right. You must take care of yourself and our child. My mother has requested your assistance in Ash Village. She values your insight, and it would be a less strenuous way for you to contribute."

Denise looked at me, a mix of reluctance and understanding in her eyes. "Very well, my king. I will join your mother in Ash Village. But please, keep me informed of all developments."

I nodded, relieved that she would be taking a less demanding role. "Of course, my queen. Your wisdom will continue to guide us."

As Denise gracefully excused herself from the meeting, the commanders and I returned to our discussion, each of us aware of the delicate balance between duty to the kingdom and personal responsibilities.

I sighed, feeling the weight of the decision. "Arrange a meeting with King Yrome. We must address these concerns directly and seek a resolution. Our hope for peace depends on it."

19
Twin Fates Collide

As the memory faded, and I returned to the present as Ezekiel, I was left with a sense of the complex challenges Ytfen faced. His intentions for peace and unity were clear, but the path to achieving them was fraught with obstacles and the unpredictability of human ambition.

We ventured deeper into the heart of Bryson Village. The devastation around us was heart-wrenching. Buildings reduced to rubble, streets eerily silent, a haunting reminder of the vibrant community that once thrived here. The air was thick with the scent of loss and decay, a profound disparity to the memories of laughter and life that once filled these streets.

Ahead, a solitary figure stood amidst the ruins, his black cloak billowing in the wind, a stark silhouette against the backdrop of destruction. In his hand, he held the crown, its ominous presence palpable even from a distance.

"Elijah," I whispered, my voice barely audible, a mix of disbelief and sorrow.

We approached cautiously, the tension rising with each step. Elijah remained still, his back to us, as if lost in his own thoughts or perhaps waiting for this very confrontation.

Papa Yamah's hand rested on my shoulder, a silent gesture of support. Camila, Gaianor, and Aria stood ready, their expressions a mix of determination and apprehension.

We stopped a few feet away, the distance between us charged with unspoken emotions and questions. The air seemed to grow colder, the wind carrying whispers of the past, of choices made and paths diverged.

The silence stretched on, a heavy cloak that threatened to suffocate us with its weight.

Elijah's voice, laced with a mixture of bitterness and nostalgia, broke the silence. "So the rumors are true, Papa Yamah. You're still alive," he said, his back still turned to us. His words hung in the air, heavy with unspoken accusations and pain.

He continued, his voice growing more intense. "We had a beautiful childhood, didn't we? Raised by you, nurtured in a village that was a haven of innocence and joy." His words painted a picture of our past, a time of simplicity and happiness.

Then, his tone shifted, darker, filled with anguish. "But everything changed that day. The day Vajra invaded our home." He paused, the silence punctuated by the distant rustling of the wind through the ruins. "I saw you transform, Ezekiel. I saw you unleash your draconic fury, destroying everything in your path. I thought you were dead... I thought both of you were gone."

His voice cracked slightly, revealing a glimpse of the vulnerability beneath his hardened exterior. "But you weren't. You survived, and yet, you never came back for me. I was left alone, abandoned, forgotten. How could you? How could you leave me behind?"

The accusation stung, a sharp reminder of the pain and loss that had shaped Elijah's path. His words echoed in the desolate village, a lament for a brotherhood shattered by tragedy and misunderstanding.

Elijah turned slowly, his face a mask of resolution and pain. "It doesn't matter anymore," he said, his eyes meeting mine. "Yrome... he's going to change everything. He's going to create a new world, a better world."

I stepped forward, urgency in my voice. "Elijah, Yrome is not the hero you think he is!"

But Elijah cut me off, his voice rising. "No, Ezekiel! You're wrong! Yrome has shown me the truth. He's shown me memories of the past, the real past. Villages burned to the ground, innocent lives taken. Atrocities committed in the name of power and fear."

His words were like a torrent, a flood of conviction and belief. "Yrome understands the pain, the injustice. He's the only one who can make things right. He's the only one who can bring order to this chaos."

The intensity in his eyes was unwavering, a reflection of a belief so deeply ingrained that it had reshaped his very being. In that moment, I realized the depth of his conviction, the extent to which Yrome had influenced his thoughts and his heart.

Elijah's gaze fell to the crown in his hand. "With this," he said softly, "everything begins. The final piece of the puzzle."

Papa Yamah stepped forward, his voice filled with a mixture of sorrow and urgency. "Elijah, please, listen to me. I'm so sorry you felt abandoned. If I had known you were alive, if I had any idea... I would have never stopped searching for you."

Elijah's expression hardened, but there was a flicker of something else in his eyes – a glimpse of the pain he had carried for so long. "Words, Papa Yamah. Just words. You left me. You chose Ezekiel over me."

Papa Yamah's voice cracked with emotion. "It was never about choosing one over the other. You were both my sons, in every way that mattered. I loved you both equally. The day I lost you both was the day my world shattered."

Elijah shook his head, a bitter laugh escaping his lips. "And yet, here we are."

Papa Yamah reached out, his hand trembling. "It's not too late, Elijah. We can fix this. Together. We can heal the wounds of the past."

But Elijah stepped back, the crown clutched tightly in his grasp. "It's too late for apologies, too late for healing. Yrome has shown me the path, and I will follow it to the end. For a new world. For justice."

I took a deep breath, steeling myself for what was to come. "Elijah, I'm sorry for everything. But if this is the path you choose, then we have no choice but to stop you."

Elijah's eyes narrowed, a cold determination within them. "I'd like to see you try," he challenged. With a swift motion, he placed the crown on the ground and, using his powers over ice and earth, encased it in a protective shell, making it nearly impenetrable.

He then assumed a fighting stance, his body poised and ready. The air around him crackled with elemental energy as he unsheathed his sword.

I looked at him, my heart heavy with the weight of the moment. "It won't be like our last battle, Elijah. This time, we'll stop you. We have to."

Papa Yamah, Camila, Gaianor, and Aria stood by my side, a united front against the impending conflict. The tension was palpable, a silent understanding passing between us. We were ready to do whatever it took to prevent Elijah from unleashing whatever plan he had in mind with Yrome's crown.

Elijah's expression was a mix of defiance and sadness, a reflection of the path he had chosen. "Then let's see who the fates favor," he said, his voice a whisper in the wind.

With that, the air around us erupted into a maelstrom of power, the clash of elemental forces echoing through the ruins of Bryson Village. The battle for the future had begun.

Camila summoned a swirling vortex of water, sending powerful jets towards Elijah, attempting to throw him off balance. Gaianor raised his hands, and the ground beneath us trembled. Massive stone pillars erupted from the earth, aiming to trap Elijah in a stony grasp.

Papa Yamah, though devoid of elemental powers, was a powerful fighter. His years of experience as a Dragon Slayer had honed his skills to near perfection. He moved with a speed and precision that belied his age, his sword a blur as he engaged Elijah in close combat.

I focused my energy, feeling the dragon within me stir. I channeled my power into my sword, the blade glowing with a fiery intensity. With each swing, I unleashed waves of searing heat, aiming to counter Elijah's ice and earth attacks.

Elijah was a force to be reckoned with. His control over ice and earth was masterful, creating barriers of ice to block Camila's water attacks and countering Gaianor's stone pillars with his own earthen constructs. His movements were fluid and calculated, a dance of destruction that was both beautiful and terrifying to behold.

The battle raged on, a symphony of elemental fury. Water clashed with earth, fire with ice, each of us pushing our abilities to their limits. Elijah's determination was evident in every move he made, his powers a reflection of his inner turmoil and pain.

In a moment of teamwork, Camila and Gaianor combined their powers, water and earth merging to create a mudslide that swept towards Elijah, attempting to immobilize him. I seized the opportunity, leaping into the air and bringing my sword down in a fiery arc, aiming to break through his defenses.

But Elijah was quick to react. With a wave of his hand, he summoned a wall of ice, deflecting my attack and countering with a barrage of earthen spikes. We dodged and weaved.

As the fight continued, Elijah's mastery over his multiple elements became increasingly evident. In a sudden shift, he unleashed a torrent of fire, the flames roaring towards us with a ferocity that matched his own inner rage. The air heated up rapidly, the intense blaze threatening to engulf us.

Camila, quick to react, countered with a powerful surge of water, creating a steam barrier that momentarily held back the flames. But Elijah was relentless. He raised his hands, and bolts of lightning crackled in the sky above, striking down with precision and power. The air sizzled with electricity, each bolt a deadly dance of light and energy.

Gaianor, undeterred, used his earth powers to create a dome of rock above us, shielding us from the lightning strikes. The stones absorbed the electric energy, but the strain was evident on Gaianor's face as he struggled to maintain the barrier.

Papa Yamah saw an opening. He signaled to us, and we followed his lead, coordinating our movements to create a combined assault. I focused my energy, channeling the fiery power within me, while Camila and Gaianor prepared their own elemental attacks.

In a synchronized move, we unleashed our powers. A torrent of water, a barrage of earthen projectiles, and a wave of fire converged on Elijah. The elements collided with his defenses, creating a flurry of chaos and power.

Elijah, however, was not easily defeated. He absorbed the fire into his own, augmenting his flames, and redirected the lightning to shatter Gaianor's rock dome. He then manipulated the earth to launch a counterattack, sending a wave of jagged rocks hurtling towards us.

We scattered, each of us dodging the deadly projectiles.

Elijah's movements were a blur, his body crackling with lightning as he propelled himself towards Gaianor. The air hummed with the energy of his charge, a tangible force that made the hairs on the back of my neck stand up. In an instant, he was beside Gaianor, his sword, now a conduit for his lightning power, slashing through the air with deadly precision.

Gaianor, caught off guard, managed to twist away, but not before the blade grazed his side, leaving a searing mark. The smell of singed fabric and skin filled the air. Before Gaianor could recover, Elijah conjured a fireball, its intense heat warping the air around it, and hurled it with unerring accuracy.

Reacting instinctively, I stepped forward, extending my hand towards the incoming fireball. Drawing upon the water training I had undergone with Papa Yamah, I summoned a surge of water, creating a barrier between the fireball and Gaianor. The water hissed and steamed as it collided with the flame, extinguishing it in a cloud of vapor.

Camila, witnessing my intervention, gave a nod of approval.

Gaianor gave me a grateful look before refocusing on the fight. "Thanks, Ezekiel. Let's not give him any more openings," he said, his voice tinged with pain but resolute.

Elijah, seeing his attack thwarted, let out a frustrated snarl. He conjured another fireball, this one aimed directly at Papa Yamah. The ball of flame roared through the air, its intense heat distorting the space around it. Papa Yamah, caught off guard and without any elemental powers to defend himself, was in imminent danger.

"No!" I screamed, my heart racing with fear. I stretched out my hand, but I was too far to intervene in time. The fireball was mere inches from striking Papa Yamah when, suddenly, a small portal materialized in its path. The fireball disappeared into the portal with a whoosh, vanishing as quickly as it had appeared.

Aria, standing a short distance away, had her hand extended, her face a mask of concentration. She had opened the portal just in time, redirecting the deadly attack away from Papa Yamah. Her quick thinking had saved him from certain harm.

Papa Yamah, realizing how close he had come to being hit, gave Aria a nod of gratitude. "Thank you, Aria. That was close," he said, his voice steady but with an underlying note of relief.

Aria, still focused on the battle, replied without taking her eyes off Elijah. "Stay alert. He's not holding back," she warned.

Elijah, frustrated by the interruption, glared at Aria. His expression twisted into one of anger and determination. "Clever trick, but it won't save you," he growled, preparing for his next move.

As Elijah's attention momentarily shifted to Aria, Gaianor seized the opportunity. He lunged towards the crown, his movements swift and determined. The crown, encased in its elemental barrier, seemed almost within reach.

"Nice try," Elijah sneered, noticing Gaianor's attempt. With a swift gesture, he manipulated the elements surrounding the crown. Suddenly, sharp spikes of ice and earth erupted from the encasement, creating a deadly barrier around the crown.

Gaianor, caught off guard by the sudden defense mechanism, tried to pull back, but it was too late. The spikes struck him, causing him to cry out in pain. He stumbled backward, clutching his side where a spike had grazed him, leaving a visible wound.

Papa Yamah and I rushed to Gaianor's side. "Are you alright?" Papa Yamah asked, examining the injury.

Gaianor grimaced, trying to downplay the severity of the wound. "I'll be fine," he grunted, though the pain was evident in his eyes.

Elijah, watching us with a cold, calculating gaze, prepared for his next move. "You can't stop me," he declared, his voice echoing with confidence and malice.

We regrouped, ready to continue the fight. It was clear that retrieving the crown would not be easy, but we were determined to stop Elijah at all costs.

Elijah's demeanor shifted, his eyes narrowing with a newfound tenacity. "Enough games," he hissed, his voice laced with venom. "Yrome will appreciate it if I end this here and now."

With a swift, deliberate motion, he plunged his sword into the ground. The air around us began to crackle with raw energy, the atmosphere charged with a palpable tension. The earth beneath our feet trembled, sending vibrations through the ruins of Bryson Village.

Elijah's body convulsed as he screamed, a sound that was both human and something else entirely. His eyes, once a familiar shade, now glowed a deep, menacing red. The transformation was beginning.

His form grew, expanding and contorting in an unnatural, terrifying display of power. Scales emerged, covering his skin, shimmering with the colors of the earth and fire. His limbs elongated, his fingers and toes morphing into sharp, deadly claws.

Massive wings unfurled from his back, tearing through his cloak with a sound like thunder. His face elongated, forming a snout filled with razor-sharp teeth, and his eyes burned with an intensity that was both mesmerizing and horrifying.

Elijah, now in his dragon form, towered over us, a creature of immense power and fury. The transformation was complete.

We stood there, momentarily stunned by the sheer magnitude of his transformation.

Papa Yamah, Camila, Gaianor, Aria, and I exchanged glances, a silent agreement passing between us. We had to act, and fast. The battle was far from over, and now, it had reached a new, terrifying level.

"Guys, he can't control his dragon form," I said. "Please be careful."

Elijah's laughter, deep and resonant, echoed through his dragon form, a chilling sound that reverberated through the ruins of Bryson Village. "Control it?" he roared, his voice a blend of human and draconic tones. "Yrome has shown me the true potential of my power. He has taught me to embrace it, not fear it."

Papa Yamah, his face etched with concern and frustration, stepped forward, his voice rising above the din. "Elijah, listen to yourself! Yrome is using you. He's manipulating your pain, your anger, for his own twisted goals!"

Elijah's dragon eyes narrowed, a flicker of uncertainty passing through them before being quickly replaced by resolve. "No, Papa Yamah," he spat, the ground trembling with each word. "You're the one who's been blind. Blind to the truth of this world, to the lies we've been fed about dragons and humans. Yrome has opened my eyes."

I clenched my fists, feeling a surge of desperation. "Elijah, please," I pleaded. "Think about what you're doing. This isn't you. This isn't the brother I grew up with."

But Elijah seemed beyond reach, his gaze fixed on some distant point, a place where his pain and Yrome's promises had twisted his perception of reality. The air around us crackled with tension, a storm brewing that threatened to engulf us all.

We braced ourselves. We had to find a way to reach Elijah, to break through the veil of manipulation and bring back the brother I once knew. The fate of our world depended on it.

Determination set in my heart, I turned to Camila and Gaianor. "We have no choice," I said, my voice resolute. "We do what must be done."

Understanding flashed in their eyes, a silent agreement passing between us. We stepped back, giving ourselves space, and focused on the essence of our dragons within. The air around us began to shimmer with energy, a tangible manifestation of the transformation that was about to take place.

I closed my eyes, feeling the familiar surge of power coursing through me. My body began to change, growing larger, muscles expanding, skin giving way to black scales. I could feel my wings unfurling, powerful and majestic, ready to take flight.

Beside me, Camila and Gaianor underwent their own transformations. Camila's form shifted gracefully into the elegant and fluid shape of her Water Dragon, scales glistening like the surface of a serene lake. Gaianor's transformation was more grounded, his body taking on the sturdy and robust form of an Earth Dragon, scales as tough as the ancient rocks of the mountains.

Together, we stood, three dragons ready to face my brother, who had lost himself to the darkness. Our forms were a testament to our resolve, a display of the power we wielded, not for destruction, but for the hope of saving what remained of our fractured world.

Elijah watched us, his red eyes burning with a mix of anger and challenge.

With a final glance at each other, we launched ourselves into the air, our wings beating powerfully against the wind.

The sky above the ruins of Bryson Village became an arena for an epic confrontation. Elijah, in his multi-elemental dragon form, exuded an aura of raw power, his scales reflecting the elements of fire, ice, earth, and lightning. His roars echoed through the air, a symphony of fury and might.

I, in my Dark Dragon form, felt a surge of energy. My scales, dark as the night, absorbed the light around me, creating an aura of ominous power. My wings, vast and imposing, cut through the air with ease, ready to engage in this dire battle.

Camila, embodying the fluid grace of her Water Dragon form, maneuvered around Elijah with agility, her attacks a dance of water and motion. She unleashed torrents of water, attempting to douse the flames of Elijah's fire and counter his earth attacks with her fluidity.

Gaianor, as the Earth Dragon, withstood the brunt of Elijah's assaults, creating openings for us to strike. He launched boulders and earthen spikes, aiming to ground Elijah and disrupt his fiery and electrical onslaughts.

The battle was a tempest of elements, each of us using our strengths to counter Elijah's multifaceted attacks. Fire clashed with water, lightning with earth, darkness with the raw power of a dragon consumed by vengeance.

Elijah's mastery over his elements was formidable. He conjured walls of flame, hurled bolts of lightning, and summoned icy spears, all while maneuvering with a speed that belied his size. His control over his dragon form was unnerving, proof of Yrome's influence and teachings.

In a coordinated effort, Camila and I created a diversion. She summoned a massive wave, forcing Elijah to focus on countering it with his fire, while I swooped in from above. My claws, imbued with the essence of my Dark Dragon form, aimed for a critical strike.

But Elijah was quick to react. With a thunderous roar, he unleashed a burst of lightning, repelling my attack and sending me spiraling through the air. The force of the impact left me dazed, but I quickly regained my bearings, knowing that any moment of weakness could be our downfall.

The battle raged on, a test of endurance, skill, and will. We fought not just to stop Elijah, but to reach out to the brother who had lost his way, hoping that somewhere within that raging dragon, the brother I once knew still existed.

Elijah's control over his elements was a sight to behold, yet it was clear that his rage fueled his actions. He unleashed a devastating inferno, attempting to engulf us in flames. But Camila countered with a massive wave, dousing the fire and creating a thick mist that temporarily blinded him.

Seizing the moment, Gaianor and I launched a coordinated assault. Gaianor, with a mighty roar, shattered the ground beneath Elijah, causing him to lose his footing. I swooped in, my dark energy pulsating, and delivered a powerful blow to his side. The impact sent him crashing into the ruins, causing a cloud of dust and debris to rise into the air.

But Elijah was far from defeated. With a defiant roar, he rose from the rubble and charged at us with renewed fury, unleashing a relentless assault. After successfully parrying his assault, he let out a roar. He conjured a massive storm of ice, a blizzard so intense it threatened to encase us all in a frozen tomb.

Camila and Gaianor struggled against the icy onslaught, their powers pushed to the limit. Camila's water attacks turned to ice before they could reach Elijah, and Gaianor's earthen defenses crumbled under the sheer cold. I could see their forms waning, the strain of the battle taking its toll.

In that moment, I realized what I had to do. The memory of my encounter with the enigmatic figure in the mindscape of Yrome's Crown flashed through my mind – the moment I had tapped into the fire element. I focused on that memory, on the sensation of heat and power that had surged through me.

Closing my eyes, I let go of my dark dragon form and embraced the fire within. The transformation was intense, a burning inferno that consumed my being and rebirthed me as a Fire Dragon. My scales turned a bright, fiery red, and flames danced along my wings.

I roared, a sound that was both a challenge and a declaration of my newfound strength. I soared above the blizzard, my body radiating intense heat. With a powerful beat of my wings, I sent a wave of fire cascading down, melting the ice and turning the blizzard into a harmless mist.

Elijah, caught off guard by my transformation, hesitated. His eyes, filled with a mix of shock and anger, locked onto mine.

Taking advantage of his momentary distraction, I dove towards him, a trail of flames in my wake. I unleashed a torrent of fire, aiming to subdue rather than harm. Elijah countered with a blast of lightning, but I was ready. I twisted in the air, dodging the attack, and closed in on him.

I could sense Elijah's steadfastness weakening. The fire in his eyes was flickering, giving way to the brother I remembered.

I knew then that this battle would not be won by force alone. It would take something more to reach Elijah, to bring him back from the brink. With that realization, I pulled back my attack, hoping to find a way to end this conflict without further bloodshed.

Elijah's voice, now a deep, rumbling growl, echoed across the battlefield. "Don't stop now, brother! You're adapting, learning. You're stronger than before. But it's not enough!" With a sweep of his massive claw, he unleashed a torrent of earth and fire, a deadly combination that hurtled towards us with devastating speed.

Aria, quick to react, opened a portal in an attempt to divert the attack. But it was clear that the sheer magnitude of Elijah's power was overwhelming her abilities. The portal flickered and warped under the strain, unable to fully contain the onslaught.

In that critical moment, I knew what I had to do. Drawing upon the memory of my recent training, I focused on the essence of water within me. If I could do it with the fire element, then I am sure I could do it with water. The transformation was swift, my Fire Dragon form giving way to the sleek, fluid form of a Water Dragon. My scales shimmered with a deep blue hue, and a sense of calm clarity filled me.

As the wave of fire and earth neared, I countered with a powerful blast of water. The two forces collided, steam hissing into the air as fire met water. My attack quenched the flames and turned the hurtling earth into mere mud, which splattered harmlessly around us.

Elijah, now hovering mid-air, watched with a mixture of frustration and curiosity. "You continue to surprise me," he admitted grudgingly. "But how long can you keep this up? How many forms can you take before you exhaust yourself?"

I hovered in my Water Dragon form, my eyes fixed on Elijah. "I will do whatever it takes to stop you, Elijah. This isn't the way. You know it deep down. Yrome is using you, just like he used others before."

Elijah's expression hardened, but I could see a flicker of doubt in his eyes. The battle was taking its toll on him too, both physically and emotionally.

Suddenly, I heard Aria speaking into her ring, her voice carrying a sense of urgency, "Are you guys ready?" she asked. She then glanced at Papa Yamah and gave him a nod. With a nod from him, she opened a swirling portal, and they both stepped through it, disappearing from the battlefield. I was left bewildered, unsure of their plan but trusting in their judgment.

Elijah, seizing the moment of confusion, let out a roar that echoed across the ruins of Bryson Village. He soared high into the sky, his massive dragon form casting a shadow over the land. High above, he began to gather a swirling mass of energy, a sphere that crackled and sparked with the raw power of fire, ice, earth, and lightning. The air around him vibrated with the intensity of the elements, a dangerous dance of nature's most primal forces.

"This ends now," Elijah declared, his tone laced with a chilling finality. "I will show you the true power of the elements!"

As he spoke, the energy sphere above him grew even larger. Elijah's display of power was a terrifying sight to behold. The sphere of energy he conjured above him was a swirling maelstrom of elemental fury, each component clashing and intertwining in a chaotic dance.

Realizing the imminent danger, I quickly reverted to my Dark Dragon form, feeling the familiar surge of power and strength course through my body. My scales shimmered with a dark sheen, and my eyes glowed with a fierce determination. I knew that we had to counteract Elijah's attack with everything we had.

"Gaianor, Camila, we need to combine our powers!" I shouted, my voice booming across the battlefield. "We can't let that hit the ground!"

As the sphere reached its peak, Elijah hurled it towards the ground, aiming directly at us. The sphere descended like a meteor, its impact imminent. In that moment, time seemed to slow. I knew we had to act fast.

Camila, her scales shimmering with the luster of the deep sea, drew upon the vast oceans' depths, releasing a glistening torrent of water, her beam reflecting the fluid dance of her dragon form.

Gaianor, his form as sturdy as the bedrock, summoned the earthen armor of the oldest mountains, his power emanating in a solid, resolute beam of stone and mineral.

And I, enshrouded in the night's embrace, unleashed the darkness woven from the void's very fabric, a dark energy beam that was the antithesis of light.

Together, as dragons, we breathed out our might. The water, earth, and darkness twined, a serpentine helix of primal forces, a tri-elemental spear set against the sky, hurtling towards Elijah with the full intent of our strength.

The collision was cataclysmic, a deafening roar filling the air as the two forces clashed. The ground beneath us trembled, and the air was filled with the scent of ozone and burning.

The sphere of fire, ice, earth, and lightning began to push against our combined beam. We pushed harder, our energies straining against the overwhelming power of Elijah's attack. It was a battle of wills, a test of our strength and resolve against the corrupted might of Elijah's dragon form.

As the struggle intensified, I could feel the strain on my body and spirit. But I knew we couldn't give up. We had to stop Elijah, no matter the cost. The fate of our world depended on it.

But slowly, Elijah's sphere began to overpower our beam of energy. His mastery over the elements, enhanced by Yrome's influence, was proving too much. The sphere inched closer, threatening to engulf us in its destructive embrace.

Straining against the overwhelming force of Elijah's sphere, I roared to Camila and Gaianor, "We need to push harder! Combine all your strength!"

"Ezekiel, we're with you!" she shouted, her voice resonating with the power of the oceans. She focused her energy, intensifying its strength and adding additional swirling torrents of aquatic force.

Gaianor grunted with effort. His earth dragon form, robust and grounded, radiated a deep, earthen energy. "We won't let him win!" he bellowed, his voice like rolling thunder. He amplified his beam and added a surge of rocky might to our collective effort.

"We can do this!" I encouraged, feeling the unity of our spirits in this desperate struggle. "Together!"

The beams clashed with Elijah's sphere, the impact sending shockwaves through the air. The sphere wavered, flickering with the intensity of our combined assault. For a moment, it seemed as if we were gaining ground, our powers inching the sphere back towards Elijah.

But then, the sphere surged forward again, its elemental chaos roaring with a renewed ferocity. We gritted our teeth, pouring every ounce of our strength into the beam, our bodies trembling from the exertion.

It was a battle of wills, a clash of powers that would determine the fate of all we held dear. And as we pushed against the overwhelming might of Elijah's sphere, I felt the world around me begin to blur, reality slipping away as I was once again drawn into the depths of Ytfen's memories.

20
The Usurper King

I found myself in Ignicia. The air was hot and dry, filled with the scent of smoldering embers and the distant sound of forges. I was in a heated discussion with Pyrus, strategizing our approach to address Yrome's aggressive expansions.

Pyrus, his face illuminated by the flickering flames of a nearby brazier, spoke with intensity. "We must confront Yrome, my king. His actions threaten the balance we've worked so hard to maintain."

I nodded, my mind racing with thoughts of diplomacy and the potential consequences of our actions. "I plan to meet with him, Pyrus. We need to resolve this peacefully, for the sake of both our peoples."

Just then, a guard burst into the room, his face etched with urgency and fear. "My king!" he exclaimed, out of breath. "The humans... they've invaded Ash Village!"

As the guard's words echoed in my ears, a single name escaped my lips, a whisper filled with fear and desperation: "Denise..."

Denise was in Ash Village tending to the gardens. The thought of her, possibly in danger or worse, ignited a fire within me, a burning urgency that could not be contained.

Without a second thought, I launched myself from the ground with a force that shook the very foundations of Ignicia. The air thundered around me as I propelled myself skyward, my body cutting through the atmosphere with staggering speed.

Pyrus's voice, calling out to me, warning me that it could be a trap, was lost in the roar of the wind and the tumult of my own thoughts. My mind was a whirlwind of fear, anger, and worry. Images of Denise, her smile, her laughter, the way she looked at me, flashed through my mind, each one a sharp reminder of what I might lose.

As I flew, the landscape below became a blur, a mere backdrop to the storm of emotions raging within me. "What if I'm too late?" I thought, the possibility sending a chill through my heart.

The possibility that I might not make it in time to protect her and our unborn child was unbearable. The thought of Denise, so full of life and love, possibly in harm's way, sent waves of dread crashing through me. "She must be safe," I thought desperately. "She has to be."

As the wind howled around me, I recalled the moments we had shared, her gentle touch, her radiant smile, and the way her eyes lit up when we talked about our future child. These memories, once sources of joy, now fueled my urgency and fear.

The pregnancy had filled us with such hope and happiness. The prospect of welcoming a new life into the world, our child, was a dream we had cherished together. Now, that dream was threatened by the harsh reality of war and betrayal.

With each passing second, as I drew closer to Ash Village, my heart raced with a mix of hope and terror. "Please, let me be in time," I pleaded inwardly. "Let Denise and our child be safe."

Then, as Ash Village came into view, my worst fears seemed to materialize before my eyes. Smoke and flames engulfed the village. The sight was a physical blow, a stark reminder of the fragility of life and the cruelty of war.

As I descended into the heart of Ash Village, the scene that unfolded before me was one of utter devastation. The once vibrant and lively village was now a landscape of destruction and death. The ground was littered with the bodies of villagers, innocent lives caught in the merciless grip of war. Children, adults, animals – all lay still, their lives extinguished in an instant. The air was thick with the acrid smell of smoke and the stench of death.

My heart pounded in my chest, each beat a drum of dread and despair. I made my way towards the gardens behind the shrine, a place that once symbolized life and growth, now consumed by flames. With a wave of my hand, I summoned a powerful gust of wind, extinguishing the fires with a forceful sweep. The flames died down, revealing the scorched earth and the remnants of what once was.

My eyes frantically searched the devastation, looking for any sign, any hope that Denise might have survived. The gardens were unrecognizable, the beauty and tranquility they once held now replaced by chaos and ruin.

Then, amidst the charred gardens, something caught my eye – a piece of fabric, partially burnt, lying close to the ground near a set of unidentifiable charred remains. My heart skipped a beat as I recognized it. It was a piece of a scarf, a scarf I had given Denise on one of our anniversaries. The fabric was singed and torn, but the pattern was unmistakable.

I knelt down, my hand trembling as I picked up the scorched remnant. The fabric felt brittle and fragile in my fingers, a stark contrast to the warmth and love it once represented. A wave of emotion crashed over me, a torrent of grief, anger, and despair.

Tears blurred my vision as I clutched the piece of scarf, the reality of the situation sinking in. Denise, my beloved queen, the mother of my unborn child, was gone. The future we had dreamed of, the life we had planned to build together, had been snatched away in a cruel twist of fate.

Sobs wracked my body as I knelt amidst the ashes of the gardens. The pain was overwhelming, a deep, limitless agony that consumed my very being.

Then suddenly, a sharp, searing pain ripped through my chest. I gasped, looking down in disbelief to see the blade of a katana protruding from my body. I screamed, a primal sound of pain and disbelief echoing through the devastated gardens.

Struggling to turn, I saw him – Yrome, standing a few paces behind me, his hand still on the hilt of the katana. He withdrew the blade swiftly, creating a distance between us, his eyes cold and calculating.

"Why?" I managed to gasp out, my voice a mix of pain and confusion."

Yrome's smirk was chilling, devoid of any remorse. "You were a fool to give me power, Ytfen," he said, his voice laced with contempt. "I have always despised dragons. Your kind thinks you are superior, almost god-like. I could not stand it."

His words cut deeper than the blade. The realization of his betrayal, the depth of his hatred, was overwhelming. I had trusted him, believed in the possibility of peace and unity. But it had all been a ruse, a ploy to gain power and turn it against us.

"You thought you could control us, make us subservient with your gifts of power," Yrome continued, his voice rising with fervor. "How dare you make a mockery of me! A king!" he proclaimed, his hands reaching up to touch his crown. "But I will use this power to end your reign, to wipe dragons from the face of this planet."

I staggered, the pain and loss of blood making it difficult to stand. The world around me seemed to spin, the gravity of his words sinking in. Denise, our unborn child, my mother, my people – all victims of this man's deep-seated hatred and ambition.

"You've destroyed everything," I whispered, my voice barely audible. "For what? Power?"

Yrome's expression hardened. "For a world free of dragons. For a world where humans are the true rulers."

At that moment, hundreds, if not thousands of human soldiers marched into view from the horizon.

The world around me began to blur, the memory began to fade, and I felt a pull back to the present.

21
Ytfen's Legacy

As the world around me solidified, I was left with a profound sense of Ytfen's pain and the magnitude of Yrome's betrayal. The loss, the deception, and the realization of Yrome's true intentions were a bitter and painful revelation, a moment that defined the tragic turn in Ytfen's life and the beginning of the war.

I quickly noticed that I did not return to my battle with Elijah. I found myself enveloped in a familiar darkness, a vast and empty expanse that stretched infinitely in all directions. It dawned on me that I was not in the physical world but had somehow been transported to the mindscape,

Gloria was there, but something felt different this time. Her form seemed to waver, like a reflection on water disturbed by a gentle breeze. I reached out to her, my voice tinged with confusion. "Gloria, what's happening?"

But she didn't respond. Instead, her image continued to blur and shift, transforming before my eyes. My heart raced as the figure before me changed, morphing into someone else entirely. The transformation was gradual yet profound, and when it completed, I was left staring in disbelief.

There, standing where Gloria once was, was a figure clad in regal attire, the same attire I had seen in my memories of a wedding. The realization hit me like a wave – it was Ytfen, the man whose life I had been reliving in my dreams, the man whose memories had become a part of my own journey.

Ytfen's eyes met mine, and in them, I saw a depth of wisdom and a shared understanding. It was as if I was looking into a mirror of the soul, seeing a reflection of myself yet knowing it was someone else. His presence was commanding yet gentle.

"Ytfen," I whispered, my voice barely audible. The emotions swirled within me – awe, confusion, a sense of connection that transcended time and space.

He simply gazed at me, his expression one of calm acknowledgment. There were no words spoken, yet the silence between us was filled with unspoken communication. It was a moment of profound realization, a bridging of two lives that had become intertwined through the tapestry of memories.

Ytfen's voice broke the silence, calm and resonant, echoing through the mindscape. "I know this is overwhelming, Ezekiel. You must have countless questions," he said, his eyes reflecting a deep understanding of the turmoil within me.

I struggled to find my voice, the shock rendering me almost speechless. "How... how is this possible?" I managed to stammer out, my mind racing to comprehend the revelation before me.

Ytfen's expression softened, a hint of sadness mingling with his wisdom. "Gloria, as you knew her, was never a separate entity. She was the embodiment of my Light Dragon's essence, the manifestation of all that was good and kind in me. She appeared as a nurturing figure because that's what my dragon's spirit represented – protection, guidance, and maternal care."

He paused, allowing the information to sink in. "Did you never wonder why Gloria never left Ash Village? It's because she couldn't. My Light Dragon's essence was bound to that place, waiting for someone worthy to inherit its power. That someone is you, Ezekiel."

His words sent a wave of realization crashing over me. Gloria, the maternal figure who had been a constant presence in my journey, was a part of Ytfen all along, a guardian spirit watching over me.

Ytfen continued, "When Yrome betrayed me, in my final moments, I made a desperate decision. I infused my Light Dragon essence into Ash Village, hoping that one day, someone worthy would come along to carry on my legacy. And that person is you."

I stood there, still trying to process the enormity of what he was saying. Ytfen extended his hand towards me, a gesture of invitation and trust. "Take my hand, Ezekiel. Embrace the legacy that awaits you."

Hesitantly, I reached out, my hand trembling as it moved towards his. As our hands touched, a surge of warmth and energy flowed through me, a connection that transcended time, linking me to Ytfen and the legacy he had entrusted to me.

As Ytfen's form began to fade, his essence flowed towards me, a stream of light and energy that seemed to carry the very core of his being. I felt it merge with my own, a powerful and overwhelming sensation that coursed through my veins. It was as if a dormant part of me had suddenly awakened, filling me with a strength and clarity I had never known.

In the midst of this transformation, I was abruptly pulled back into the present, right into the intense struggle against Elijah. Our powers were still locked in a fierce battle, but something within me had changed. I could feel the surge of new energy, a force that was both foreign and intimately familiar.

My Dark Dragon form began to undergo a startling metamorphosis. My scales, once a deep, shadowy black, started to shimmer and pulse with a brilliant white light, flickering between darkness and radiance. My body grew larger, more powerful, each movement resonating with the newfound essence of the Light Dragon.

As I completed the transformation into the Light Dragon, a sense of immense power and serenity enveloped me. I felt as if I could see the world in a new light, understanding the delicate balance between darkness and light, and the role I was destined to play in maintaining it.

With a deep, resonant roar, I unleashed a beam of pure, radiant light from my maw, a torrent of energy that was terrifying in its intensity.

This beam of light, brilliant and unyielding, joined the combined powers of Camila and Gaianor, further amplifying the trinity of elemental forces that surged towards Elijah's sphere of energy.

As the beam of light met Elijah's sphere, there was a moment of resistance, a battle of wills and power that seemed to hang in the balance. But the purity and intensity of the light began to overpower the elemental sphere. The light, infused with the essence of the Light Dragon, was not just a physical force; it was a manifestation of hope, resilience, and the unbreakable spirit that Ytfen had passed on to me.

With a final, determined push, the beam of light broke through the sphere, shattering it into a million fragments of dissipating energy. The explosion that followed was blinding, a burst of light that illuminated the ruins of Bryson Village like a second sun. The shockwave from the impact sent ripples through the air, shaking the ground beneath us.

As the blinding light from the beam enveloped Elijah, his massive dragon form began to shrink and contort, transforming back into his human form. He was now unconscious, his body limp and falling through the air.

Reacting instinctively, I shifted back to my human form, feeling the rush of the Light Dragon's power coursing through me. With a burst of speed that left a shimmering trail of light in my wake, I darted through the air. The sensation of moving at such incredible speed was exhilarating and new, yet it felt as natural to me as breathing. The world around me seemed to blur, the ruins of Bryson Village passing by in a whirl of colors and shapes, but my focus was solely on ensuring Elijah's safety.

I reached Elijah just in time. My arms wrapped around him, slowing his descent, as I carefully maneuvered us towards the ground.

As we touched down, I gently laid Elijah on the ground, his body still and peaceful in its unconscious state. I knelt beside him, a mix of emotions swirling within me. Relief that the battle was over, sadness for the brother who had lost his way, and a deep sense of responsibility for what lay ahead.

The air around us suddenly shimmered, and a massive portal tore open the fabric of reality. From within its swirling depths, Papa Yamah and Aria emerged, their expressions a mix of relief and determination. Behind them, the elders of Serenity's Edge stepped through, their faces etched with determination, followed by a formidable procession of villagers.

These were no ordinary villagers. Each one bore the unmistakable mark of a former Dragon Slayer. Their eyes held stories of battles past, their stances exuded a readiness for combat long ingrained in their muscle memory. They were a force to be reckoned with, a testament to the village's hidden legacy.

As they fanned out around the portal, forming a protective circle, their gazes fell upon the scene before them. The ruins of Bryson Village, the aftermath of our epic battle, and Elijah, now defeated and vulnerable, lying at my feet.

Papa Yamah's eyes met mine, a silent question passing between us. I nodded slightly, confirming the battle was over. The tension in his shoulders eased, but his gaze remained wary, scanning the surroundings for any further threats.

Aria moved to my side, her eyes wide with a mix of awe and concern. "Is he...?" she began, her voice trailing off as she looked down at Elijah.

"He's alive, just unconscious," I replied, my voice tinged with a mix of relief and sadness. "We managed to stop him before it was too late."

The leaders approached, their expressions a blend of relief and disbelief. "We came as fast as we could," Gabriel said, his voice heavy. "We thought you might need our help."

I looked around at the assembled crowd, at least one hundred, their faces a mosaic of courage and readiness. "Your arrival means more than you know," I said, my voice carrying across the silent ruins. "Even though the battle is won, your willingness to stand with us speaks volumes. This unity, this coming together of dragons and Dragon Slayers, is what we need to face the challenges ahead. To stop Yrome, once and for all."

The villagers nodded in agreement, a sense of purpose uniting them. The elders exchanged glances, their faces reflecting a newfound hope. "We may have been Dragon Slayers once," one elder spoke up, "but today, we stand as protectors of peace, alongside our dragon allies."

I looked down at Elijah, his chest rising and falling with each breath. "We need to ensure he's safe," I said, turning to the group. "He's still my brother, and despite everything, I believe he can be redeemed."

Aria knelt beside Elijah, checking his condition. "He'll need care, but he'll recover," she confirmed.

"We'll take him back to Serenity's Edge," Papa Yamah decided. "There, he can heal, and we can keep him safe."

As Elijah's eyes fluttered open, a flicker of the brother I once knew seemed to return. But it was quickly overshadowed by a glare of defiance and anger. "I will kill you all," he rasped, his voice weak yet filled with a lingering threat.

I turned to him, my heart heavy with the pain of seeing my brother so consumed by hatred and vengeance. "Elijah, it's over," I said softly, my voice a mixture of sorrow and resolve.

"You need to understand why we're fighting, why we're on this side."

He tried to turn his head away, but I gently held it in place. "I'm going to show you something," I continued, "something that will help you see the truth."

I wasn't sure how I was going to do what I wanted to do, but I would try.

Placing my hand on his forehead, I closed my eyes and focused. I could feel the connection between us, a bond that went beyond blood, a bond forged in the fires of our shared past and the trials we had faced.

Slowly, I began to channel Ytfen's memories into Elijah's mind. It was a delicate process, like weaving a tapestry of thoughts and emotions, each thread a memory of Ytfen's life – his joys, his struggles, his love, and his pain.

The memories flowed from me to him, a stream of consciousness that painted a vivid picture of Ytfen's journey. The moments of his wedding, filled with love and hope; the training sessions with Yrome, marked by a growing sense of unease; the devastating betrayal that shattered his world.

As the memories unfolded, I could feel Elijah's resistance waning, his rigid body beginning to relax. His breathing, once shallow and rapid, deepened and slowed. The anger in his eyes was gradually replaced by confusion, realization, and then, a dawning horror as he began to comprehend the magnitude of the deception he had fallen victim to.

As the last of the memories faded, I removed my hand and looked into Elijah's eyes. They were no longer filled with rage, but with tears.

"Elijah," I whispered, my own voice choked with emotion, "do you understand now? Do you see why we must fight Yrome, not join him?"

He didn't respond immediately, but the look in his eyes told me he was beginning to see the truth. The truth about Yrome, about us, and about himself.

Papa Yamah approached the crown, his steps measured and solemn. He paused before it, his gaze lingering on the ancient artifact that had caused so much turmoil. The air around us seemed to still, as if in anticipation of his next words.

"This crown," he began, his voice resonating with a deep, unwavering conviction, "has been a symbol of division and despair for far too long. It has pitted brother against brother, dragon against human, and brought untold suffering to countless lives."

He reached out, his hand hovering above the crown, yet not touching it. "For generations, this crown has been used to manipulate, to control, and to wage wars. It has been a tool for those who sought power at the expense of peace and harmony."

His eyes met each of ours, a silent call to witness his vow. "No more. We will take this back to Serenity's Edge, and together, we will find a way to end its dark legacy. We will work to heal the wounds it has inflicted and forge a new path – one of unity, understanding, and hope."

He finally picked up the crown, holding it with a reverence that belied its ominous history. "This is not just the end of the crown's reign of terror. It is the beginning of a new era – an era where dragons and humans, and all beings, can coexist in peace. An era where power is not used to dominate, but to protect and to nurture."

Papa Yamah's speech, filled with passion and hope, seemed to echo through the ruins of Bryson Village, a promise to right the wrongs of the past and to build a better future.

Elijah's voice was barely audible, strained with effort as he struggled to speak. "Aria," he gasped, his eyes meeting mine with a desperate urgency. "She's… she's been working with us…"

22
Echoes of Betrayal

The revelation hit me like a lightning bolt. I turned towards Aria, my heart pounding in my chest. But before I could process the truth, her expression changed. Gone was the hesitant, unsure Aria we knew. In her place stood someone cold, conniving, and smirking with malice.

In a swift, unexpected movement, she pulled out a knife – its blade glinting ominously in the sunlight. Before any of us could react, she lunged at Papa Yamah, plunging the knife into his back. The act was so sudden, so brutal, that for a moment, time seemed to stand still.

"Noooo!" I screamed, my voice echoing through the ruins of Bryson Village.

Papa Yamah's eyes widened in shock and pain. He stumbled forward, a hand reaching towards the wound. The betrayal, more than the physical wound, seemed to drain the strength from him.

The crown tumbled from his grasp, rolling in slow motion. Aria immediately seized the fallen diadem.

We stood frozen, disbelief and horror etched on our faces. The sound of Papa Yamah's pained gasps filled the air.

His eyes, once full of wisdom and kindness, now stared blankly into the distance. His lifeless body slumped to the ground. A collective gasp rose from the crowd, a chorus of shock and sorrow.

I felt something within me ignite. A surge of light, pure and blinding, coursed through my veins, propelling me forward instinctively.

With a cry that was both a war cry and a lament, I charged at Aria, my hands alight with the power of my light dragon essence. The villagers watched as I became a bolt of vengeance, aiming to slash at Aria with the full force of my grief and rage.

But in that critical moment, as my light sought to find its target, Aria turned, her eyes locking onto mine with a smirk that spoke of secrets and lies. With a flick of her wrist, she conjured a portal, stepping back into its swirling depths. The portal snapped shut behind her, leaving me slashing at empty air, my light dissipating into the shadows of the village ruins.

Nina, her face a mask of shock and grief, rushed to Papa Yamah's side, her hands trembling as she reached out to him. "Yamah!" she cried, her voice breaking. "No, this can't be happening!"

Caius, usually composed, stood frozen, his eyes wide with disbelief. The betrayal, so sudden and brutal, had shaken him to his core. "How could she...?" he muttered, more to himself than anyone else.

Joren clenched his jaw, his fists balling at his sides. The pain in his eyes was palpable, a deep sense of loss for a man he had respected and fought alongside.

Gabriel let out a low, anguished growl. "We will avenge you, brother," he vowed, his voice thick with emotion.

As Papa Yamah lay there, his life slipping away, the elders gathered around him, their faces etched with sorrow and anger. They had lost a leader, a mentor, and a friend.

In that moment, as I watched Papa Yamah's eyes go blank, a part of me shattered. The man who had been a father to me, who had guided and protected me, was gone. The pain was overwhelming, a searing agony that threatened to consume me. But amidst the grief, a burning resolve took root. Aria's betrayal, her alliance with Yrome, had changed everything. The fight was no longer just about survival; it was about justice, about honoring the memory of a man who had given everything for us.

Moments later, another portal tore open in the sky above us. Aria's voice, now laced with malice and triumph, boomed from the portal. "Oh, foolish Elijah," she taunted. "If only you had stuck to the plan."

Her words hung heavy in the air, a bitter reminder of the deception and manipulation that had led us to this point. "You see," Aria continued, her voice echoing ominously, "Yrome's vision is the only path to true order. A world cleansed of dragons and their sympathizers. And I, Aria, am his devoted servant, his instrument of change."

The portal shimmered with a sinister light, framing her silhouette against the backdrop of an unknown realm. "Your resistance is futile. Yrome's power is beyond your comprehension. And with the crown now in our possession, nothing can stop us from reshaping this world."

A heavy weight settled in my chest, as I began piecing together the fragments of betrayal that had led us to this devastating moment. It all made sense now, a cruel puzzle finally coming together.

Aria... she was the key. She was the one that brought Yrome to us in the Whispering Woods. And it was her who had betrayed the location of Serenity's Edge to Elijah.

I felt a surge of anger and disbelief. How could we have been so blind? Aria, who we had trusted, who had fought alongside us, was the architect of our downfall. She had played us all, manipulating events from the shadows, her loyalty not to us, but to Yrome and his twisted vision.

She had been with us every step of the way, privy to our plans, our strengths, and our weaknesses. And we had welcomed her, unsuspecting of the viper in our midst.

I stood there, numb with shock and grief. Papa Yamah lay dead because of her treachery. And now, with the crown in their possession, Yrome and Aria posed a threat greater than we had ever imagined.

We had been outmaneuvered at every turn.

"Oh, and Camila, Gaianor," she sneered, her words laced with venom, "thank you for unwittingly revealing the locations of your villages. While you've been playing heroes here, Yrome has been... busy."

Her laughter echoed through the ruins of Bryson Village, a chilling sound that sent shivers down my spine. Camila and Gaianor's faces twisted in horror and disbelief. "No... You traitor!" Camila shouted, her voice breaking with anguish.

Gaianor's fists clenched, his body shaking with a mix of grief and fury. "How could you? Our people..." he trailed off, unable to finish.

Aria's smirk widened, her eyes gleaming with a cruel satisfaction. "Your villages are no more. Yrome has seen to that. His power is unmatched, and your little resistance... a mere inconvenience."

The air around us grew heavy with despair and rage. The loss was unimaginable – entire villages, countless lives, wiped out.

"And now, for the grand finale," Aria announced, her tone dripping with anticipation. "My king, Yrome, will be joining us shortly. I'm sure he'll be delighted to see the mess you've made."

Her words hung in the air, a dire prophecy of the chaos to come. Camila and Gaianor were consumed by grief, their faces etched with pain and shock. The villagers, once ready to fight, now stood in stunned silence, grappling with the magnitude of Aria's betrayal.

Yrome was coming, and with him, the battle for our very existence.

The air around us grew heavy, charged with an ominous and familiar energy that seemed to press down on us like a physical weight. Every instinct screamed of danger, of a power so immense it was almost suffocating. And then, in a blink, he was there.

Yrome stood before us, his presence commanding and terrifying. His long silver hair flowed in the wind. His eyes, a piercing red, scanned the crowd with a cold, calculating gaze. He exuded an aura of absolute power, a force that was barely comprehensible, yet undeniably real.

We all stood frozen, our eyes locked on this figure who had brought so much pain and destruction. The villagers, once proud Dragon Slayers, now looked on with a mix of fear and defiance. Camila and Gaianor, their faces etched with anger and sorrow, stood ready to fight, despite the overwhelming odds.

I felt a surge of emotions battling within me – fear, anger, grief, and an unyielding determination. Papa Yamah's lifeless body lay just a few feet away, a stark reminder of what Yrome represented and the cost of standing against him.

Yrome's lips curled into a sinister smile as he took in the scene before him. "So, this is what remains of the resistance," he said, his voice smooth and chilling. "A pathetic gathering of broken souls and shattered dreams."

His gaze finally settled on me, and in that moment, I felt as if he was peering into the very depths of my soul. "Ezekiel," he said, his tone almost mocking. "The last hope of a dying breed. How quaint."

As Yrome's chilling words hung in the air, another portal materialized beside him, and Aria stepped through, the crown in her hands. Her face bore a look of triumph mixed with a disturbing reverence for the man beside her. She approached Yrome with an almost religious zeal, her betrayal now complete in its final act.

Yrome's eyes lit up with a dark glee as he took the crown from Aria. "You have done well, my faithful servant," he praised her, his voice dripping with satisfaction. "In my new world, there will indeed be a place for those loyal to me."

The crown seemed to pulsate with a life of its own as Yrome placed it upon his head. Its jewels glowed ominously, casting eerie shadows on his face. A deep, resonant hum filled the air, growing louder with each passing second. The ground beneath our feet began to tremble, a subtle vibration at first that quickly escalated into a violent shaking. The wind, previously a gentle whisper, transformed into a howling gale, whipping around us with ferocious intensity.

The crown settled onto Yrome's brow, and for a brief moment, there was a terrifying stillness. Then, with a suddenness that took our breath away, a spectral figure emerged from the crown. It was the same figure I had fought in the mindscape when I first touched the crown. The same mysterious figure that haunted my nightmares. The same enigmatic figure that came out of me and Elijah and fused to unleash Yrome. It was a being of pure energy and darkness, its form shifting and undulating like smoke.

The specter hovered above Yrome, its presence casting a pall over the landscape. Then, in a movement that was both graceful and horrifying, it descended, merging with Yrome in a whirl of dark energy. The air crackled with power, the atmosphere thick with the scent of ozone and the unbridled force of the elements.

The earth continued to quake, the wind screamed, and the very air seemed to warp and twist around Yrome.

We stood frozen, our hearts pounding in our chests. Yrome raised his arms, and the elements responded to his will. Fire danced at his fingertips, lightning crackled around him, and the ground beneath his feet cracked and groaned.

The villagers, now looked on in horror, their faces etched with fear. Camila and Gaianor, stood ready to fight, but even they could not hide the uncertainty in their eyes.

Yrome looked down upon us with a gaze that promised destruction and despair. "Behold," he proclaimed, his voice echoing like thunder, "the dawn of a new era, an era where I reign supreme. Your resistance is futile."

"We cannot let him win!" proclaimed Joren, with a rallying cry that echoed through the air. The villagers, their faces set with determination, surged forward.

The battlefield before us transformed into a frenzy of chaos and power as over a hundred villagers, once Dragon Slayers, charged towards Yrome. Each warrior, a master of their element, unleashed their abilities with a ferocity born of desperation and determination.

"He can't be stopped," whispered Elijah, his voice barely audible over the din of battle.

Aria stepped forward, perhaps to join the fight. But Yrome, with a simple gesture, halted her in her tracks. He raised his hand, palm forward, signaling her to stay back. It was a clear message: he needed no assistance; he was a force unto himself.

A group of former Dragon Slayers, their hands ablaze, hurled torrents of flames towards Yrome. The fire roared like a living beast, seeking to engulf him, but with a mere flick of his wrist, Yrome summoned a gust of wind that snuffed out the flames as easily as one would extinguish a candle.

A second group of Dragon Slayers, crackling with electric energy, launched bolts of lightning, their jagged arcs seeking to strike Yrome down. Yet, he stood unscathed, the lightning bending around him as if repelled by an invisible shield, then harmlessly dissipating into the air.

A faction of villagers, their fists and weapons encased in rock, charged, attempting to pummel Yrome with the force of the very ground beneath them. But their attacks were futile; Yrome's aura of power shattered their earthen constructs before they could even touch him.

Another group of Dragon Slayers, manipulating the moisture in the air, created whips and torrents of water, aiming to bind and drown Yrome in their aquatic embrace. However, with a mere glance, Yrome turned their water into steam, vanishing into thin air.

Amidst the onslaught, a group of villagers tried a coordinated attack, combining their elemental powers in a spectacular display of teamwork. Fire and wind merged to create a scorching tornado, while lightning and earth combined to form a charged, rocky spear, all directed at Yrome. But to our disbelief, Yrome absorbed their combined assault, his body glowing brighter, as if feeding off their energy.

The villagers' attacks, though fierce and relentless, seemed to barely touch Yrome.

One by one, the villagers fell before him. A fire slayer, her flames flickering defiantly, charged at Yrome, only to be met by the swift arc of his dark energy blade. In an instant, her fire was extinguished, and she collapsed, lifeless, to the ground.

A lightning slayer, his body surging with electricity, launched a high-voltage attack, hoping to catch Yrome off guard. But Yrome parried with his dark katana, the blade absorbing the electrical energy and redirecting it back at the Dragon Slayer, electrocuting him in a blinding flash.

An earth slayer, his arms encased in rock, swung with all his might, aiming a crushing blow at Yrome. But Yrome's blade moved faster, slicing through the rock as if it were mere clay, and then through the slayer himself, leaving him to crumble in a heap of stone and flesh.

A water slayer, tears mingling with the water she commanded, created a tidal wave, a desperate attempt to wash Yrome away. But Yrome simply stepped into the wave, his blade cutting through the water, splitting it in two, and with a flick of his wrist, he sent the divided waters crashing down upon the Slayer, drowning her in her own element.

With each passing second, the hope of victory dimmed. The villagers' attacks, once coordinated and fierce, now seemed like mere whispers against a storm. Yrome's laughter, cold and devoid of any humanity, echoed across the ruins, a chilling reminder of the power he wielded.

I watched, horror-struck, as one by one, the villagers met their end.

The battlefield, now a grim landscape of fallen warriors, echoed with the haunting silence of defeat. Yrome, towering above the few survivors, turned his gaze to Aria. "Show me your worth," he commanded, his voice resonating with a dark authority. "Prove to me that you deserve a place in the new world I will create."

Aria, her eyes alight with a mix of fear and ambition, nodded. "Yes, my king," she said, her voice trembling with a mixture of excitement and trepidation. She stepped forward, her posture shifting from that of a hesitant ally to a determined adversary.

As she approached us, the air around her crackled with energy. "I'm sorry, Ezekiel," she said, her voice cold and devoid of the friendship I thought we once shared. "But this is my path now. Yrome has shown me the truth, the power that lies beyond our petty squabbles."

I stared at her, disbelief and anger warring within me. "Aria, how could you?" I asked, my voice laced with betrayal. "You've seen what he's capable of, the lives he's taken. How can you stand by him?"

She smirked, a twisted smile that was a far cry from the Aria I knew. "Power, Ezekiel. He offers power beyond our wildest dreams. And I intend to seize it."

The leaders, weary and battered, stood beside me, their expressions a mix of sadness and resolve. "Aria, you were one of us," Joren said, his voice heavy with sorrow. "You've been blinded by his promises. He's using you."

But Aria's resolve was unshaken. "No, Joren. I'm finally seeing clearly. And now, I'll do what must be done." Her hands began to glow, the air around her shimmering with the energy of her portal magic.

Camila and Gaianor, though still exhausted from their fight with Elijah, readied themselves for what was to come. "We won't let you do this, Aria," Camila said, determination etched on her face.

Aria's laughter, cold and devoid of any warmth, filled the air. "Let's see if you can stop me."

The air around us grew dense with a malevolent energy as Aria chanted the incantation of a forbidden spell. Something felt different about this. It wasn't just her portal magic. No, it was something else.

As Aria's voice crescendoed to the climax of her spell, she uttered the chilling words with a twisted glee, "Forbidden Magic, Black Hole!" The air around us crackled with dark energy, and a massive vortex of swirling darkness erupted into existence. Its pull was immediate and overpowering, a gravitational force that threatened to consume everything in its path.

The vortex's edges shimmered with an eerie light, the very fabric of space seeming to warp and twist around it. The ground beneath our feet trembled, and the air was filled with the sound of reality tearing apart.

The remaining villagers, already weakened and disheartened, struggled futilely against the inexorable pull of the vortex.

The elders, realizing the gravity of the situation, mustered their remaining strength in a desperate attempt to reach Aria. "Stop this madness, Aria!" Gabriel shouted, his voice filled with a mix of anger and despair.

But Aria was beyond reason. "It's too late for that," she replied, her eyes gleaming with a dark triumph. "Yrome's new world awaits, and I will be at his side."

As the leaders charged towards her, Yrome intervened with a casual flick of his wrist, unleashing a wave of dark energy that struck them down with ruthless efficiency. One by one, they fell, their hopes and dreams extinguished in an instant.

I stood there, paralyzed by the horror unfolding before me. The people I had come to respect and admire, the villagers who had once been proud Dragon Slayers, were now being consumed by the vortex or cut down by Yrome's merciless power.

In that moment of despair, I felt a deep sense of helplessness. The world I knew was crumbling around me, and the future seemed nothing but a dark abyss.

I moved quickly to Elijah, gripping him tightly, determined not to let the vortex claim him. His body was limp in my arms. Despite everything, he was still my brother, and I couldn't abandon him to the dark abyss that Aria had summoned.

Camila and Gaianor were fighting their own battles against the pull of the vortex. Camila's feet were planted firmly on the ground, her water powers creating a barrier around her that seemed to lessen the vortex's pull. Gaianor summoned pillars of rock to anchor himself, his face strained with effort.

As the vortex's pull grew stronger, Elijah's voice cut through the chaos, resonant and clear. "Now it's time to put your trust in me, brother," he said, his eyes meeting mine with an intensity that conveyed more than words ever could. "It's time for me to protect you, like you've tried to protect me. Let me go, brother."

His words echoed in my mind. Let him go? How could I let him go? The idea of releasing Elijah during such a critical time clawed at my soul. My grip on him tightened instinctively, the fear of losing another loved one overwhelming my senses.

"Trust me." Elijah's voice pierced through the din, calm yet filled with an unwavering steadfastness.

Looking into Elijah's eyes, I saw a determination that I couldn't ignore. It was a look that spoke of sacrifice and trust—a trust he had in me.

With a heavy heart and a deep breath, I released my grip on Elijah. It felt like letting go of a part of myself, a leap of faith into the unknown. As he was pulled towards the vortex, his body began to crackle with an intense electricity.

In a flash, Elijah transformed into a bolt of lightning, his body a streak of pure, electric energy. He shot towards Aria with incredible speed, the sound of thunder echoing in his wake. As he neared the vortex, his lightning form intensified, illuminating the dark maw with flashes of brilliant light.

With a swift strike, Elijah slashed at Aria. The surprise and shock on her face were palpable as she struggled to maintain control over the vortex. Her concentration faltered, and the vortex began to waver, its pull weakening as her spell started to unravel.

In that moment, Elijah's sacrifice became clear. He had chosen to risk everything to protect us, to stand against the darkness that threatened to engulf us all. Despite the turmoil and conflicts that had marred our relationship, in this crucial moment, Elijah had chosen to stand with us, to fight for a cause greater than himself.

The vortex, now unstable from Aria's loss of focus, began to dissipate, its dark energy waning. The pull lessened, and we could feel the force of its grip releasing us. Aria, wounded and weakened by Elijah's attack, struggled to regain her composure.

Her strength waning, she turned her desperate eyes towards Yrome. "Yrome, please," she begged, her voice a mix of fear and hope. "I can't hold it much longer. Help me!"

Yrome's expression remained impassive as he observed the scene before him.

Then, in a sudden movement, Yrome teleported, appearing directly in front of Aria. Her face lit up with a flicker of relief and hope, believing her pleas had been heard. But the look in Yrome's eyes told a different story. There was no compassion, no hint of mercy – only disdain.

"Pathetic," Yrome uttered, his voice devoid of emotion. With a swift motion, he unleashed a powerful shockwave from his hand, a burst of energy that hit Aria with the force of a tempest.

Aria's body was thrown back violently, her form spiraling uncontrollably towards the vortex. Her cries were lost in the roar of the vortex as she was consumed by the very darkness she had summoned.

With Aria's disappearance, the vortex began to close, its dark energy dissipating into the air. The threat of the vortex was gone, but the cold, ruthless action of Yrome left a chilling silence in its wake.

We stood there, stunned and horrified, witnessing the true nature of Yrome's merciless ambition. His willingness to discard even his most devoted follower like a pawn was a chilling testament to his ruthlessness.

I felt a surge of anger and disbelief. "How could you?" I demanded, my voice echoing amidst the desolation. "She was loyal to you, and you just... threw her away!"

Even though I couldn't forgive Aria for what she had done, Yrome's coldness was more than my heart could fathom.

Yrome's gaze met mine, cold and unyielding. "Loyalty is a tool, Ezekiel," he said, his voice dripping with disdain. "A tool that serves its purpose until it becomes expendable. Aria served her purpose. Nothing more."

Elijah, his face etched with pain and betrayal, confronted Yrome. "You showed me memories, visions of atrocities committed over the years," he accused, his voice trembling with emotion. "You said you were here to fight against those who caused them."

Yrome's response was a cold, mocking laugh that echoed through the ruins of Bryson Village. "Oh, dear Elijah," he said, his tone dripping with sarcasm. "Did I forget to mention? Those atrocities, those horrors that I showed you... they were my doing."

Yrome, the man who had positioned himself as a savior, as a beacon of hope against the darkness, was in fact the architect of the very atrocities he had decried. His laughter continued, a sinister sound that chilled us to the bone.

"You see, Elijah," Yrome continued, his eyes gleaming with malevolence, "I have been orchestrating this for longer than you can imagine. Every village burned, every innocent life taken... it was all by my hand. And you, my naive pawn, you believed every word I said."

Elijah staggered back, his face a mask of horror and disbelief. The realization that he had been manipulated, used as a tool in Yrome's grand scheme, was a bitter pill to swallow.

"You're a monster," Elijah whispered, his voice barely audible.

Yrome's smirk widened. "Monster? No, Elijah. I am a visionary. I am the one who will reshape this world, purge it of its weaknesses. And you... you were just a means to an end."

I clenched my fists, feeling a mix of fear and determination. "We will stop you, Yrome. We have to. For the sake of everyone you've hurt, for everyone you've betrayed."

Yrome's smirk widened.

"I see you now for what you truly are," Elijah said, his voice laced with a newfound clarity. "A tyrant, a destroyer. I was blinded by my pain, by my anger. But no more. I stand with my brother, against you."

Yrome's expression remained impassive. "Regret is a weakness, Elijah. You were a useful tool, but now you're just another obstacle. Your newfound conscience changes nothing."

Elijah moved to my side, a grim determination settling on his features. "I was wrong, brother. I let my pain and anger cloud my judgment. But I see the truth now. Yrome must be stopped for the sake of our world."

Yrome laughed, a sound devoid of warmth. "Such touching sentiment. But it changes nothing. You stand before me, divided and weakened by your own follies. You cannot hope to defeat me."

Elijah's gaze never wavered from Yrome. "You may have power, Yrome, but you lack something crucial – the strength that comes from fighting for something greater than oneself. We fight for our world, for its people. That's a strength you'll never understand."

Yrome's eyes narrowed, his aura of confidence unshaken. "Idealistic words from a broken soul. Let's see how far they take you."

I stepped forward. "This ends now, Yrome. We won't let you destroy everything we hold dear."

Yrome's response was a cold, humorless smile. "Then come. Show me the strength of your resolve."

As I stood there, facing Yrome, a sense of unity and purpose filled me. "Together, then," I declared, feeling the power within me surge. I began my transformation into the Light

Dragon form, a radiant energy enveloping me. My body grew and shifted, scales shimmering with a brilliant white light that seemed to pierce the darkness around us. Wings unfurled majestically, casting a glow that illuminated the ruins of Bryson Village. The transformation was a manifestation of hope, a beacon in the face of despair.

Camila and Gaianor exchanged a determined glance. "For Aquaria and Terra," Camila said, her voice resolute. She began her transformation, her form shifting into the Water Dragon, a creature of grace and fluidity. Her scales glistened like the deepest ocean, and her presence brought a sense of calm amidst the chaos.

Gaianor nodded in agreement, his expression hardened by the memories of his fallen village. "For Terra," he echoed, as he transformed into his Earth Dragon form. His body expanded, taking on the robust and rugged appearance of the mountains themselves. His scales resembled layers of rock and soil, embodying the strength and resilience of the earth.

Lastly, Elijah, who had been torn between two worlds, now stood with us, a changed dragon. "For redemption," he whispered, his voice carrying a weight of newfound purpose. He began his transformation, his body crackling with the combined energies of fire, ice, earth, and lightning. His dragon form was a magnificent amalgamation of the elements, a creature of raw power and elemental fury. His scales sparkled with an array of colors.

Together, we stood as a united front against Yrome. The air around us crackled with energy, the tension palpable as we prepared for the final confrontation. In that moment, we were more than just dragons; we were the embodiment of hope, unity, and the unyielding spirit of those who had fallen. Our roars filled the air, a chorus of defiance against the darkness that threatened to engulf the world.

Yrome seemed unfazed by our transformation. His eyes glinted with a dark amusement, as if relishing the challenge we presented. "Impressive," he said, his voice dripping with disdain. "But ultimately futile."

The air around Yrome began to shimmer with a dark energy. He raised his hand, and the ground beneath us trembled. "Witness the true power of a god," he declared, a sinister smile spreading across his face.

With a collective roar, we charged towards Yrome, ready to face whatever darkness he wielded. The fate of our world hung in the balance, and we were determined to fight until our last breath.

As we charged towards Yrome, the air crackled with the clash of elemental powers. I, in my Light Dragon form, led the charge, my scales shimmering with a radiant glow. Each beat of my wings sent waves of light cascading through the air, illuminating the ruins of Bryson Village.

Camila, embodying the essence of water, moved with fluid grace and precision. Her scales glistened like the surface of a serene lake, and as she roared, a torrent of water spiraled around her, ready to strike.

Gaianor's massive frame shook the ground with each step. He roared, and the earth responded, rocks and boulders levitating around him, orbiting like satellites ready to be hurled at our foe.

Yrome stood his ground, the crown upon his head glowing with a sinister light. He raised his hands, and dark energy swirled around him, forming a barrier that absorbed our initial attacks. He laughed, a sound that echoed ominously through the ruins.

Undeterred, we pressed on. I unleashed beams of intense light, aiming for any weak points in his defense. Camila's water attacks flowed like a raging river, trying to find a way through his barrier. Gaianor's earth powers sent a barrage of rocks and boulders, each strike resonating with the power of the land. Elijah, with his mastery of multiple elements, launched a relentless assault, his attacks a whirlwind of fire, ice, earth, and lightning.

Yrome, however, seemed to be toying with us, his barrier effortlessly deflecting our combined assaults. With a flick of his wrist, he sent a wave of dark energy towards us, forcing us to scatter and regroup.

I soared high, dodging the tendrils of darkness that snaked through the air, seeking to ensnare me. From above, I could see the scale of the battle – a clash of titans, each blow shaking the very foundations of the earth.

Camila, weaving through the air with agility, launched water spears that crystallized into ice upon contact with Yrome's barrier, trying to find a crack, a weakness to exploit. Gaianor, grounded and unyielding, summoned the earth to rise up in walls and spikes, attempting to break through Yrome's defenses.

Elijah, a storm of elemental chaos, was a blur of motion. His attacks were unpredictable, a fusion of fire and ice, thunder and earth, each strike more ferocious than the last.

Despite our efforts, Yrome remained unscathed, his barrier impenetrable. He laughed again, the sound sending a shiver down my spine. "You cannot hope to defeat me," he taunted. "I am beyond your petty powers. I am a god!"

In that moment, I realized brute force alone would not be enough. We needed to be smarter, more strategic. I signaled to the others, and we began to coordinate our attacks, combining our elemental powers in ways we had never attempted before.

Our new strategy began to show promise. The combined force of light, water, earth, and the raw energy of Elijah's multi-elemental form started to strain Yrome's barrier. Cracks began to appear, and through them, we could see Yrome's expression change from amusement to concern.

The battle raged on, our newfound unity giving us hope.

As our attacks intensified, the cracks in Yrome's barrier widened. We could sense his control wavering, his confidence faltering. Elijah, seizing the moment, unleashed a ferocious combination of lightning and fire, a storm of energy that illuminated the sky. Camila followed with a massive wave, its power amplified by my beams of light, turning it into a radiant tsunami. Gaianor's earth powers shook the very ground Yrome stood on, destabilizing his stance.

Yrome roared in frustration, his barrier finally shattering under our relentless assault.

As Yrome's barrier shattered, we surged forward with renewed vigor, sensing our opportunity. But Yrome, far from defeated, revealed the true extent of his power. Dark energy swirled around him, coalescing into a maelstrom of malevolent force. His eyes, now glowing with an unholy light, fixed upon us with a predatory gaze.

The air crackled with raw power as Yrome unleashed a barrage of dark energy blasts. We dodged and weaved, countering with our own attacks, but it was clear that Yrome was toying with us. With each passing moment, his strength seemed to grow.

Camila, ever brave and determined, charged at Yrome with a powerful stream of water. But Yrome, with a flick of his hand, turned her attack against her, freezing the water mid-air and shattering it into a thousand shards. Camila, caught off guard, was hit by a blast of dark energy. She let out a pained cry as the force of the blast sent her crashing to the ground.

I watched in horror as Camila lay motionless, her once vibrant form now still and silent. A deep, gut-wrenching pain tore through me. "Camila!" I screamed, my voice echoing through the ruins.

Gaianor and Elijah, shocked and enraged, redoubled their attacks, but Yrome seemed invincible. He moved with terrifying speed and precision, his dark energy cutting through our defenses.

I rushed to Camila's side, hoping against hope that she was still alive. But as I reached her, I knew it was too late. Her eyes were closed, her body lifeless. A sense of despair washed over me. We had lost another one of our own.

Yrome's laughter filled the air, a sound devoid of any humanity. "You see? You cannot win," he taunted. "I am unstoppable. I am the future!"

In that moment, something within me snapped. A burning rage, fueled by grief and loss, ignited in my heart. With a roar that shook the heavens, I channeled everything I had into my Light Dragon form. Elijah and Gaianor, fueled by their own grief and determination, joined me.

We launched ourselves at Yrome with a ferocity born of desperation and loss.

Yrome, surprised by our sudden surge in power, struggled to fend off our relentless assault. His dark energy, though formidable, was met with the combined might of our elemental fury. Lightning, earth, and the pure energy of light clashed with the darkness, creating a spectacle of chaos and power.

In the midst of the battle, I caught a glimpse of Camila's fallen form, a striking reminder of the stakes of this fight. Her sacrifice fueled my resolve, lending strength to my attacks. I unleashed a torrent of light beams, each one striking with the force of my anger and sorrow.

Gaianor's earth attacks became more potent, the ground responding to his command with unprecedented force. Rocks and boulders pummeled Yrome from all directions, each hit a blow for justice.

Elijah, his emotions a tempest of rage and regret, became a living storm. His lightning crackled with a raw intensity, each bolt a strike against the tyranny Yrome represented.

Together, we pushed Yrome back, our combined powers slowly overwhelming his defenses. We could sense his uncertainty, his realization that he was not as invincible as he had believed.

Yrome, though battered by our combined assault, was far from defeated. His dark energy surged, a relentless tide seeking to sweep us away.

Gaianor launched a massive upheaval of the ground beneath Yrome. The earth rose like a vengeful titan, but Yrome, with a cruel sneer, unleashed a wave of dark energy that shattered the earthen giant into dust.

In that moment of distraction, Yrome saw his opportunity. He lunged towards Gaianor with a speed that defied nature, his dark katana gleaming with a sinister light. Gaianor, caught off guard, barely had time to react. He raised his arms in a futile attempt to shield himself, but Yrome's blade cut through his defenses like a scythe through wheat.

The impact sent Gaianor crashing to the ground, his form reverting to his human shape upon impact. A deep wound marred his chest, the life rapidly draining from his eyes. I watched in horror as another one of my closest allies, a friend and a fellow warrior, lay dying before me.

I was fueled by grief and rage. My attacks became more desperate, more ferocious. I unleashed a blinding barrage of light beams, each one a piercing lance of pure energy.

But Yrome, now seemingly invigorated by our despair, met my attacks with a chilling calmness. His movements were precise, his counters deadly.

"We need to change tactics," I gasped, struggling to regain my footing. "He's too strong. We can't beat him like this."

Elijah nodded. "We need to find a weakness, anything that can give us an edge."

But even as we regrouped, Yrome advanced, his every step resonating with the power of the crown. The air around him seemed to warp and bend.

"We need to separate him from the crown," I suggested, dodging another wave of dark energy. "That should hopefully weaken him enough."

Elijah nodded, his eyes scanning for an opening. "Easier said than done. He's not going to let it go willingly."

In a flurry of motion, we launched another series of attacks, each one more desperate than the last. I focused my light beams, trying to blind and disorient Yrome, while Elijah used his lightning to disrupt Yrome's connection to the crown's energy.

But Yrome was relentless. With a sweep of his hand, he unleashed a barrage of dark energy blades, each one aimed with deadly precision. We dodged and weaved, but the onslaught was unending. With each passing second, our hope of victory dimmed.

Then, in a moment of clarity amidst the chaos, I caught a glimpse of the crown. It pulsed with a malevolent light, its power almost palpable. A plan began to form in my mind, a risky gambit that might just turn the tide.

"Elijah," I called out, "cover me. I have an idea."

Without hesitation, Elijah redoubled his assault, drawing Yrome's attention. I used the distraction to close the distance, my every sense focused on the crown. If we could just separate Yrome from its influence, we might stand a chance.

But as I neared, Yrome turned, his eyes narrowing. "Foolish," he sneered.

I didn't respond. Instead, I poured every ounce of my power into one final, desperate strike. The fate of our world hung in the balance, and I knew that this might be our only chance to save it.

As I wrenched the crown from Yrome's grasp, a fleeting sense of triumph washed over Elijah and me. We exchanged a brief, hopeful glance, believing we had finally turned the tide in this dire battle.

But our triumph was short-lived. Yrome's laughter, deep and menacing, filled the air, echoing off the ruined walls of Bryson Village. "Do you truly believe that removing the crown would weaken me?" he taunted, his eyes gleaming with dark amusement. "The crown's power was mine long before you even knew of its existence. It has merely returned to its rightful master."

Elijah and I exchanged a look of disbelief and horror. "What do you mean?" I managed to ask, my voice barely above a whisper.

Yrome's smirk widened. "The crown was but a vessel, a means to an end. I am beyond the need for such trinkets now."

Before we could react, Yrome unleashed a devastating barrage of attacks. Waves of dark energy, interwoven with the raw elements of fire, ice, earth, and lightning, crashed down upon us. The force was overwhelming, and despite our best efforts to defend ourselves, we were no match for his might.

The impact sent us hurtling to the ground, our dragon forms dissipating as we reverted back to our human selves. We lay there, battered and bruised, our bodies aching from the assault.

I looked up at the sky, the clouds swirling ominously above. Despair gripped my heart. I mustered the strength to confront Yrome. "Why did you betray Ytfen?" I asked, my voice strained but resolute. "He sought peace, an alliance. He was never a threat to you or your people."

Yrome's expression shifted subtly, a flicker of something deeper passing across his face. It was a look that hinted at a complex past, one filled with more than just malice. "You fools," he said, his voice low and tinged with an emotion I couldn't quite place. "You know nothing of the truth, of the real reasons behind my actions."

His words piqued my curiosity, despite the dire situation. "What truth?" I pressed, trying to understand the motivations of the man who had caused so much pain and destruction.

Yrome's eyes narrowed, and he took a step closer. "Allow me to enlighten you," he said, his tone ominous. He reached out, placing his hands on our heads. A familiar sensation washed over me, the edges of my vision blurring as the world around me began to fade.

In that moment, I braced myself for what was to come. The sensation was unmistakable – the onset of memories, not my own, being poured into my consciousness. I could feel Elijah beside me, experiencing the same invasion of thoughts and images.

23

The Usurper King, Part II

A flood of memories washed over me. Each memory was a vivid reminder of the life I had built, the love I had cherished, and the dreams I had nurtured. The joyous moments of my wedding with Denise, the wise counsel of my mother Sonia, the laughter and hopes of my people – all these memories swirled within me, a maelstrom of happiness and love that had defined my existence.

But amidst these memories, the most poignant were those of Denise. I recalled her radiant smile, the warmth of her touch, and the gentle swell of her belly as we anticipated the birth of our child. Her last words echoed in my mind, a reminder of the person I had strived to be – kind, just, and benevolent.

As I stood there, pierced by Yrome's blade, surrounded by his soldiers, something within me began to shift. Denise's words, her hopes for me, clashed with the harsh reality of the betrayal and loss I had just endured. "I'm sorry," I whispered to myself, to Denise, to the memory of what I once was. "I can no longer be that kind person. He is gone."

In that moment, a profound and ominous transformation began. One that was both familiar and yet utterly different. The ground beneath my feet started to tremble, the very earth responding to the turmoil within me. Lightning crackled in the sky, a visual manifestation of the storm raging in my heart. The air grew heavy, charged with a palpable tension that seemed to press down on everything around me. Dark clouds gathered rapidly, and a heavy rain began to fall.

The initial stages were those of a typical dragon transformation – my bones elongated, my muscles expanded, and my form grew larger, a physical manifestation of the dragon power within me.

But amid this metamorphosis, something unprecedented occurred. A massive pillar of darkness descended from the sky, enveloping me in its shadowy embrace. This was no ordinary transformation; it was something more, something born of the uncontrollable rage that had taken hold of my very soul.

The darkness around me pulsated with energy, and as it did, the dragon transformation reversed. My bones and muscles began retracting, molding back into a human form, but not as before. This was different. My muscles tightened, becoming more defined, and a surge of power unlike anything I had ever felt coursed through me.

The world around me shifted into startling clarity. Every detail, every droplet of rain, every grain of ash from the destroyed village became vividly apparent. It was as if time itself had slowed down, allowing me to perceive the world in a way I never had before.

I stood there, a changed being, my gaze fixed on Yrome and the soldiers arrayed behind him.

In that instant, a palpable force emanated from me, an invisible yet overwhelming power that seized the soldiers. They began to choke, their faces contorted in terror as they were lifted high into the air by an unseen force. Suspended in a macabre dance, they were helpless, their fate now in the hands of the very being they had sought to destroy.

With a mere snap of my fingers, the soldiers' bodies exploded in a gruesome spectacle. Blood rained down, mixing with the raindrops, a crimson shower that painted the village in the colors of death.

Yrome, his face a mask of fear and disbelief, witnessed the carnage. Then, summoning the courage borne of desperation, he tapped into the dragon power I had once bestowed upon him. With a burst of speed, he dashed towards me, his katana drawn, gleaming with pure energy, a silver streak in the rain.

But his attack was futile. As he swung his blade with all his might, I raised a single finger, stopping the sword's descent instantly. The impact of our powers meeting sent a massive shockwave rippling through the air, an earthquake that shattered the ground and obliterated everything behind me.

We stood there, locked in a moment of confrontation. Our eyes met, his filled with fear, mine with an unyielding resolve.

The battle between Yrome and me was a one-sided affair. Yrome, despite the dragon power I had once given him, stood no chance against the wrath I unleashed. The rain continued to pour, a fitting backdrop to the relentless onslaught I delivered.

Yrome tried to defend himself, his movements desperate and erratic, but they were futile against my overwhelming might. With each strike I landed, the ground trembled, and the air crackled with raw energy. My attacks were brutal, a manifestation of the rage and pain that consumed me.

I grabbed him by his armor, lifting him effortlessly off the ground. His struggles were weak, his eyes wide with the realization of his impending doom. I threw him against the remnants of a shattered wall, the impact echoing through the desolate village.

Yrome, battered and broken, tried to crawl away. I advanced, my steps heavy with intent. Each blow I delivered was a release of pent-up anger, a response to the betrayal and loss he had caused. I was no longer the just and kind ruler I had once been; I was an avenger, a force of retribution.

His cries of pain were drowned out by the thunder and the relentless rain. With every hit, I felt a release, but it brought no solace, no peace, just a deepening of the dark void within me.

Finally, Yrome lay at my feet, barely conscious, his body a testament to my fury. He was defeated, his dreams of conquest and power shattered by the very power he had sought to wield against us.

I paused for a moment, my breaths heavy with exertion and rage. The rain continued to fall, each drop a cold reminder of the chaos that surrounded me. It was then that I caught a glimpse of my reflection in a puddle – a sight that momentarily arrested my fury.

In the water, I saw my own eyes, glowing a sinister red, filled with a rage and pain that seemed to consume my very being. My hair now hung long and silver down to my waist. The reflection was a mirror to my soul, revealing the transformation that had taken place within me.

Looking down at Yrome, his body broken and spirit crushed, I felt a surge of dark satisfaction. But it was not enough. The betrayal, the loss of Denise and our unborn child, the loss of my mother, the destruction of my village – it all fueled a desire for vengeance that went beyond one man.

With the rain beating down, I spoke, my voice resonating with a cold, merciless resolve. "This is just the beginning, Yrome. Your suffering will pale in comparison to what I will unleash upon your people. I will make sure that every human, every loved one you hold dear, experiences the pain and despair you have brought upon me."

I leaned closer to him, my red eyes burning into his. "I will eradicate your kind, just as you sought to eradicate mine. You thought dragons were gods? I will show you the wrath of a god. Your kingdoms will fall, your people will perish, and your legacy will be nothing but ashes and sorrow."

As I stood over Yrome, a dark resolve took hold of me. With a flick of my wrist, I conjured a katana, not of steel, but of pure dark energy, its blade shimmering with a malevolent light. The weapon was a manifestation of my anger, a tool of vengeance forged from the depths of my despair.

I raised the katana, its dark energy crackling in the rain-soaked air, and slowly, deliberately, I pierced Yrome with it. The blade slid into him with a sinister ease, and I watched, unflinching, as the life drained from his eyes. His last breath was a whisper in the storm, a final surrender to the inevitable.

But my fury was not sated. With Yrome's lifeless body beneath me, I began to stomp on him relentlessly. Each hit was an outpouring of my rage, a physical release of the torment that had consumed me. The impact of my blows sent shockwaves through the ground, each one creating a larger crater around us.

The rain continued to pour down, but it was as if I was beyond the reach of the elements, lost in my own world of vengeance and destruction. All sense of sanity, all remnants of the just and kind ruler I once was, had left me. I was no longer Ytfen, the benevolent dragon king; I had become something else entirely, a creature driven by grief and a thirst for revenge.

Beneath a weeping sky, I knelt by Yrome's fallen form. In my hands, I clasped the weight of his legacy, the crown that had commanded nations. With solemn reverence, I crowned myself amidst the downpour, the rain washing away the remnants of battle, baptizing me in the role I was to play next. The raindrops, like a chorus of the fallen, drummed a somber rhythm as I rose, the crown's new bearer, under the gray, mourning heavens.

As I stood amidst the destruction, my fury unabated, the arrival of my Pure Elemental Commanders broke through the haze of my rage. They approached cautiously, their expressions a mix of shock and disbelief at the scene before them.

Zephyra was the first to speak, her voice trembling with concern. "My king! You must try to calm down."

I turned to face them, my eyes still burning with an unquenchable fury. "We will kill all the humans," I declared, my voice resolute and unwavering. "They must pay for what they've done."

Pyrus stepped forward, his face etched with pain. "But, my king, this is not right. We cannot condemn an entire race for the actions of one man. There must be another way."

"I am your king!" I screamed, my voice echoing through the devastated village. "You will obey me!"

The commanders exchanged glances, their loyalty to me now at odds with their sense of justice and morality. The air was thick with tension, the weight of the moment palpable.

"We cannot let you do this," said Glacius, "we cannot follow you down this path."

"Please," added Joaquin, his voice barely above a whisper. "Let's talk through this."

Aquarion and Tarn stood in silence.

I looked at each of them, my heart now a void where compassion and reason once resided. "Is this your choice? To stand against your king?" I asked, my voice cold and devoid of emotion.

Their silence was the answer I needed. "Very well," I said, a dark resolve settling over me.

In an instant, I charged at them, my powers unleashed in a torrent of rage and betrayal. The memory ended abruptly.

24

Legacy of the Lost

As the flood of memories receded, I found myself back in the ruins of Bryson Village, the harsh reality of the present crashing down on me. My mind was reeling, struggling to comprehend the staggering revelation.

I stared at him, my eyes wide with disbelief. "Y-Y-Ytfen?" I stammered, my voice barely above a whisper. The implications of this truth were overwhelming, reshaping everything I thought I knew.

Ytfen, once a figure of wisdom and kindness in my memories, now stood as the embodiment of the very force we had been fighting against. "How... why?" I managed to ask, my mind racing with questions.

"That's right," he confirmed, his voice heavy with unspoken pain. "The memories you've seen, they are mine. The truth is far more complex than the legends and tales that have been passed down through generations."

I struggled to process his words, the shock of the revelation still fresh. "But the war, the destruction... how could you let it happen?" I asked, my voice rising with emotion.

Elijah's gaze softened as he observed Ytfen, the weight of realization settling upon him. "It's the grief, isn't it?" he said, his voice carrying a blend of empathy and sorrow. "The unbearable pain of losing everyone you cherished... Denise, your mother, your entire kingdom, your unborn child. That's what pushed you down this dark path, wasn't it?"

Ytfen seemed momentarily vulnerable. His eyes, a mirror to his tormented soul, briefly met Elijah's before looking away, unable to hold the gaze. The silence that followed was heavy, filled with the unsaid and the unbearable. It was a moment of raw, unguarded truth between them, a recognition of the deep wounds that had never truly healed.

I could see the torment in his eyes, the internal struggle between the man he once was and the being he had become. "But Yrome... how did you convince everyone you were him?" I asked, trying to piece together the fragmented history.

Ytfen looked up, his eyes meeting mine. "Yrome was a facade, a persona I continued, in order to manipulate events from behind the scenes."

Ytfen's demeanor shifted, the brief glimpse of vulnerability replaced by an intense, almost malevolent presence. "Curious, isn't it? That you don't remember our battle all those years ago. The battle where you both managed to seal me and my powers within you. But, you see, before the seal was complete, I released a fragment of myself, a sliver of my essence, into the crown."

His voice grew colder, more detached, as he recounted the events. "It was a desperate move, born from the realization that my end was near. That fragment, that piece of my soul, it lingered within the crown, waiting, biding its time."

He stepped closer, his eyes locked onto mine, a sinister glint in them. "Over the years, that fragment grew, fed by the ambitions and desires of those who sought it. It became a separate entity, one that eventually took on a life of its own. Yrome, the persona I had created, was no longer just a mask I wore. It became a reality, a being with its own will, driven by the darkest parts of me."

Elijah and I exchanged a look of confusion, our brows furrowed in an attempt to grasp the gravity of Ytfen's words. "What battle?" I whispered, both to Elijah and myself. The pieces of this intricate puzzle were slowly coming together, yet there were gaps, missing memories that eluded our understanding.

I did, however, begin to connect the dots. The mysterious figure that plagued my nightmares, the shadowy presence that had haunted my dreams, was in fact a fragment of Ytfen, a piece of his essence that had been sealed within me all along.

It was the same with Elijah. That figure was another fragment of Ytfen, a part of him that had been lying dormant, waiting for the right moment to emerge.

The figure from the crown, the entity that had given the Dragon Slayers their powers all these years, was also a part of this complex tapestry. It was all Ytfen, or rather, fragments of him, scattered across time and space, each playing a role in this grand, tragic narrative.

Then it suddenly dawned at me. During my fight with Ytfen's fragment in the crown, I experienced some sort of vision or memory. I was fighting alongside another mysterious figure. We fought together against Ytfen. Could this have been the elusive memory of the battle Ytfen mentioned?

Yet, try as I might, the fragments remained jumbled, a puzzle refusing to yield its final picture.

"Any final words?" Ytfen demanded, his intent clear and lethal.

I steadied my voice against the tide of fear. "And what of the Light Dragon?" I challenged.

Ytfen's gaze softened momentarily as he contemplated my question about the Light Dragon. "The Light Dragon," he began, his voice tinged with a hint of melancholy, "was indeed a fragment of my essence. A part of me that clung to nobility, to the ideals of a just and benevolent ruler. But that part of me... it's no longer needed. It only serves to hold me back."

He paused, his eyes drifting skyward as if lost in a distant memory. "The Light Dragon was the embodiment of all that was good and pure in me. But now, I see the futility of such ideals. This world... it doesn't reward nobility or kindness. It only respects power."

With those words, Ytfen began to levitate, his body rising effortlessly into the air. The atmosphere around us grew tense, charged with an impending sense of doom. "Enough of this chatter," Ytfen declared, his voice resonating with a newfound authority. "It's time to end this once and for all."

As he spoke, the air around him crackled with energy, a swirling vortex of elemental power that seemed to emanate from his very being.

His body started to contort and expand, growing larger and larger, until it was obscured by a swirling mass of energy. The ground beneath our feet trembled, and the sky above darkened as if the very heavens were reacting to the monumental shift in power.

High above, where Ytfen had risen, a colossal barrier formed, enveloping him completely. It was a cocoon, a chrysalis within which something unimaginable was taking shape. It's sheer size and presence warped the very air around it. This cocoon seemed to draw in the energy of the world, creating a gravity that tugged at the fabric of reality itself.

For a moment, there was an eerie silence, a calm before the inevitable storm. The cocoon began to pulsate rhythmically, each throb sending ripples through the air.

Then, without warning, the cocoon erupted in a blinding explosion of light and power, a cataclysmic release of energy that shook the very foundations of the earth. The light was so intense, so all-consuming, that it momentarily blinded us, forcing us to shield our eyes.

As the blinding light from the cocoon's explosion faded, a new form took shape in the sky, casting a shadow that blanketed the land. Before us stood a dragon of unparalleled magnitude, its presence so overwhelming that it seemed to consume the very air around us.

Dominating the center of this colossal entity were three heads. Each head was a masterpiece of draconic design, distinct yet harmonious in their terrifying beauty.

The central head, regal and commanding, bore a crown of twisted horns that arched back like the branches of an ancient tree. Its eyes, deep and penetrating, glowed with a fiery red intensity, burning like embers in the night. The scales on this head were a deep, lustrous black, absorbing light and reflecting a spectrum of dark reds and purples.

The head to the right was slightly smaller, sleek and serpentine, with a row of sharp, backward-curving horns that gave it a menacing appearance. Its scales were a darker shade of red, like blood spilled on a moonless night. The eyes of this head were narrower, more cunning, flickering with a malevolent intelligence.

The left head was broader, more brutish, with a jaw lined with rows of razor-sharp teeth, each one gleaming like a polished dagger. The horns on this head were shorter but thicker, resembling the jagged rocks of a treacherous mountain peak. The scales here were a mix of black and deep crimson, creating a pattern that seemed to shift and change with the dragon's movements.

Together, they formed a trinity of power, a perfect union of terror and grace that stood as a herald of the apocalypse.

Ytfen's body was colossal, each muscle defined and powerful, rippling under the thick, armored scales that covered him from head to tail. The scales themselves were a tapestry of darkness and fire, interlocking plates that moved with a fluid grace despite their formidable appearance.

The dragon's wings were vast, so wide that they blotted out the sun when fully extended. They were like twin canopies of darkness, each membrane taut and strong, lined with spines and ridges that added to their intimidating presence.

The tail of the dragon was long and prehensile, ending in a spade-like tip that crackled with energy.

As I gazed up at the colossal dragon form of Ytfen, a sense of helplessness washed over me. Beside me, Elijah shared the same look of disbelief and despair. Our eyes were fixed on the monstrous being that loomed above, its presence overwhelming and its power seemingly boundless.

"Elijah," I whispered, my voice barely audible against the backdrop of Ytfen's ominous growls and the crackling energy that surrounded him. "We... we can't stop that. It's too much."

Elijah, usually so full of determination and strength, could only nod in silent agreement. His eyes, wide with a mix of fear and resignation, reflected the gravity of our situation. We stood there, rooted to the spot, as the realization of our powerlessness against such a force sank in.

I had faced many challenges, overcome many obstacles, but this... this was beyond anything I had ever imagined. In the face of such might, what could we possibly do?

The sky above us transformed into a canvas of impending doom as Ytfen's new form began to gather an unfathomable energy.

The very air around us crackled with raw, untamed energy, as if the fabric of reality itself was being torn asunder.

Above, the heavens split open, revealing a nightmarish vision. Meteors, engulfed in flames, descended like a rain of fire, each one a herald of obliteration. Their fiery trails painted the sky in streaks of red and orange, a macabre display of the dragon's wrath.

Elijah and I, dwarfed by the scale of the impending catastrophe, found ourselves locked in a helpless embrace. In this moment of despair, our shared history, our conflicts, and our bond as brothers crystallized into a silent understanding. We stood together, not as adversaries, but as brothers bound by blood and fate, united in the face of our looming demise.

Our eyes, wide with a mix of fear and awe, followed the descent of the celestial inferno. The ground beneath our feet trembled, a foreboding prelude to the chaos that was about to be unleashed. The air grew hot, the heat from the approaching meteors suffusing the atmosphere with an unbearable intensity.

As the first of the meteors neared, its size and speed becoming terrifyingly clear, we braced ourselves. Our hearts pounded in our chests, a futile protest against the inevitable. We closed our eyes, a final, instinctive act of self-preservation, waiting for the world to be consumed in a cataclysmic blaze.

But the expected explosion, the searing pain of our end, never came. Instead, there was a profound silence, a stillness that was as unsettling as it was unexpected.

Cautiously, I opened my eyes, half-expecting to find only darkness. But what greeted me was a scene of utter desolation. The landscape around us was a wasteland of ruins and devastation.

The air was thick with dust and ash, painting the sky a dull, lifeless gray. The sun, barely visible through the haze, cast a weak, pallid light over the ruins, its warmth unable to reach the cold, desolate earth.

In every direction, the devastation stretched to the horizon. The magnitude of the destruction was overwhelming.

However, a sense of dissonance washed over me. The landscape held an eerie quality that unsettled me further. The devastation, while profound, bore the marks of age; it was not the fresh wreckage of a recent cataclysm but rather the weathered remains of a long-forgotten disaster.

The buildings and structures, or what was left of them, were overgrown with vegetation, nature reclaiming what once belonged to it. The rubble and debris were not scattered chaotically as one would expect from a recent event but were instead settled, almost integrated into the landscape, as if they had been part of it for years.

The air, heavy with the scent of decay and neglect, carried a stillness that spoke of a long absence of life and activity. The ground, littered with the remnants of what once was, was covered in a layer of dust and dirt that had clearly not been disturbed for a considerable time.

Suddenly a distant voice pierced the heavy silence. It was a call, faint yet filled with an emotion that resonated deep within me. "Ezekiel! Elijah!" The voice grew louder, more distinct, carrying with it a sense of urgency and relief.

From the haze of dust and ash, a figure emerged, running towards us with a determination that defied the surrounding chaos. As she drew closer, there was something strikingly familiar about her – the way she moved, the tone of her voice, something that tugged at the very core of my being.

She reached us, her eyes brimming with tears, and enveloped us in a tight embrace. Her arms, warm and comforting, held us as if to never let go. In that embrace, there was a sense of safety, a feeling of returning home after being lost in a storm.

Confusion and disbelief warred within me. My heart raced, and a myriad of emotions surged through my mind. There was a recognition, a connection that defied logic but felt as real as the air I breathed.

Her face, lined with the marks of time and hardship, softened as she looked at us. In her eyes, I saw a reflection of my own – the same color, the same depth.

Tears welled up in my eyes, unbidden, as a single word escaped my lips, almost a whisper, yet laden with a lifetime of longing and unspoken questions. "Mom?"

The word hung in the air, a fragile bridge between hope and reality.

To Be Continued…

As you turn this final page, I hope you find yourself a little richer in spirit and imagination. Thank you for lending your heart and mind to this adventure, for it is readers like you who breathe true life into the words.

If this tale has sparked joy, wonder, or even the thrill of adventure within you, I kindly ask you to consider leaving a review. Your thoughts and reflections not only mean the world to me but also help guide others to join us on this extraordinary journey. Each review helps to spread the word, allowing more readers to discover and enjoy this adventure.

Below, you'll find a QR code. A quick scan will take you directly to where you can share your thoughts and experiences about the book. Whether it's a moment that touched you, a character who felt like a friend, or simply the enjoyment of the escape—your review is a precious gift that supports the journey of this book far beyond its pages.

Neftali Hernandez is not only a storyteller but also a seasoned actor who has appeared in popular shows like Queen of the South, Florida Man, MTV's Revenge Prank, Fatal Attraction, Murder Calls, Homicide Hunter, and many more.

Born in Puerto Rico, **Neftali** developed a love for storytelling at a young age. This passion only grew stronger as he pursued his acting career, bringing to life a variety of characters on both the big and small screens.

To learn more about **Neftali Hernandez** and his work, visit his website or follow him on social media:

Website: www.neftali-hernandez.com

IMDB: www.imdb.me/neftalihernandez

Instagram: @neftalihernandez

Printed in Great Britain
by Amazon